EAST OF
HAITI

EAST OF
HAITI

CÉSAR SÁNCHEZ BERAS

English translations by
Mark Cutler and Rhina P. Espaillat

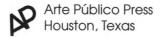
Arte Público Press
Houston, Texas

East of Haiti: Three Novellas is funded in part by the National Endowment for the Arts. We are thankful for its support.

Recovering the past, creating the future
Arte Público Press
University of Houston
4902 Gulf Fwy, Bldg 19, Rm 100
Houston, Texas 77204-2004

Cover design by Mora Des¡gn
Cover art by Dixie Miguez

Library of Congress Control Number: 2023943391

∞ The paper used in this publication meets the requirements of the American National Standard for Information Sciences—Permanence of Paper for Printed Library Materials, ANSI Z39.48-1984.

23 24 25   4 3 2 1

To Rhina P. Espaillat with deep gratitude

CONTENTS

HE MUST NOT KNOW IT

English translation by
Rhina P. Espaillat

Chapter 1

MADAME DEGÁ

"There is a kind of escape that looks like seeking."
Victor Hugo, 1802-1885

Alberto Durosier, now known as Zero-One, arrived in the neighborhood during the final weeks of winter 1970. The family had been looking around from city to city, across the whole south of the country, as if running from something malignant and unknown. They settled on Seventh Street, in the neighborhood of Villa Consuelo in Santo Domingo, after eluding, thanks to some good luck, a certain stroke of bad luck—a major mishap in their original home, Barahona.

The truck used to transport the few possessions that comprised their improvised move was not adequate for that type of service. It was a massive mastodon that looked like a big, rambling metal house with tires worn smooth by overuse; no rear lights to indicate stops, and no rear mirrors, so the driver had to work magic to know who was coming up close behind the truck.

The old motor of what was once a 1959 Leyland Hippo would snore, threatening to stop in the middle of Sanchez highway during the weekly trip it normally made from the interior of the country. Whoever saw it far away did not confer on it the nobility of its origin. When it crossed in front of the stands built

3

roadside it caused shock because of its rickety appearance and total lack of paint, its bed surrounded by a railing of tubes and a canvas for covering the merchandise it originally transported.

The truck's owner was a middle-aged man, paunchy, with narrowed, unusually lively eyes. A farmer toughened by daily work, without the mettle necessary for that kind of labor, especially for a man preceded by a well-earned reputation for being quick with a knife. He knew the country's every corner, no matter the spot or site pointed out to him, but he was born and raised in Moca, in a settlement called Estancia Nueva. His transport was, as they say, the soul of his business, since he was a seller of chickens on a grand scale, and he delivered them all over the capital during the first hours of the morning. The owner of the truck had an order of some few hundred pounds to deliver to the marketplace at Villa Consuelo, and he did the new arrivals a favor by bringing their possessions, which he dumped in front of Number 49 without even making sure that was the address to be occupied by those he had just transported.

La Turca, the name by which the woman was known who owned the little house in the back, looked with some mistrust at the woman who was to be her tenant before a breath of uncommon goodness pierced her maternal heart. She too had roamed around from place to place, without a husband to support her and her hungry children. On seeing herself in the image of another misfit she couldn't help taking pity on that very skinny woman, who had a mad look, and was carrying a child of about two astride her narrow waist.

After a long time, the neighborhood realized that Cuza, as the mother of Albertico was called, was a native of Haiti. Her birthplace was the community of Pétion-Ville, and she had found work not long before in the home of a landowner in the sugar business. In her latest job, she had been impregnated by a moneyed man who frequently visited the home where she had worked since she was a little girl until almost thirteen, when her grace—that of a black woman—initiated the *via crucis* caused by her misfortune.

Cuza's mother was Degá Durosier, a woman of medium height with round, expressive eyes. She seemed never to be tired, could do hundreds of things during the day, many at once without breathing a word of complaint. She had come into the world in a very poor village a few kilometers from the ancient city she loved with all her soul. Her desire to progress took them and her husband to Pétion-Ville in search of food for the growing family, and to build a better future. At that time the new place that took them in was a birthplace of merchants and artisans. Painters who offered works of great artistic value, but were urged by poverty to sell them for a tenth of their worth. Woodworkers who carved into cedar and mahogany indigenous landscapes that no longer existed. Nevertheless, they had no opportunity to raise a family in peace, nor to become really acquainted with their own country. Fierce pursuit by the Haitian government called for the unexpected absence of the husband. Finding herself alone and pursued, she had no option but to flee without looking back. To leave Pétion-Ville at once and cross the border to this part of the island, ending up in the settlement of the sugar works known as Batey Central de Barahona, in worse conditions than those they had left behind, and a child still breast-feeding.

She found work as a cleaning woman, but in a short time other duties were added: she served as an errand-girl who shopped twice a week for the family's food; nursemaid to the children of the lady of the house until they went to bed; hairdresser to the same lady, braiding her straight hair to embellish it; and every other night, provided sexual release to the master, who from the first day did not hide the libidinous looks he gave the hips of the worker he had hired.

Degá was the firstborn of the fourth-grade elementary school teacher, Alexandrine Chevalier, and Webert Durosier. Madame Chevalier was a natural teacher of reading and writing in creole, or, as she used to say, the language of the people, and worked tirelessly at the President Toussaint school. Monsieur Durosier was a musician and self-taught intellectual who became aware very early of the political problems of his country. Her father gave no ground when he knew he was right about some issue. His ideas, set to popular musical scores and sung, attracted the attention of the henchmen of the Duvalier tyranny, and he had to run for his life. First to France for a short stay, during which he improved his French, then to New York, to perfect his knowledge of the English language and try to earn a living performing with the Caribbean afro-jazz musicians in Harlem and, finally to Boston, where he met his death when a taxi-driver ignored a red light and drove into a tall, slender black man who was walking from his apartment to the Methodist Church to give music lessons on a volunteer basis.

When Degá saw herself in the whirlpool of widowhood, with a small child and no husband to protect her, she didn't hesitate before crossing the border to the village of Jimaní. Like hundreds of others of her countrymen, she saw a brief oasis on the eastern part of her island and put space in between, to distance herself from the tragedy of her own surroundings.

But her chain of penury was just beginning to take shape. Degá's unspeakable calvary took her to survive in a hell disguised as a country estate. The huge house of the owners, that house of the rich, that place where peons and servants die, where she sighted land, was the closest thing to slavery that she could remember. The night that they found her hallucinating that she was returning to her country she had a fever of over thirty-nine degrees Celsius. The wife of Señor Mendoza, for the first time in their married life, opposed her husband's decision and quickly sent a servant to fetch Dr. Abad.

The doctor was Dominican of Lebanese descent, and served as a veterinarian at the sugar mill. They called him for an emergency and he came under the impression that he would earn a healthy sum for taking a look at one or another of the animals on the land of the engineer Mendoza, but when he reached the house they led him through to the barracks in the dark where Degá was dying. She had contracted tetanus walking barefoot over rusty barbed wire on her way to market.

The once cheerful face that used to shine like a mirror had become almost grotesque, deformed by the grimaces provoked by increasing pain. Her muscles, as they contracted, added a load of years that she had not lived, and spasms overran her body from her feet to her tangled hair. From afar she seemed to be laughing inside her sadness, but seen more closely it was evident that it was her suffering that produced that twisted smile with what remained of her full lips. Her pharynx had begun to narrow, introducing a desperate asphyxiation. She had not eaten for several days, and only moistened her lips slightly in her struggle against the fever. The tension of her fists and arms had shrunk her to a stain on the white sheet that covered the bed. It was the closest thing to death that the estate had witnessed. They wanted to avoid exposing Degá's daughter to that Dantesque scene by removing her from her mother, in a kind of quarantine imposed more out of pity than sanitary purposes.

Degá, their loyal black worker, died half an hour later, despite what the doctor, something of a good soul, attempted to do: administer intravenously a load of penicillin used for sick horses. Before closing those intensely black eyes forever on the world that had wounded her in so many ways, she regarded them all for a few seconds and fastened her eyes on the mistress to beg a favor: "Look after my daughter, madame! *Bondye ap pey ou!*

That was all she said with the few words she could articulate from the flames of fever. An overwhelming torment consumed her wholly, not so much the fear of death as leaving her defenselessness little girl an orphan.

The Mendoza home continued undisturbed, despite the absence of that woman who, for such a long time, watched over everything in the mansion to assure that all would be in order. The little girl had taken up the reins of the house before the departure of her mother, and turned out to be equally hard-working, although she had much to learn about preparing meals for her employers.

After a few years the belly of the child, who had already entered adolescence, began to expand in a way that suggested something was taking place in her body; a burden of shame and impotence kept her away from everyone and she hardly ever went out even to the patio, hiding herself in chores and duties, attending to the kitchen and the house. They forced her to say what they all suspected in some way, but no one in the family wanted to admit. Corralled among them all, she identified by both first name and last the man responsible for the violation and the resulting pregnancy that she would now endure.

They asked themselves how they would tell the society that observed them that Alberto Mendoza, the engineer, the bachelor most sought by young ladies of marriageable age, the rich man about town—he who played tennis and spent the Christmas holidays in the United States, the best partner for any matrimony, heir to a growing fortune since age thirty-five—had begotten a child with a girl, a little black girl who ran errands at the market, the daughter of a Haitian servant.

The employers wanted to blame her for a non-existent seduction and a lascivious offer that had never happened, but she had only enough strength to cry inconsolably. She cried broken buckets worth of tears. All of this in the crowded gathering in the living room seemed to be the climax of a pre-ordained curse, hearing the name of the younger brother of the engineer Mendoza, and yet no one ventured to suggest a just solution to that unspeakable assault.

They commiserated momentarily with the victim's helplessness. They tried to console her with the crumbs of a pity that lasted only a few hours. By the end of the day, they had given her some money for the impending departure, raw food in a knapsack and some used clothing for herself and for the creature not yet born. What seemed like generosity from the family was in no sense a gift inspired by goodness. The package of gifts was given to her on an unshakeable condition to "Go, and don't come back!"

With that laconic command they asked her not only to leave the town, but also to disappear from the life of the lady's brother-in-law. While she gathered the items and prepared to leave, they gave her the last instruction: "The child can't be born, and you know it very well. You are not to give birth to it. This problem should be resolved right away, today, by any means. This money is to resolve the matter. And for your own good, don't say a single word about what has happened."

They sent her with one of the peons to a doctor friend who was an expert in such matters. She traveled seated on some sacks of agave on the floor of a van of the kind used for taking the harvest from the farm to the market. For a moment she thought her employers were right, and she repeated to herself what they had said: "The child can't be born, and you know it very well." But when she placed her hand on her belly and felt a gentle movement that pushed on her ribs, a windstorm of tenderness gave her back the strength they had taken from her with their threats. At that moment, she decided to give the creature waiting to be born what they wanted to deny it, the right to live.

A few months later, everything was forgotten at the estate. Cuza, in complete solitude, gave birth to the baby in the hallway of the public hospital of Barahona, because she couldn't wait for a bed. The cries of the newborn joined her own, linking them in a pain that would accompany them forever.

On more than one occasion she intended to find the father, shame him to his face and confront him in a resolute manner, but she always ended by resigning herself to the crushing reality that she was a stranger in a world dominated by people to whom the tragedy of her lot would not matter in the least.

Before the baby was a year old, she saved the small sum necessary to register a birth, and added a few more pesos to buy the indulgence required to register it in the civil record. She wanted to call him Webert in honor of the artist grandfather she never met, but anger won out. She named him Alberto, a touch of revenge, and added his last name, Durosier, so as not to abandon a lineage that was not important even to her.

She loved the city of Barahona like a hometown. She didn't know the Haiti that her mother spoke of, nor the ancestors from Pétion-Ville, who had entered her life as stories told when her mother rested at the end of the day. Santo Domingo was far from any Haitian city where she had relatives, but she was also disconnected from her past. She was a woman without roots, without any door she could cling to in order to remain upright along the route that began with zero. She had nowhere to go, but neither could she remain where she was. Money can do everything, she thought, and they would not forgive her courage if she contradicted them, or her arrogance if she aimed to unite gold with mud through an unwanted child. She liaised with a construction worker who knew the capital, a name, a street, a neighborhood, and decided to face adversity with the only armor she had left: the smile of her son and the memory of her mother, a fighter who did not surrender even at the threshold of death.

Chapter Two
THE BIRTH OF THE REAL ZERO-ONE

Cuza spoke very little, no matter what situation she was in. If alone in the horrific poverty of the shack, the silence was almost unbroken. She did the housework talking to herself, but always internally, hardly moving the full lips which stood out on her face, as if through that circumspection peace and silence would let her listen to the other woman who lived in her.

Other than when Albertico got into trouble, as he often did, Cuza went unnoticed in the neighborhood. If the boy pulled one of his stunts, she came out of her silence and spoke, not to herself or to the neighbors, but to her son, screaming warnings at him as if he were an adult, and insisting that he behave as one.

By the time the people of Villa Consuelo, during one of those screaming sessions, realized that Cuza's accent was definitely from the western end of the island, they had already learned to respect her for her hard work. Nobody noticed at all that she was one of the few Haitian women who lived in Villa Consuelo.

Albertico was not yet Zero-One. He still used no first name at all, or any last name to identify himself. It was Miguelón who baptized him with that name, after comparing his friend's face to his favorite tile used in his favorite game, Dominoes: on one side one spot, and on the other, nothing, total absence. At first

Albertico was not at all amused by his friend's wit, and in fact found it offensive. But he ended by finding it a sign of total trust, a sign of affection that aimed only to see the least painful side of that misfortune. Much later, he became "the real Zero-One," when the obstacles to survival harassed him until he became a wild animal constantly at war. A warrior disposed to battle under the blinding sun of the tropics, or an animal pursued by the atmosphere of the street at night. His name was Alberto Durosier, but few in the neighborhood knew his name as Cuza had entered it in the official civil files of Barahona. His mother called out his pet name as a sign of love every half hour, shouting herself hoarse to see if that boy overflowing with energy could be cured of his love of mischief.

"Albertico, don't climb up that mango tree!"

A squalid human lightning bolt would obey, laughing, showing a row of such white teeth that they filled his face with a splendid smile. He descended from any tree, however intricate, with a speed that invited vertigo and with an expertise worthy of better luck. He would descend radiating a rare ecstasy, as if dreaming up the next deviltry that his head could invent, exacerbated by the impetus of youth.

"Muchacho, *ti gason sa a terib!* Come, come have some of this *Tassó con Gonbó!*"

But no sooner had he landed than they had to give him some other order.

"Muchacho! Dammit! Get down from that stranger's car! Don't look for any more trouble! If the owner comes, he may think you're a *vole mote* and accuse you of trying to steal it. . . ."

He's always been the same. Restless and happy, even if walking on the edge of a gaucho knife, daring danger to find him and laughing at the crises of daily life, like the clowns who balance, smiling, on a rope, knowing that there's no net to catch them if they fall. The night that Cuza's son became Zero-One forever, she had a premonition; she felt something terrible was going to happen. She'd had a bad night with insomnia, and a headache. When she was just grabbing the end of a light sleep not far from dawn, a violent fight broke out on Seventh Street where it crosses a bit of Daniel Henriquez Street. In the fog of drowsiness, she heard a dry blow, as if struck by a sturdy night-stick, then a long silence and the voice of someone who mentioned her family name. It took her a few minutes to gain awareness and grasp the gravity of the little she had heard in the broken quiet of night.

"*¡Pitit mwen!* My son!" cried Cuza, shocked by what she was picturing in her mind. She ran out as if possessed by a legion of bad premonitions, toward the beginning of Daniel Henriquez Street. She was half-dressed in a ragged, faded nightgown and a yellow kerchief to contain her hair, as she avoided obstacles and rubbish, running so hard that her heart threatened to shatter for lack of breath.

Fifty meters from where the two streets met, a group of four or five boys who were generally on street corners could be seen. Two of them who saw her coming ran away, afraid of Cuza's reaction, not of what was happening. Of those who remained she knew only one, Miguelón, the chubby kid with the foolish face. She had never seen the other. The one on the ground, half conscious and bleeding from one side of his face, was her son. While she hugged him and wiped his face with a piece of her nightgown, which was soon soaked and red, Miguelón described what happened, with his usual stammer, now accentuated by his commotion:

"Do . . . doña Cuza, the one who hit Albertico wa . . . was Pa . . . pa . . . polo, the son of Mariana, who has the bea . . . beauty sa . . . salon, where they fix nails on La . . . La Guardia Street." His voice became much more uneven, perhaps not because of his genetic disability, but because he was calculating whether it was a good idea to denounce the aggressor. He calmed himself a bit and went on: "May . . . maybe it was Albertico's fault, be . . . because he didn't hon . . . honor the bet they . . . they had made. Your son lost, and he refused to pay; that's how the problem star . . . started."

The left side of Albertico's face was ripped by the force of the blow he received. The crash of the nightstick crushed the left brow, fracturing the eye socket and mutilating the retina forever. Between Miguelón and the other boy they helped Cuza lift him from the ground and carried a half-conscious Albertico, complaining and on the brink of fainting, while his mother wiped away the blood that had begun to coagulate and the new flow. They lifted him onto the back seat of a motorcycle, whose chauffeur looked on stupefied at the wounded boy and the friends helping him. Cuza climbed on and held the boy upright despite the fact he was close to collapsing between her chest and the back of the driver.

"What hospital are we going to, Señora?" asked the driver, concerned over the bleeding boy they had lifted onto the seat with great difficulty.

"Get . . . get to the Darío," replied Miguelón, trying to hasten the trip to avoid the loss of more blood, giving Cuza no opportunity to decide where to go. The mother was so perturbed that she could barely think and speak at the same time. She, too, was crumbling.

The night breeze, combined with the speed they were going, finally put the wounded boy to sleep. The stripe of blood that had poured out was now a dark trail, like a whiplash across the middle of his face, from the broad forehead to the chest. When they reached the Emergency Room, they lifted him and carried him to a semi-wrecked bed, from which they had just then moved another victim from an accident in Boca Chica. The doctor on duty checked to be sure this woman was the wounded patient's mother, and proceeded to stabilize him with the necessary first aid, while he searched for a vein in which to inject an IV.

Outside, the night was full of stars that the woman could not see. Tears interfered with her vision; everything seemed wrapped in a pale curtain. While the doctor channeled the saline solution that would return a bit of life to the injured mulatto, Cuza combined her cries with the prayer she often prayed, but was now delivered in anguish: The Lord's Prayer in Creole.

The prayer directed to Providence made itself heard in Creole, and sounded anonymous and heavy with grief. The words lost their consistency and diminished with the trembling lips of a mother who was making a tremendous effort not to fade away. Her hands, her eyes and tongue had acquired lives of their own and seemed incongruous in the heart of a tragedy that had been revealed beforehand to Cuza, but that she had not been able to grasp.

Chapter Three

THIS AIN'T A HOMELAND, BUT A "GO-HOME LAND"

Zero-One is still recovering. The loss of his left eye has over-turned his life and also brought a major concern to Cuza. He has sworn to take revenge on Papolo, but the aggressor has not been seen by anyone since the morning of the fight. Sometimes Zero-One wanders the area around the house where Papolo's father has an improvised workshop where he offers services to the landowners, owners of defective tractors in need of repair, but he has not managed to see him. The earth has swallowed him. Miguelón pictures him in an area known as Los Cocos, in the outskirts of Santiago, where his maternal grandmother lives, but that hasn't been proven in the neighborhood either.

Cuza sees him leave the house in the dark glasses he wears to hide the cavity left by the absent eye, and no sooner does she see him go out the door than she is on her knees again, but now with her faith damaged by the daily misfortune. Deep down, she fears that by praying so often for the life of Albertico, she is annoying *Bondye,* God.

Beginning Thursday afternoon, a new storm shakes Cuza's mind. The boy didn't come home for the midday meal, even though she made eggplant, for his sake, because she doesn't like that local dish. Neither did he come home to sleep, but Cuza assumed he had stayed overnight at the home of his cousin Antoine, after helping him with a job he accepted—keeping an eye on a shipment of pineapples in a van in the Mercado Nuevo. But he's not there either. The transformations that Albertico's personality undergoes trouble her. Although he doesn't mention the issue, she notes that his face alters when someone says "Zero-One," an allusion to his missing eye. Before, he was accosted with racial attacks over his Haitian origin, although his skin color says mulatto, not the black that is his maternal ancestry. But this new item that generates mockery irritates him in a very particular way. Now he's not "Blackstinky" or "Pitit gason." Now all the town is morbidly focused on his lack of vision, on the physical diminution he has undergone since the day he lost the bet.

Cuza has just returned from the anthill of unemployed laborers who, like Antoine, mill about in search of day work in the stands of the old plaza on Duarte Avenue.

The disappearance of the boy causes her to fall apart. She's turned into a pile of nerves from guessing that Albertico has regained his brave high spirits in search of some new venture. On the last night he was in the hospital, after the fight with Papolo, he met a great "*bacano*," or "gentleman who likes to live high," known locally as Chino de Villas Agrícolas. The bacano was stretched out on a bed next to his, in which they were suturing a wound in the forearm, which, in addition to being painful, seems to have destroyed a tattoo that featured the twin towers in New York. The man couldn't say enough about how much he likes this country, but only for a couple of weeks at a beachside hotel, hanging out with a young girl and then returning to the streets of The Bronx after using up all the dollars he had brought with him. In fact, the bacano's name was really Martín Puello, and, like Zero-One, he had come to Villa Consuelo by chance. His mother had filled out the "papers" after marrying an Italian who was the supervisor at a factory that produced leather jackets for men. Before he was four, his mother took him to her ghastly poverty-ridden apartment in upper Manhattan, but Chino was brought up almost like an orphan. His mother would drop him off at the daycare center at 4:30 in the morning, from where he would be taken to school, and she would come by at 6 to take him home after a day's work. When the mother of Martín aka Chino became aware of the kind of life she was giving the boy, it was too late. A call from the Department of Human Services confirmed her suspicions: Chino was in deep trouble. He had been arrested for aggravated armed robbery, and deportation was only a few months away.

For Zero-One—who didn't know the background of the story Chino recited to each nurse in turn, that man whose good luck runneth over—he seemed the right person to guide him out of the neighborhood. He wanted to go too. To find the way to get the things he dreamed of having: a sports car with chrome hubcaps, jewelry to adorn his naked neck, the purchase of a house for his old lady far from that pigsty, Villa Consuelo, pay for a good doctor who would adapt a prosthesis for his lost eye—in short, to change his life. To leave, to get the hell out any way he could—but above all to come back. To show up in Villa Consuelo with the power to rebuild everything. Return, but not to get drunk in deluxe hotels nor fill up the rented car with young girls. No, to come back with all the money in the world, to ride in a respectable car in the neighborhood, dismount on the corner in front of Pupo's grocery store and let everybody know who exactly this son of Cuza was, the real Zero-One, the same who would not be held back by either misery or the sea.

When Zero-One next got together with the bacano some weeks later, both were firmly determined to embark for Puerto Rico. They were among the last to arrive at the meeting with the man who would command the ship. Chino had a small leather case with a diagonal strap that would keep it attached to his person. Zero-One, on the other hand, stuffed what few items he had in a plastic bag to protect his property from the water. He squatted to pat the sport socks he was wearing, to ascertain in which sock he had placed the money to pay the captain. In the other extremity he had camouflaged a few dollars in case of some emergency.

They trudged in silence on the trail that led to Caletón Beach, where Lolo, the man who had become captain by the seat of his pants and innate talent for navigation, stood surrounded by a multitude of beggarly types, who, like Albertico, were dreaming of departure.

"We can't go today," said the captain, and stood peering at the wide seascape that opened before his small black eyes. The others remained a few paces behind, but it was easy to hear the forced breathing that resulted from having walked a long stretch through shrubs and underbrush. They had arrived after midnight, at that indeterminate time when it was hard to decide whether it was night or day. The roosters crowed without rhyme or reason, and the next day's dew crept up, wetting their feet, having passed stealthily, secretly, through the soles of their shoes.

"Not today, it's better to wait one more day." Lolo's voice could be heard, as if he were saying what was meant for the waves the sea kept bringing to the shore, not to the battalion of paupers who had followed him from the most varied points on the island. Some said they knew him from childhood, when he already gave proof of his skill at swimming both on and under water, and still others swore they had seen him cross the Ozama many times, back when it was a raging torrent, not the slough of mud and weeds it was today. And a number were sure he had never lost a yawl.

Lolo was drawn to the fact that Zero-One had isolated himself. The boy had not asked him, as the others did, how much he charged each passenger. He seemed less interested in the cost than in the reason for the journey. He regarded the boy with pity and asked him, "Why are you leaving?"

Zero-One heard a tone of self-confidence in Lolo's voice that persuaded him to believe that they would succeed. That they would leave the asphyxiating place and reach that other coast, but the captain gave him no time to answer, and instead gave him this advice: "Think about it: this crossing is not easy."

The coast was a clearing between woods and beach. Men from everywhere had come, and although they had not been introducing themselves to each other, one could intuit that it would happen. All you had to do was observe the process by listening to the accents and watch their treatment of each other. Three very light-skinned boys with Cibao accents were discussing the sowing, the impossible agricultural loans, the undervalued sales to the producers, the burning of rice by the government. Two other young men, short and sunburned, talked about the superstitions, the cults of Yemayá, the prayers to the saints to avoid drowning, the devotional rites to avoid death at sea, the travelers who were saved because they wore Virgin del Carmen scapulars, the blessing by one's mother and the vows made to God Himself while weeping.

Two brunettes stayed very close to Lolo, as if protecting themselves from what might come. Chino squatted close, took a second breath and whispered, "Those must be prostitutes. Lolo is letting them travel for free for sure."

The younger of the two, still wearing the lushness of childhood, was clearly in an advanced state of pregnancy, which made that last affirmation unlikely. She spoke of ending the pregnancy in the United States, to have a little *gringo* baby, give birth as God wills, without having to share a bed with two or three women giving birth, to be the mother of an "American citizen" who, in time, would get the rest of them out of this hell of a country. The other spoke only of how much she wanted to join Pancho, the love of her life. He had arrived safely and for a time stayed hidden in the home of cousins in Aguadillas, but later managed to make the big leap and reach the great city. She was determined to find the man she loved. He who had told her he would love her until the end. Pancho, an assistant at a bakery, the son of Bienvenido Guzmán, her life-long boyfriend. But Pancho was now a sad sailor, adrift. He wanted to breathe a different air and became lost at sea, perhaps never to return because she never even tied him to her by bearing him a child to bring him back. When the pregnant one said "Pancho" her voice cracked and let out a flute-like wail, like the soprano of a child courting puberty.

One of the men from El Cibao fussed and fussed over the frustration of the thwarted trip; the other calmed him down, telling him that providence had most likely kept them from drowning. They took him to the rear of the port of Sans Souci, where a second lieutenant with a bad temper pushed them angrily to a cell that sheltered another group that tried leaving the same way and, like them, were taken back to firm land.

"Will you go at it again?" somebody asked amid the confusion, the chorus of lamentations and the mockery of those who also failed to make the previous trip. Another man replied with caution, since the question had been directed to him: "Maybe, but not with these people."

"And you?" asked Chino, addressing Zero-One. "Will you try again?"

"Yes, of course, yes," he said, with resolve, "I'll try again. I'm going with the same captain." Then he added, ". . . the water wasn't even moving the other day . . . when that guy says let's go, boys. God willing, we can go with confidence, secure, with our eyes closed. Lolo never went to school, but he knows how to read the sea."

Chapter Four
MARTÍN IS GONE

Martín Puello succeeded in leaving with the next attempt led by the yawl captain. Once Lolo paid the hefty sum required by M-2, a commander of lower rank spoke on short wave and the remaining subalterns looked the other way while the *Margarita* passed. Zero-One accompanied him to where the beach began and the woods ended, and then said goodbye with a faith he didn't know he possessed. He said he would follow later, and Martín could trust that his friend would catch up with him. That he would find a way to leave once he had the required sum, which back then, was a fortune for a poor person.

Chino did not entirely believe his friend's motive for staying. This was not the same resolute person with whom he had spoken, but neither did he contradict him; friendship required that he respect the other's silence. He offered to lend his friend what Lolo was charging—Lolo had given him a discount to make up for the inconvenience encountered on the previous attempt—but Zero-One refused the offer and embraced his departing friend, wondering privately if he would see him again.

"Give no thought to doubt," his friend assured him firmly, as if to encourage him, but not even that changed his mind.

"Pal, the problem is not the money. My mother is not well, and I am all she has," he said, trying to conceal the true motives that only he could fathom in his heart. He lied with a measure of pain. He hated betraying the trust and the affection of friends, but he did not want to make his friend a participant in older, more profound wounds. The health of one's mother was a more universal reason for anything, and involved less suffering over the intimate grudges that hounded him when he thought of Barahona.

A tear born of impotence threatened to make an appearance at that moment and Zero-One hastened to cover up by embracing his departing friend once again.

The captain of the yawl gave the signal and all the travelers moved in the direction indicated. Zero-One helped, as he had months earlier, to push the yawl out to deeper water, and then swam back to shore. He looked out to the group from terra firma and saw that the yawl was becoming nebulous and vanishing in the distance. A hand rose and moved with some insistence in the come and go of the tide as it grew more forceful, and a second sad hand responded, unwillingly, to that salute that was really another farewell.

Zero-One reached the neighborhood when most of the people were sleeping. He walked silently, feeling such desolation that his chest was like a huge, empty house. The streets were wider below the desert of the night that fell uninhabited. The bulb in the lamppost on Daniel Henriquez Street was the only illumination. To his surprise, the grocery store belonging to Don Pupo, the neighbor from Baní, was open. The merchant had decided to close because of the hour, but some locals who were watching the game between Licey and Escogido had ordered another jug and two Cokes to await the outcome of the match, less than another four innings.

With the streets eclipsed by the dark of night, he removed his dark glasses to become, once again, the *Ti gason* Albertico Durosier, son of Cuza and grandson of Madame Degá. It was restful, when nobody watched him, to live without the affront of being a black one-eyed man, to walk without facing hostility, without fearing the mockery of those who noted first the empty eye socket in his face rather than the eye he still had. He quietly pulled the metal latch that shut the door of the little house and dropped, clothes and all, onto the litter made of flour sacks. He clasped his hands together under the nape of his neck, and while waiting for sleep to visit him, imagined the trip he finally could not make with a touch of nostalgia.

The coolness of the night sped up his fantasy about the trip he didn't take. He saw himself seated behind captain Lolo, making plans with his *pana* as soon as they arrived in "those countries." He could see with great clarity the illuminated signs of the grand avenues that filed by in his mind. He sensed the odors and the humidity of the streets, the racket of the trains carrying factory workers and university students, the music of African Americans on the street corners of Harlem, and he could see himself wearing a frock coat with the sober colors of formal clothes, like those worn by detectives in the movie called "The Streets of San Francisco."

That's how he would have liked to be dressed when passing through the last door at the airport, where Cuza would be waiting for him upon his return to Santo Domingo.

His mother was aware of his entrance to the room, but the day's tiredness had left her no energy with which even to get up and embrace him. While he sank into sleep, she smiled, filled with good humor in the darkness of the room, thanking *Bondye* for his response to her prayer, surviving the shocks from Zero-One and putting off for a few more hours the kiss she would give her son on the following morning.

Chapter Five

WHO WILL LEND ME A TONGUE
WITH WHICH TO SAY IT?

───────────

"All the great cultures have blossomed from forms of
crossbreeding."
Gunter Wilhelm Grass, 1927-2015

Cuza has been humming—though her rhythm is off—a
merengue in the *kompa* style since last night. She doesn't even
know how she came to remember that song; Degá sang it on
those few occasions when she was happy, but she recovers it in
memory, dancing with pleasure in that cloister of a kitchen
where she worked until her death. Sometimes she murmurs the
sticky melody that she believes belonged to Nemours Jean-Bap-
tiste, when he performed with the group called Ensemble aux
Calebasse, or maybe it's one of the *kompa merengues* by Webert
Sicot, but she's not sure. Meanwhile she balances on the sound
of the percussion she imagines, because she has totally forgotten the lyrics and she makes up for the lack of words by moving her shoulders and hips rhythmically.

She goes out to the sidewalk to see the sun, half-hidden behind some clouds; today will be radiant. She squats with her
torso stretched toward the front, blowing forcefully on the
chunks of firewood that will catch fire at any moment, and then

she'll be able to place on it the pot containing the foods she will offer her local customers.

She invested a bit of money that Zero-One gave her, when the trip was canceled, on a variety of root vegetables for the construction workers who mill around in front of the two-story house being built next to hers.

It's been only three days that she's had her own small business, which is modest but important. At first, naturally, her only customers were the Haitians who, like her, had emigrated and perhaps for similar reasons would not return to their place of origin. On the second day, some young men ventured to taste her seasoning and asked for *tostones* with salami for lunch: something both familiar and economical. Later on, some older men joined in, who even announced their favorite dishes and expressed wishes, to see if Cuza would oblige them.

A short mulatto with a shaved head wearing multicolored clothing pushes a tricycle to the very front of the little table where Cuza places her offerings for the day. The menu consists of parboiled plantains, boiled yucca, dumplings with bacalao and a pot of spaghetti. The greengrocer has not yet met the owner of the food stand, but he intuits that she must be very close. She has run to the kitchen to fetch the salt for the fried eggs, and on the way tells her son to come out and give her a hand so as not to leave anything unattended.

"Merchant, here is the man who brings the food," says the newly arrived vendor, in Spanish under stress because of the speaker's difficulty with pronunciation. And he adds, after a pause, to make his claims as clear as possible, "Today I have yucca, avocado, good carrots, plantains and white ñame."

"*¡Mesi anpil fre!* Thanks, dear friend!" she replies, with a smile as white and magnificent as her son's. The vendor smiles, and his face lights up with pleasure. He had not noticed Cuza's looks and assumed she was a Dominican mulatta, with curly hair and prominent hips. Now, recognizing her as Haitian, he switches the announcement of his merchandise, and improves it with the confidence he gains in his own language: "*Cheri . . . Mwen gen bannann, yucca, zaboca, kawot, yanm. Tout bagay pou ou.*"

Cuza hands him a few coins, which the salesman thanks her for, more with his gaze than with words. He smiles at her again and kisses the metal disks, offering them to the sky, to convey that they are his first sale of the day.

Zero-One watches him climb on his tricycle and pedal with enthusiasm, under the bright light of an ineffable joy. It surprises him that joy should be so costly for some and so easily acquired by others. It moves him that the smile of the greengrocer is the result of a few coins that won't go very far, the tone of his mother and a few words he may not grasp fully because he doesn't master creole.

Maybe that happy black man pushing the tricycle has had far fewer opportunities than he himself has been given. He notes the salesman's clothes, which are clean but tattered, the cap announcing support for a candidate the wearer probably doesn't even know, but which shields him from the merciless climate of the Antilles, rubber boots handy in the fickle Caribbean weather, hands calloused from cutting the grass and on one side of the tricycle a small tricolor flag without shields or mottoes, but symbolic of the place he's from.

Zero-One watches him ride into the distance and silently compares himself to that poor man who demonstrated unreservedly the awards of legitimate joy. He approaches his mother to hold her close, surprising her customers—and her—with inexpressible feelings.

He embraces her warmly, as if trying to pay a debt of affection contracted with her for her devotion and love. Then he looks at the greengrocer again, who, wearing the same expression as before, offers another client his supply of food from the market.

He has a sudden enormous impulse to run and embrace that man who has no hope of achieving prosperity, but holds such a courageous attitude toward life. He wants to tell him that a few minutes in his presence has returned to him the desire to confront whatever might await him. To tell him, "Thank you, brother, for pointing out the way," but he is frozen in place knowing he cannot say so in his own language. He becomes rigid with shame because he cannot speak to the other in the language of their shared heritage. Again, he feels even poorer than before over the devastating truth that although he is Haitian, son of Cuza and grandson of Degá, he cannot say in creole, "A man's smile has taught me the way."

Cuza watches him from the side and goes back to the *kompa* that charmed her the night before, but now she recalls the lyrics to the song, "Mal de Amor," and can sing it with her lips and hips at once.

Chapter 6

THE ART OF WEARING THE MASK

Being born in Barahona in the Jaime Mota Hospital did not entitle Albertico to call himself a Dominican citizen under the law. That would have required birth in some eastern part of the island, and would need to be proved on every occasion. One had to be more Dominican than any other, in all aspects of life, as much in the house as in the woods, which sometimes replaced the street. It was always so, as it was when, trying to get to school on time, one had to stop in the middle of the street out of respect for the Dominican National Anthem by José Reyes and Emilio Prud'Homme, which was sent loudly into the air at seven-fifty every morning by the school principal, who had installed a loudspeaker on the second floor for that purpose.

Yes, you had to stand at attention out of respect, as your mother reminded you to do every day, although lateness to the earliest class, taught by the mathematics teacher Clotilde Andujar, entailed the denial of recess as punishment. He proved his Dominicanhood unreservedly when, during the carnival festivities that followed Lent, he trailed after the costumed devils down whatever lane they chose to Dr. Delgado Street, took a left there to Independence Street, then to the Malecón beside the sea wall, and there he danced with abandon while no one watched him, just one more member of the crowd beside the blue strip of the Caribbean.

He was undoubtedly from that part of the island when he danced *bachatas* with the natural beat to those born on the east side of the Massacre River or while enjoying the *merengue* with the same swing as the people from the Cibao Valley, who also called it *"perico ripiao."* He was pure Dominican, although in school he was "the screwed-up Haitian," or "the Congo stinker" when, later, while playing basketball, his armpits proved that he had entered puberty.

For Zero-One it was not easy being the same all the time. He carried on his shoulders the double obligation of a fragmented identity and the power to demonstrate who he really was. In front of Cuza and those few friends who visited them from time to time, he had to be as Haitian as the imitative paintings sold on the sidewalks of Mella Avenue, in front of the Model Market, as creole as Jacques Stephan Alexis and Jacques Roumain had been, but above all, he had to sense the moment when he had to wear the right mask to please others.

He had to like the Christmas pig roasted on a spit and later eaten with baguettes, but also please his mother, who had already cooked, with a great deal of trouble, the traditional Griot, the *Gombo con pesé banan* and the *joumou* made with yellow calabash, just like the ones prepared by his ancestors to celebrate their liberation from the yoke of the French on what was then their colony.

Neither Cuza nor anyone else imagined how hard it was to be two people at the same time. Dance, until fatigue set in, the Christmas *merengues* of Johnny Ventura, and gracefully shake when some friend of Cuza managed to bring a tape of *kompa* like those they used to listen to over on the other side of the border. Zero-One was inebriated by the sensation of being two people. A smile would appear, and outsiders would never imagine that what had been a sharp, persistent pain had suddenly become a pleasure disguised as a bell clapper. He would go to the left, and need to sound like *pitit gason* without question, like a Nigerian drum at the celebration of *gagá*. But he also had the obligation to revert with the same force in the opposite direction, swing toward the right to make his Dominican sound free of half-tints and warmth, the Quisqueyan sound of those drums made with the skins of two different goats. He was threatened by the double fate of having to be the whole person in both places; clapper of that one bell that was his daily life.

That bifurcation of his origin always kept him on the defensive in school. He attended the morning session of the lyceum, which bore the name of the founding father of the Dominican nation, but for some reason that Zero-One could not fathom some of the boys in the neighborhood who attended the night session, when asked where they went to school, would identify it as the Miguel Ángel Garrido school. It took him a long time to understand that both schools occupied the same rigid location with its marble stairs, its carved caoba banisters with balusters lathed by expert woodworkers and high ceilings of a soft white faded by time alongside vertical blinds made of aluminum resistant to the passage of time. The two educational centers were merged into one, since they offered two faces of the same past, but since it was neither Miguel Ángel Garrido nor Juan Pablo Duarte, instead it was made to honor the tyrant of San Cristóbal; it was baptized the President Trujillo Teacher Training School for Boys.

The same sanitary facilities and washrooms for both sessions, the same rows of rickety desks where amorous students hid their names on the backs of seats in hopes of allowing love to survive in the wood fiber, perhaps far beyond student life.

Zero-One couldn't understand why the school had had different names in the short span of a few hours. Didn't both sessions share the same lush almond tree out front, just to the right of the metal tube that served as the flagpole, the place where they lined up to enter the building every morning?

Why call them by different names if they share the Gina tree next to the wall that divided the old building from the playroom of the Training School, where there was also a coliseum for boxing and wrestling events?

Maybe the two schools that worked in the one building enacted the duality of a personality like the one that was his fate. He tried to reason through the doubt. Just as some attended secondary school in the Juan Pablo Duarte Lyceum, while others, barely out of this group, crowded into the Miguel Ángel Garrido night school. The son of Cuza, like the lyceum, faced a double life each day.

He entered the neighborhood certain that he would be two injured boys. He greeted the "Big Guys" who, as always, were talking baseball on the school sidewalk in front of Pupo's grocery, and up to that moment of the day he was still "the real" Zero-One. However, a few seconds at most, the fast-walking Dominican mulatto with the incisive gaze and the broad smile would vanish. The little black boy he had been outside would reincarnate. He would enter his house as one finding refuge after a rough battle. He would open the curtain that separated the little living room of the tiny house and the bedroom he shared with his mother, and as soon as he saw Cuza going about her daily chores, he would cease to be that phantom who removed one mask to put on another. He was transformed into *pitit* Alberto Durosier, grandson of Grandma Degá, bastard son of a stranger who had his same name.

Chapter Seven
Solving the Puzzle

Cuza is no longer the same as she was a few weeks ago. She has lost the wide smile that stretched her very red lips when she offered an illuminated window with the very white, very perfect teeth she's always had. The customers who buy the food she offers daily and the vendors who leave her their offering and return later for payment have noticed that Cuza no longer laughs. She doesn't hum between her teeth the old *merengues* from the other part of the island that she left behind. Neither does she try to dance. She walks in her own atmosphere, as if drunk with some feeling that dulls her sense. She goes from the alley to the sidewalk, from the kitchen door to the space that serves as living room. She barely walks from the little house to Pupo's grocery, trying to see if her boy is back in the neighborhood.

It's been eight days since she last embraced him. Since she heard his voice, that voice that is rough when he speaks to others but is a stream of water that eases her soul. A sound that becomes a song, at least for her, and no other sound exists that gives her back peace and promises happiness like when her boy calls her *Maman*.

Her countryman Antoine told her that he saw him working with a team of masons on a building they're putting up on Paraguay Street, in Máximo Gómez Avenue. He's sure it was him, although he was many meters away. "Yes, sister, it was your boy," he's said effusively, and Cuza doesn't let him finish before running off like a windstorm in the direction he's indicated. But Albertico is not among those who assist cement mixers, whose faces all look alike under the layers of dust that cling to them. She's climbed some rudimentary stairs to see if she'll find him among the beam layers who are squatting two floors up, but they're all over thirty. She goes back to the first floor and checks the young men who shape the inner walls of the structure, and asks them in a slow creole and a choppy Spanish, but receives the same answer: "No, madame, we're very sorry, but we don't know him."

She returns home even more remorseful than before. Nothing comforts her out of this hopelessness and everything conspires to increase her suffering. Miguelón, who—thank God—has luckily run into her, is the only one who offered a ray of hope to Cuza'a tormented soul. He says he saw Albertico in the New Market area of Duarte Avenue, and that calms the agony that is consuming the mother. As she walks toward the market, she thinks that maybe he wants to sell coconuts or root vegetables and start his own business with the few pesos he has saved. Maybe he's rented a tricycle, as Antoine did a few months ago, and has decided to sell yucca and avocados to the neighbors around Villa Consuelo. She shakes her head as if to say no, trying with that brusque gesture to remove from her mind an image that comes back to injure her. She tries not to think the worst, but like a flood of hurt, the memories return of that night she saw Albertico strewn on the ground, bleeding from one side of his face, in the darkness of the street.

The owner of the truck, who delivers root vegetables from the locales in the south to the capital has told Cuza words that have returned her soul to her body.

"Yes, Doña, he was here. But he's already left," he says, sipping Presidente from the bottle. And he adds, "I've just hired him. Seems like a good worker, I hope he turns out to be one, but one thing's for sure: if he's a *mane* I'll split him in four. Tell him that good and clear!"

Cuza hasn't heard a word of the stream of warnings from the trucker, she wants him to stop so she can keep looking for her boy. She hasn't even asked what kind of work he's going to be doing for this man or what his pay will be, or if his life will be in danger on the job. She leaves in great haste toward the neighborhood without saying goodbye to the man who has given her the news that her son is well and has a job. She gets home when it begins to turn into night. From afar, she sees the light that twinkles through cracks in the wooden fence that forms a wall to the street. The joy has not yet reached her heart, knowing that he's alive *and* in the house.

"*Muchacho*, you're going to kill me from anxiety," she says, her legs still trembling from the long and fast walk, and also from the tense nerves that have kept assaulting her chest. "And what's this about your going to work for a trucker?"

After embracing her and without denying the recriminations of his mother, he asks for forgiveness for taking off without telling her anything. He says, "Yes, Ma, that's how it is. He offered me good pay, three meals and a place to sleep for delivering and unloading the trucks in Tamaya and Barahona. I have to take them to the tables at the market." He smiles triumphantly. His breast swells; he feels more adult than he really is, and softens the news that has displeased Cuza with one more highlight: "He also says he can give me a load of plantains or bananas at a better price so I can resell them and earn more money."

"But . . . what about school? Aren't you planning to study? Are you going to end up like me, dammit, with no future to wait for and no past worth telling? Don't tell me you're planning to be a poor vendor of plantains all your life. I can be a cook until I die, because I took no other route to get ahead, but you! Nobody is hunting for you, no government wants to kill you for what you think. Look at you, you don't deserve that! You were born to be something more than a poor black man shouting from house to house selling your youth and at the end of the story become the same as all those others who came before, those who crossed the Massacre River to leave their lives in the cane field or dying on a farm, old and broken down, after working for a few pesos that won't be enough even to treat the tuberculosis that for sure will kill them all."

"No, Ma, I'm not going to end up like them. Just give me a few more months to achieve some things, and I promise you, by *Bondye*, that I'll go back to school." Cuza regards him with compassion, between tenderness and reproach.

"Yes, Ma, believe me, I'm not going to fail; I know how much you've suffered and how much you've sacrificed. I only need a little time; have faith in me and in what I do." In truth she wanted to believe him, because she understood that she was approaching the moment when she would let him go, give him an opportunity, but her maternal heart resisted.

She embraces him gently to see if the caress can do what her words have not. She tries to be tender so he won't leave. So he will stay in school, not leave the neighborhood, not leave home for so long. A thought that hammers at her mind has overwhelmed her ever since the conversation with the trucker who is employing Zero-One.

She looks at the boy. Fear invades her mind and bruises her body, which is troubled simply anticipating what could happen. "*Muchacho*," she says, and tries to choose her words precisely so as not to stir too wildly the hornet's nest she foresees. "Do you know if your employer has other routes to sell plantains that aren't so close to the capital?"

"Yes, he does," he says cheerfully, as if assuming himself already an employee with responsibilities. "He makes some trips bringing bananas from Valverde Mao and Monte Cristi to San Cristóbal, and twice a week he takes trucks of plantains to San Pedro de Macorís and La Romana."

"Well then, you should have chosen one of those routes," says the anguished voice of the mother, as if she could point out a way that would keep him from encountering the ghosts that torment her.

"No, Ma," replies Zero-One, "the boss offered me the same kind of work and the same pay for any of the places I preferred to work in. But I was the one who chose to go to that city."

"Go back, my son! Go to him and ask him to assign you another route . . . tell him that you've changed your mind, that you hadn't thought it through, that you made a mistake and you're not going to the south . . . that you want to work on the route to San Pedro or La Romana."

Cuza's words fall drop by drop like a prayer. It should be an order, but she knows this is a push and pull situation. Zero-One looks at her with grief in his eyes, thinks about the options he considered when he chose the work he asked for and fires a reply: "I'm going to Barahona not only for the plantains to sell, Ma. I'm also interested in finding the pieces that are missing from my past. I want to see the face—even if it's only for a few seconds—of the youngest of the Mendoza brothers."

Cuza falls unto a chair that creaks under the weight of her collapse. The slight happiness that had reached her with the return of the boy is snuffed out. She rises, tries to keep herself busy so as not to think, to silence the voices she hears in the depths of herself. For the first time in years, she doesn't know what to do with her trembling and sweaty hands. Her face has become distorted. She has the look of shock and heaviness she had when the Leyland truck threw her possessions on the sidewalk, the day she arrived in Villa Consuelo.

Chapter Eight

THE DRUM AND THE BLOOD

The neighborhood is deserted. The silence that covers the city for the moment has transformed the atmosphere of Villa Consuelo into a series of little houses laid out erratically on the sinuosity of narrow streets. Everything seems drowsy under the heavy dullness of the hours and the Caribbean sun. This is the calm Ash Wednesday brings, which awaits an even deeper quietness beginning Thursday. All this will surely end at dawn on Monday, when homes and people return to normalcy.

Many of the neighbors have taken advantage of these days to visit the interior of the country, where relatives live who almost never come to the capital. Others return to towns they came from, if only to learn that their generation is dying and few remain from the original group that founded the community they abandoned in order to come to the Distrito Nacional in search of a better life.

The youngest choose something more in keeping with their contemporary tastes and set out to enjoy the holiday. As always, they face rejection from their parents and the disapproval of elders who adhere to the church's mandate and never depart from spiritual withdrawal and absolute tranquility. But youth has always been rebellious and always will be. That is its natural, essential right, its unique prerogative granted by time. To be rebellious is its own reason for being, at least for the duration of that divine madness, the young years.

They're young precisely to oppose everything, since they have more than enough time for regret. Therefore they go, against all orders and without regret, to dive into the waters of the island's southeast. There, the young rebel as their nature demands, in full defiance of what has been imposed on them as the norm. They frequent feasts and drinking parties with an energy that bewitches them, pushing them to celebrate love with the beloved of the moment, or to court the next one. Precisely a year later they will revindicate the anniversary of that day with another spree on the banks of another river that will welcome them.

Cuza also pauses during that week and sets out to celebrate the passage from death to life, as do the followers of the European religion. She invited Zero-One to a celebration, but he said he doesn't want to go anywhere. He ends up accepting but is not interested in what she tells him he will see.

"Where are we going?" asks Albertico. His words convey as much indifference as lack of interest and rejection.

"I want you to accompany me to visit a sugar mill near a place called Guerra." She replies with less joy than at first; Albertico has taken the edge off her desire to make the trip. She also knows that this coming experience may help him know his roots. It was precisely there that many years ago thousands of Haitians arrived to harvest the sugar cane, and she remembers that one of her father's brothers labored at the Central Ozama mill. She herself always returns to the sugar mills of San Luis, Los Llanos and San Pedro de Macorís, where hundreds of emigrants are housed, and where every year they gather there during the feast of Lent.

The minibus that transported them took them only as far as the meeting of four roads, leaving them at the entrance to the mill. It looked like a shortcut rather than a real road toward the settlement. Zero-One followed two steps behind her, using his left hand to stop any leaf of the grain from getting too close to his face. *That could be fatal, given his disability, because if it were to enter his one eye it could result in total blindness.* Cuza goes before him, clearing the way with both hands to prevent that from happening. Every so often, she stops a moment and pauses to listen to her instinct and the still-distant drums, so as not to lose the way to the celebration. She sharpens her hearing, tells him to be still for a moment, then takes the more traveled route, which is surely the one that will lead them to the mill after the Caleta. She's not too sure if this year the *gagá* celebration will be held where it says "Enjuagador" and then past Hato Viejo or the community of La Joya. Last year, she went only to Mata de Palma for lack of time to get to the *gagá* at Andrés, and then it became too late to dance at the community known as El Toro.

The rhythmical sound seems to be getting louder as the distance decreases. The beat of the *batá* drums crosses the cane fields and makes Zero-One think it is much louder. He doesn't hide the timid smile that breaks through as the sound begins to entrance him. The growing sound of the *yom* invites Cuza to move her waist, but that's only a rehearsal for what follows. The catharsis occurs when they approach the maracas, and her blood and the wind instrument called the "fotuto" join before the dancers, and all of it pours into the rhythm and the cadence of hips that stall between sweating and dancing.

A multicolor circle occupies the little park known as Hato Viejo. A beehive of boys and girls dancing with complete abandon goes first into the center of the ceremony, which has begun. Cuza pulls vehemently on Zero-One, who is looking about in all directions, as if searching for something that is inside him that he has been unsure of. The boy's one eye enlarges, as opposed to Cuza's inward look, which follows the music. She lets herself flow into the melody and her childhood along with it. She revisits how her mother used to take her to Batey Central during Holy Week and how she taught her the way to move her waist and shoulders to perform the dance, the joy of the rite that delights body and soul.

The elderly women dance and sing with solemnity. They wear white and cover their heads with small yellow and black handkerchiefs. The adolescents move with more eroticism and their contortions attract boys of their own age to pair up in a dance that may go on to include amatory gestures. An aged man wearing a cardboard crown adorned with shiny dust carries a cane that serves as a leader's baton. When he lifts it, the music stops and everyone listens reverently to what he says to the deities; when he lowers his cane, the music resumes, in the same place as when it halted. The group that sponsored the festival seems to have a special petition for someone very young. Yellow prevails, and that is the case when the petition involves the health of a child or newborn. The religious majesty of the occasion goes in tandem with the carnival-like celebration. It's a dual world in which one both entreats the saint with a promise to worship and also delights the flesh with the motion of bodies and the recently distilled cleren, which lifts the mind toward paroxysm and clears the throats that will sing hymns to enhance the performances of the masqueraders.

Those not participating in the celebration watch from the front windows of their homes so as not to miss the precise moment when the *gagá* leaves the *batey*, where the sugar mill's personnel reside. Some lament that they cannot follow it as the multitude crosses the shortcut and takes up the pebble trail that leads to the next neighboring town. At the head is the spiritual chief, known as the King or Master. Beside him the Queen, who moves like a serpent and dances continuously. She is a very young woman, moves with grace. She is followed by the musicians and a dozen members known as believers and dancers. Zero-One watches the celebration as if his life depended on it. The musicians speak in correct Spanish, and only a few of the dancers have said anything in creole. Maybe the celebration came from there, he thinks, a daughter of the Haitians who came during the beginnings of the sugar industry, but born in the Dominican *bateyes* of the south and east. He imagines that the *gagá* is from there and from here at the same time, like him. And that its origin hardly matters compared with the magnitude of the joy that overflows from the rite of the drum and the dance.

He looks at Cuza, who is dancing with a happiness he did not know existed in her. He watches her with amazement, noticing that around her throat she is wearing half a dozen handkerchiefs given to her by the musicians who have seen her at the *batey*, year after year, during the last decade. He approaches her to dance with her, imitating the step that she keeps up, although she is not young. They look like two children who have discovered a new game; he strokes her hair with a loving gesture, and tells her with a jubilant air, "Ma, thanks for bringing me! You know I didn't want to come, but the truth is, it's marvelous being here!"

Cuza embraces him with ineffable tenderness, and while kissing him whispers into his ear, *"Byenveni nan kay gason.*Welcome home, son.*"* She hugs him against her chest, where pride and happiness accelerate the rhythm of her heartbeat. She smiles sweetly and murmurs in a slow Spanish, *"Bienvenido a casa."*

Chapter Nine
THE POOR MAN'S I.D.

Don Patricio's Mercedes Benz truck leaves the La Aurora farm before five in the morning on Thursday, July 15. It had been loaded the night before, but a personal matter affecting the owner prevented its departure on the scheduled date, so the farmworkers, including the foreman and the two stevedores, who loaded and unloaded the merchandise spent their time sleeping and waking, and waiting for the boss.

The foreman, a short man with slanted eyes and very straight black hair, hoped to remove all blame from the delay of the day's work by alleging that the matter involved a sick member of the family, but one of the sowers on the farm—thanks to some alcohol he had imbibed—said, loudly enough to be heard by all, "The boss' sickness can't be cured with aspirin or menthol. What that man has is a male fever he's been suffering with for a couple of months now, and the sick family member he refers to is a little peahen not yet twenty, a pretty little thing who's got him spinning out of his mind and pulling stunts."

They all paid attention, with a degree of surprise, to the swift candor of what had been revealed by the farmworker. He was the oldest member of the group. When sober, he was a very quiet person given to slow gestures and a tendency to solitude or isolation. But he could not deal with alcohol. A single drop of rum dismantled that parsimonious character and transformed him into a gossip, a teller of spicy stories and a man likely to offer women corrosive compliments. Drinking also changed his reserved gaze; his eyes acquired a brilliant flash. After imbibing three fingers of Brugal rum he was a very different man all together.

Some laughed heartily over the wit of the news reported by the oldest employee, but the more recently hired feared celebrating high-biting humor and chose to pretend not to understand it, so as to avoid finding themselves out of work.

When Don Patricio returned someone had to awaken one of the stevedores, who was sleeping face down on one of the big boxes used as beds on the ground. The boy had been overtaken by the drowsiness of fatigue, hunger and the boredom of waiting. They all noticed the disheveled condition of their employer, but nobody had the courage to repeat the alleged reason for the delay of the trip, much less comment on the wrinkled clothing and disordered hair of Don Patricio when he returned from his visit to his supposedly bedridden relative.

The distance from the farm entrance to the market area took a bit more than four hours. Traffic was no heavier than usual, but Don Patricio had a sudden attack of vomiting and convulsions, perhaps due to alcoholic intoxication, and that called for a halt to the journey when they reached Azua de Compostela. Some looked at the boss with a touch of mockery and even some laughter, but noting that the stomach problem was serious they went from sarcasm to sincere concern for the man, who seemed about to throw his soul out through his mouth.

Albertico was seated in the rear of the truck, with his back to the road. He just watched the landscape fly past, marveling at the greenness that rose up on each side of the road. Children playing on the roadside shouted names at the workers alluding to their skin color, the dimensions of their noses and the gross proportion of their lips.

For lack of some better way to respond, Zero-One answered by making obscene facial gestures and throwing orange peels and bits of tender guava at them. Later he saw them from afar, when they reverted to being good children playing at the edge of the poor southern path. He watched them exude a cheerfulness that did not seem to be aware of their poverty. He drew near the palm bark that served as walls for the ill-made huts and offered a clean smile to the strangers who burst into the solitude of the road. He had a yen to get out of the truck to play with them. He watched them pushing an ancient tire, pretending that they, too, were drivers. Observing the precarious pleasure of those children, he himself returned to a childhood and waited anxiously to encounter another group of children to shout at them the nicknames they had screamed out to him.

They had barely reached the capital when the truck was unloaded, but only by half, as there was not enough room in the stalls of Mercado Nuevo. Don Patricio put off unloading the remaining merchandise for the next day, because Albertico was overwhelmed with fatigue and the other carrier, now advanced in age, was too frail to do a good job.

They obeyed the orders of the boss as if they were two robots, and sometimes didn't even wait for orders and instead fulfilled the demands of the peddlers, who, when they saw the truck, cried out loudly the order they had already agreed on with Don Patricio.

"Hey, you, darkie, it's my turn. Leave a thousand big plantains at house number four—the little one; I already paid Don Patricio." The merchant's shout could be heard all over the neighborhood, calling attention to that toothless man whose wavy gray hair contrasted strongly with his very black, very disorderly mustache.

They had just unloaded the last order when an obese lady with a baritone voice called out, "*Gason,* give me two thousand, bananas and plantains—but they must be from Barahona; if they're not from there I don't want them. If you have white *name,* leave me an order of five hundred—or five hundred and half—and tell me what I owe."

When they unloaded that last load and spread the heavy canvas to cover the merchandise, Don Patricio signaled for all of them to gather around the armchair where he drank sips of a bitter soda to calm his upset stomach.

He was passing around a little roll of bills in a rubber band, having already identified it with the workers' names. They were arranged in the order in which he called them to collect their pay. Albertico was the last to walk off with his money. When Don Patricio handed him his bills, the boy smiled weakly, too tired to demonstrate his joy over receiving his day's pay.

"Good work, young man. We'll get together the day after tomorrow to make another trip I've already been paid for." Don Patricio sounded enthusiastic and cheerful, as if recovered from the mishap to his health the night before. Albertico nodded, and added with gratitude, "Yes, I'll be here, just as you say. Thanks, Don Patricio."

He walked toward his neighborhood with a certain air of pride. He would be home early and Cuza perhaps had not yet sold all the food to the greengrocers who tend to gather around, hungry, looking for the traditional dishes she prepared. He should have stopped on the way somewhere to buy her a dress, or sandals, to spoil her with his first salary, but the yearning to see her, as well as his fatigue, made that impossible. He thought that Saturday would be a good day to go with her so she could try on her new clothes right in the store. Maybe Sunday would be even better because she didn't work that day, and, together, they could go to buy the dress and whatever else she might need.

As he was approaching Duarte Avenue, right where it crosses Barney Morgan Street, a Brigade of the National Army ordered him to stop for an impromptu roundup. Ostensibly checking for identity papers, they confiscated knives or guns or maybe some electric home appliance not accompanied by a sales slip.

They weren't really after identification or weapons or the source of confiscated items. They were after the few pesos that pedestrians might be carrying, and hoping that fear would persuade them to hand those over in order to avoid being arrested, or beaten up in the worst case.

"Search him carefully . . . that one looks suspicious to me!" a sergeant said angrily, in a hoarse voice and unfriendly face. He had a nervous, convulsive tic that drove his hand to his gun holster every ten seconds. His grotesque appearance may have been due to the obesity accompanied by his lack of height and the oversized clothes he wore. The sergeant issued orders indistinctly with both his voice and his hands, and some squalid, beardless rookies rushed to obey them.

"What's your name, darkie?"

He tried to stay calm. He knew he had to be still. Common sense told him to count his words and say only what was necessary. The order to search him had been issued in a sing-song voice, but the man had an impenetrable face, as if he were a concrete wall capable of speaking.

"Alberto Durosier. My name is Alberto Durosier, sir," Zero-One said, guardedly.

He emphasized his first name, trying to draw attention away from his foreign last name. The corporal didn't even really listen to his name. He was more interested in the other questions to be asked in order to complete the prepared ritual and get to the bite, the real purpose of the investigation.

"Give me your I.D. . . . . Where are you coming from now?"

The soldier went on with his work, like a robot programmed to ask questions. He waited for the proof of identity and paid no attention at first. He noted slyly how other young men had been detained for identical reasons and questioned by other members of the squad with the same diatribes with which inquisitions are carried on.

"I have no I.D. yet, sir, because I'm a minor . . . I've been working at the market. My boss is named Don Patricio."

He began to sweat, although the temperature was cool. His voice trembled a bit over the uncertainty of what might happen to him. His weariness after a day's work now vanished and was replaced by growing fear, and his sleepiness had gone while his heart raced madly in his chest.

Albertico thrusted his hand in his front pants pocket and drew out a few bills that he had separated from the rest of his day's pay. He wanted to give the larger portion to Cuza so she could save it, and with what he had separated he planned to buy some fried snacks and enjoy a little fun with his few friends. He showed the singles to the corporal to prove that he was a working man, but hoping that the poverty of the soldier would lead to a chance for an accord.

"Look, chief!" he said, showing the bills as if they were making a contract. "I'm telling you the truth, I've just come from working for twelve hours at the market."

The soldier reached with his right hand without looking him in the face and closed his fist around the three pesos with unusual speed, trying to avoid being seen by other members of the patrol, who were engaged in the same work.

"Go, *piti!* Go quickly, and don't look back," he said faking an authority he didn't have. When Albertico was about ten meters away, he opened his fist, counted the money again and said to himself, "Black boy, it was only three pesos. Not much, but that's as much as your proof of identity requires."

Chapter Ten

The Peon and the Queen

"This obsessive heart that is disconnected from my tongue
and my habits, and is bitten by feelings like grappling irons."
León Laleau, 1892-1979

Don Patricio looks very angry. He slammed his hands on
the little table that serves as a desk, and tens of pending invoices
have flown away, but he hasn't even bothered to pick them up.
He notes carelessly the surrounding that is his office, which he
sometimes feels becomes a cell that imprisons his wandering
spirit. He looks over his shoulder at the receipts, still unpaid,
that rise, twirl and fall, like torn paper tossed into the air by
some child.

He's given his work, to supply merchandise to a new business that's hired him, but he still doesn't have the necessary
workers to load and unload the goods. It's not all their fault. The
order reached him on Sunday night, and in such a short time
he's been unable to put together a team to handle the delivery.

One of the peons fractured his wrist and forearm when he
fell off a motorcycle on a return trip from the south, where he
had gone to see his parents.

"He's alive by pure luck," they told him when he called, furious, asking about his absent worker, swearing.

Another of his steady workers asked for permission to leave for a few days and still has not returned. He said, to justify his three-day absence, that he had been chosen to be the best man at the wedding of his youngest sister living in El Cercado, and could not refuse such a request. Don Patricio has no complaints on them. They're good workers who throw themselves into the tasks asked of them, so he's not angry. They have very valid reasons for their absence, and this was an unforseen order.

The worker's accident was genuine; he went to see for himself. Without any warning, he showed up in the little room where the poor man lived, and could barely recognize him. The wretched man had, beside the two fractures, a great swelling of the head, and a scrape, still bleeding, that covered the entire left side of his face. Only a miracle had prevented the loss of an eye or several teeth.

"Come back when you're better," he said in a friendly tone and with genuine concern.

He put some rolled-up bills on the little pine table, gave the injured man another glance and left with a wave of the hand and a nod. By the time Don Patricio disappeared through the tin door that opened to the main street, the accident victim had already counted the gift with certain joy and, gazing at the sky, crossed himself without putting down the pesos, which, to him, were unexpected mana under such circumstances.

The only one left to speak to was Zero-One. Don Patricio had not heard from him since the last delivery to the Mercado Nuevo on Duarte Avenue, and he wanted to be sure he could be counted on for help with the rush delivery of plantains. While he headed for Villa Consuelo, he wondered if maybe the pay had not been enough for the boy, and he no longer wanted the work. Young people have flighty temperaments, and can easily choose to leave a job and find some other occupation, or simply live the lazy way, waiting for luck to rain down on them from the sky. He also thought that maybe the pay was enough but the work was too strenuous for an adolescent without children or a wife, nor any other urgent need to work for a living.

When he thinks of Albertico he sees himself and remembers his hard initiation into the role of peon on a farm. What it cost him to leave the ramshackle bed at four-thirty in the morning—dawn—to oversee the La Gloria farm, owned by Don Anselmo Valdez, before he dedicated himself to politics and become the richest landowner in the whole town of Pimentel. It was a job for a hardened man, not for the sickly creature he was then, when it was his duty to inspect, from head to tail, long before the sun rose in the east, the installations on that land whose thousands of divisions were circled with barbed wire. Days without rest on those interminable rambles for a boy just rounding his fourteenth year: out looking for the best cows for the first milking, clearing the plantings where the plantain rootstocks grew, so the plants would reach maturity, clean and even. Bringing on the mule's back five-hundred pound loads of cacao and setting them to dry on the sheds, on the flat surfaces of masonry. Picking the ripe coffee so the good selection led to plentiful sales. Filling the pig nurseries to fatten them. Feeding the workhorses, then bathing and combing the manes of the saddle horses. Cleaning the gates of the cock roosts and gathering the eggs of the quality hens, and finally breathing deep when free to leave the farm, or when he was sent to town on an errand on condition that he return before sundown.

He leaves behind the reverie of memory and realizes that he's lost the address of the place where he took his worker home some weeks before. He's come to the neighborhood alone and doesn't recognize these houses that all look the same to him. Neither does he recognize the businesses, the mix of bars and grocery stores, sounds of an extremely loud *bachata* playing the voices of Luis Segura and Leonardo Paniagua. He stops the truck to make sure he's going in the right direction.

"Listen, brother!" he shouts, greeting with a wave of his hand. "Do you know where a young man by the name of Albertico lives?" Thinking that more information may be necessary, he adds that the boy is dark skinned and is missing one eye.

The stranger wonders if he should share Zero-One's address with an unknown person who's come to town asking questions. He hesitates, but Don Patricio's look of wealth suggests that he may be looking for the boy for a good purpose.

"Don, I think you're looking for the son of Cuza, the Haitian woman who sells food on the corner of Seventh Street and Daniel Henriquez."

Don Patricio stares at him, more confused than before. He recalls that Albertico mentioned his mother's little food business, and the name "Cuza" sounds familiar, but he doesn't believe this is the person he's looking for.

"Thanks for the help, friend. But the boy I'm looking for is not Haitian."

"If I were you, I would look in at house firty-nine on this same street, behind the little house with two doors that's painted blue and white. Maybe the person you're looking for isn't Haitian, but his mother may be. You never know."

Don Patricio steps lightly on the accelerator while arranging his thoughts. He turns left on Máximo Grullón Street and lets himself be distracted by the smell of fresh-baked bread from the Vinicia bakery. He crosses La Guardia Street, takes a left toward Marcos Ruiz, goes three corners, passes the Hora Buena Hotel, takes Manuel Ubaldo Gómez to where it ends and returns at Seventh Street, but from its beginning. He stops at the number indicated to him five minutes before and sees, at the end of an alley, a woman peeling an enormous pile of plantains in front of a cauldron. He sees a blue and orange flame from a rustic burner made of a grayish metal.

"*Bonjou, madame.* I'm Patricio, owner of the stand at the market. Do you remember me?" he says. Now he knows that Albertico and the son of the Haitian are the same person.

"*Bonjou, mesye*," she replies, removing the apron she wears to avoid staining her clothes.

"I'm looking for your son," says Don Patricio, observing Cuza's huge black eyes. He speaks in pure Spanish, as if to signal that the conversation would be carried out in his language. Cuza understands. She makes an effort to pronounce her words clearly and precisely, since she knows that she is at a disadvantage using a language other than native creole. She is already used to speaking slowly, repeating what she says more than once and even being told that she is not being understood, as if it were a reproach.

"He is not here now," she replies. "Can I help you?"

"Please tell him that he should go to the market as soon as possible. To look for me among the merchants who own the stands or in the administration office. I'm waiting for him to help me with an urgent delivery I need to make this same week. Tell him not to delay and to show up in work clothes. Ah, yes, one more thing: don't worry about him, madam. I'm going to pay him very well. I will also feed him and bring him home."

"Please . . . *mesye* Patricio . . . after this trip wait a few months after giving Albertico more work. Thanks for all your help, but . . . *silvouple* . . . don't take him with you to Barahona."

Don Patricio listens but can't fathom her request or the pleading expression on her face. Given the need they must have for the pesos her son can earn, he finds it odd that she is asking him not to give the boy work. He tries to understand, but he can't.

"Why don't you want your son to work for me?"

"There's nothing wrong involving you, *mesye*," Cuza replies, and adds one of her reasons, to smooth whatever anger her words might have aroused. "The thing is, I want my *gason* to stay in school and earn his bachelor's degree, so he can enter a profession, something that will pull his life out of this poverty."

Don Patricio regards her with amazement and a degree of undeserved resentment. He expected any other reason for the boy to leave the job, but not the one he had just heard. He was prepared to offer Albertico two pesos more for each trip, give him a bonus at year's end and even let him drive one of his trucks when he'd had some experience at steering heavy vehicles. He looks at Cuza with contained rage, imagining how she wants for her son what he could not acquire for himself, although he had yearned for it hundreds of times.

"And since when do Haitians attend the university?"

His voice conveys inquiry and sarcasm at once. But not any negative feeling toward her. His bitterness is not aimed at Cuza's valor in the face of adversity, but toward his own inability to cast aspersion on the effort she is making to change her son's life.

"Since forever, *mesye* Patricio, since forever," she repeats slowly, convincing herself of what she says. She regards him without exasperation, and from within a sense of pity forces her to say the words she doesn't want to say: "The problem is that you only know the *madame* who came to be the cook for the farm's owner, the boy who loads plantains onto your truck and the old ones who were brought in trucks to harvest the sugar cane that sweetens the coffee you like."

"Neither they nor you, Madam, were forced to come. You crossed the border of your own free will and more or less knew what to expect."

"That's true, *mesye* Patricio, I was not forced to come. But poverty always pushes. Maybe you don't know that because you've never suffered hunger."

"Forgive me, *madame* Cuza," replies Don Patricio, visibly repentant, noting that his words may have conveyed some prejudice and contempt, "truly, believe me, *madame,* I never meant to offend you."

"Don't concern yourself, *mesye.* I know very well where I come from."

When Don Patricio climbed into the truck and started the motor to leave, Cuza, wholly undisturbed, approached to tell him quietly, "And I also know who I am, *mesye* Patricio."

Night fell as if in secret, under the intoxicating fragrance of the flowering almond trees lining both sides of the street. Cuza's last words buzzed and hovered incessantly in the head of the old trucker. He opened a half-full bottle he kept on the right-hand seat near the morning paper, looked for a station playing some popular song. At that moment any record would do, no matter who sang it, so long as it was cheerful enough to dissipate from his mind the sense of defeat that weighed heavy on his soul.

Chapter Eleven

HE MUST NOT KNOW IT

Cuza is very sick. Nevertheless, she greets the morning with a certain vigor and lies to herself with false joy, trying to dismiss the sickness that she knows lives in her body. During the day she experiments with a kind of occupational release, and the pain that has lacerated her body for three months now gives her a break that last a few hours. She takes refuge in the thousands of chores it takes to prepare the daily meals, but only delays her decline, which falls on her shattered anatomy like an avalanche just as she washes the last pot, takes the little sales table back out to the alley and collapses on her side of the "sandwich bed." She looks to the ceiling to interrogate *bondye,* but receives not a word in reply. Her faith is immovable, so she leaves in the hands of the deity the future of her health and tries to organize plans for the following day as the night passes.

She doesn't want Albertico to discover everything, just now when he's returned to school and is giving signs of wanting to achieve his bachelor's degree. Cuza is happy over her son's decision and full of legitimate pride in her insistence that the boy resume his studies. She has made Antoine and Miguelón swear by all the saints never to tell him that she is taking medications to fight the infection, nor that she fainted a few days ago and that they discovered her half-conscious on top of the stove, which, luckily, she had not yet been lit.

Some weeks past, during her first visit to the hospital center, a recently graduated internist took charge of her lovingly, but somewhat hastily in the emergency clinic of the Moscoso Puello Hospital. He observed her eyes, gave her a routine stress test and several times listened to her lungs with a silver stethoscope. He ordered an X-ray of her thorax to validate his initial diagnosis, which was supported by her lackluster eyes and the weakness of her extremities. She returned to the doctor a few days later. When they brought him the negative of the image of her torso and lungs, he looked at her with profound sorrow; grief forbade his identifying her condition, but he said, soberly, "Doña Cuza, you're not in good health. You must take care of yourself, or you will give us a fright."

On her way back to the neighborhood she stitched together excuses she would use to avoid discussing the matter. The coughing fits would not be hard, as she had always had asthma and her attacks of hoarseness were frequent all year round, with or without some virus or other in the town. To justify her fatigue, maybe she could blame the fact that more and more clients were asking for unusual dishes she had not prepared, so she had to run back and forth to and from the kitchen to look for the ingredients required by the diners.

Back to the patio to boil *auyamas* because the bananas are spoiled. Scramble some eggs with salami, because the chicken is all gone and the rice has nothing to go with it. Fry eggplants because she bought the wrong peppers and the ones she prepared were too hot and spicy. "The fatigue is easy to explain away," she said out loud, as if speaking with someone else, and went on to reinforce her strategy by adding, "You've been tired your whole life."

What troubles her is how to cover up the cold that takes over her body entirely. She has always liked wearing light clothing and doesn't know what to do about the frozen demon that is consuming her life. Sometimes she wears a double scarf, supposedly to keep her curly hair in order, but really to keep out the chilly wind that nests in her head and interferes with her thinking and calculation. A cold that hurts. As if there were some endless warfare between her body temperature and the surrounding air, and she were the battlefield of that once-pleasant coolness that had become the bearer of bad news. Her hands were cold, despite their eternal position near the fire that cooks the rice she stirs to make sure it comes out evenly. Cold that tortures her arms, although she's been moving them since five in the morning, when her day begins, before the cock's crow to awaken the crowds off to their daily work. Cold that swells her feet and freezes her fingers, although she wears the heavy socks Albertico wears to play basketball. She who has always wished that the sun would set a few hours earlier, so as not to sweat buckets in front of her customers, now prays for it to rise early and remain in the sky until she finishes the dishes and throws herself into bed to ride out the storm.

She has reached the neighborhood, which, luckily, is deserted. She doesn't know where she got the strength to keep her from disintegrating halfway to her home. It's cost her a life to walk each block, on feet that weigh on her as if they were not part of her body. She pants at each crossing. Her heart is beating at great speed, but she doesn't hear it. She tries to decipher, in the flute-like sound of her chest, if the antibiotics have brought about any improvement, but when she breathes deeply to hear the resonance of the bronchi, she has to stop suddenly because of the sharp pain that drills her ribcage.

The sound of her son returning home calls for a change of activities. She throws herself into bed again, covers herself completely and pretends to be asleep—a state which, as on so many other nights, will evade her until a few moments before the day begins anew.

Albertico asks for her blessing very quietly. She will give him the blessing if she is awake, and if she is asleep he is left with the satisfaction of having asked for the divine intercession, as he has been taught to do. She hears him but does not answer. She has not moved a muscle and is praying that the cough doesn't return and reveal that she is not asleep.

Albertico approaches the jar that is keeping hot over the slowly extinguishing coals. He notes that the leaves are almost touching the bottom, beyond boiling. As he sets about looking for an old rag to handle the tea he means to drink, he murmurs to himself what he would never say to his mother: "Damn, the old lady is beginning to forget things."

Cuza hears him and is amused by his remark but has no strength to laugh. She feels a gust is rising from her feet and freezing her body. Only her eyes, once black, are now the red of lit fire, as in the abrasive forge of rising fever.

Chapter Twelve

THE NEIGHBORHOOD WANTS TO
BID THE GYPSY GOODBYE

The neighborhood is as dark as a wolf's mouth. A light rain relieved, for only a few instants, the soporific weather of October on the hot pavements. The air becomes hazy with the steam that rises from its contact with water, spreading its hallucinatory odor over all those who cross the street just as the mist creates the illusion that the asphalt is breathing in the smoky air.

Cuza closed her sales four hours earlier than usual, even before all the food for the passersby had been consumed. Those who arrived late were somewhat annoyed, and some customers approached the entrance of the alley leading to the yard and asked loudly why there was no food for them. With absolute calm she answered the casual clients—those who approached the table doubtfully and asked for the menu, even though it was spread out on aluminum trays—with an excuse that sounded reasonable but was a lie: "Thank you, come tomorrow; almost all the food went very quickly today. Tomorrow without fail I'll have rice with pork and yucca dumplings with anise and oat gravy."

For the loyal customers with whom she shared the news of the day and the health of children, she had a different excuse that, while true, was not the true reason for closing her little enterprise so early: "I don't feel well. I have body aches. Maybe it's the flu. My head is one big ache."

The truth was something else. A violent outbreak was nearing the neighborhood and she didn't want to be in the middle of the fracas, carrying tables, putting away things and on the lookout for the safety of her son.

She became aware of it by accident, because, although there had been hints in the midday news, she'd had no chance to hear what precisely was taking place. She had forgotten the little transistor radio she always put under the table to listen to romantic music, and none of her customers commented on the news that had been aired.

It was old Pupo who alerted her. They were alone in the grocery store and he, who had seldom spoken to her, although she shopped in his establishment for condiments and oil, this once called her by name and spoke with her briefly as evidence of a belated friendship.

"Doña Cuza, don't let your son out of the neighborhood. Tell Albertico to stay in the house and not to go out except for an emergency. Things are going to get rough for the Dominicans, and I think for him even worse. You know he's black, poor and Haitian."

She looked at him with startled eyes and settled her hands on the counter, to be steadier before hearing what else he had to say, but Pupo didn't give her a chance, and told her in a friendlier tone, "I'm fond of the boy. He's more hard-working than many Dominicans and he respects his mother. That's why I'm telling you this, I don't want anything to happen to him if I can prevent it. I'm warning you beforehand so you can be prepared."

Cuza doesn't understand what it is that she must protect Albertico from. It occurs to her that Papolo discerns some threat to Albertico's life, but dismissed the thought at once, because some days earlier someone said, while buying an order of *tos-*

tones with salami, that he had seen him in the Victoria peniten-
tiary, and added, unasked, that he looked stout and healthy, although in prison, and that filled her with mixed emotions.

The grocer moves away slightly as if to give her time to consider what he told her. He lowers the metal rolling door with a
frightening squeal, inserts two iron bars to keep out the thieves
that roam freely at night and heads toward the side door. He repeats the process mechanically, but this time adding, between
his physical efforts, a bit of information to be sure that Cuza understood the situation.

He checks one of the locks and says, "All the neighborhoods
in the north are on guard. There isn't a single grocery open.
They're burning tires, breaking electric meters and spilling
garbage in the middle of Padre Castellanos Avenue."

Pupo breathes deeply and relaxes his lungs and his tired
heart. He's elderly, and obesity doesn't permit him to move with
ease. He maneuvers another metal pike and while looking for
the lock for that door, imparts one more item of information.

"The chief of police ordered a lockup of all members of the
institution. There are mixed patrols checking both incoming and
outgoing bridge traffic. They're taking away arms from civil-
ians, even if they have valid permits and sales receipts. But the
hoodlums got ahead of them, and the revolution is bigger than
it seems."

Pupo has left only the main door open. He wants to be protected in case of a scuffle, but like all the folks from Bani he
considers business sacred and plans to be ready to continue giving his customary service and sell his neighbors whatever they
may need. His elderly clients are buying flashlight batteries,
bread, sardines, chocolate, coffee and sugar. A few young people under twenty greet Cuza, recognizing her as the mother of
Zero-One, and ask Pupo for two bottles of rum, a box of
matches, three large candles in glass cups and a dozen small

white ones. Cuza is even more confused than before her conversation with the grocer. She doesn't grasp the magnitude of what's approaching, but she wants to get home as soon as possible to see if Albertico has already returned.

Anxiety consumes her breath, not knowing where her boy is. She goes from the door to the kitchen; out to the mouth of the alley and back to the patio; round and round in circles and swiftly to the grocery door, only to return full of anguish because she hasn't seen him come home yet.

The silhouette taking shape in the distance gave her back her peace of mind and quieted her hands, which had not ceased trembling. For another it would have seemed only a shadow, but she recognized with precision her son's walk, balanced on his long legs, turning his head to one side to situate himself better despite his lack of complete vision.

"Yes, it's him," she said with a timid smile, as if reaffirming that no one knows Albertico better than the firstborn daughter of Degá.

Five minutes after he entered the room they shared, the spiral of violence that Pupo had warned of so mysteriously exploded.

Someone hurled bottles at a police car. From the terraced roofs of some distant houses, they threw rocks and pieces of iron pipes, an out-of-tune chorus screamed: "The National Police is a gang of criminals!" Later, a burst of machine-gun fire, isolated shots from revolvers, the squeal of car brakes; the sound of hasty steps and military orders were followed by curses and obscenities.

Cuza jumps as if on springs and places a thick wooden plank across the supports on both sides of the door, to prevent the sudden entry into her house of anyone running from pursuit.

She questions Albertico, who having come from the fringes of the neighborhood might have some explanation for the warning issued by Pupo. "Son, what is it that's going on out there? Do you know anything about what's happening?"

"I'm not too sure, Ma," he simply replies, and then adds, "I got here on foot from Enriquillo Park, and there's no light anywhere. The entire city is in the dark, but on the sidewalks, there are thousands of small candles and tall yellow candles. They're also playing a *merengue* that's driving the guards patrolling the streets crazy. They've beaten up some of the boys who were lighting the candles, and have taken others out of their parents' homes, pushing them with their nightsticks. Miguelón was walking next to me and asked a girl who was shouting insults at the police what was happening, and she said, as if we were the only people left who didn't know, 'Those cowards killed Tony, the leader of the Gypsies!'

"Then she told us, with a voice full of sorrow, that they set a trap for Tony, that a jealous and very powerful man turned his love of some woman into a tragedy. She said that Tony was a very entertaining guy, and that cost him his life."

"The leader of the Gypsies?" asked Cuza, obviously still in the dark over the story she had just heard. "Is that a guerrilla troop or a political party?" she adds.

"Neither, Ma," says Albertico, who shared his mother's astonishment when the girl told him. "I asked the same thing, but according to the girl, Tony, the leader of the Gypsies, was a singer."

Chapter Thirteen
GRANDFATHER'S BOOKS

———

Cuza knows that at any moment death will come to call her name. She knows her body very well, and senses that what little strength she has left must be spent on important things still left to do. Her anatomy, lacerated by disease, reveals the damage done by viruses and malnutrition—they have left her worn out as by a storm that has stolen her youthful vigor. What was once her pure ebony skin has become loose hide barely sealing the bones that are beginning to show through. But not everything has been a defeat: Albertico earned his high school diploma, and although he gives no sign of registering at the university, he has promised to pursue a vocational career or some specialized field.

"How well my boy has turned out!" she murmurs out loud, as if comforting herself in advance of what lies ahead. Daily she begs *bondye* not to take her yet, before she can see her *petit* headed toward the future she has dreamed for him.

Albertico is also transformed since learning of the illness of his mother. The smile he wore in the past has vanished, and not even a grimace has taken its place. He barely opens his mouth. He asks for things with gestures that strike others as brusque, because they don't know of the storm raging in his chest, nor the wounds he hides every day. Miguelón extends his unfailing embrace whenever he can, reminding him that they are brothers, although he is not Cuza's son, and tells him that "love is what lets you know who is family and who is friend," handing him a sports sock in which he has a little money.

Gently, he says, "Take this, my brother. It's all I have. It's not much, but it will help somewhat with Doña Cuza's medications."

Albertico feels like crying while they hug, but tears fail to follow his melancholy. They remain like his words, caught in his throat, a knot that renders even his breathing a difficulty. The friend understands without seeing any tears. He leaves, sorry that he can't be of more use, recalling in the other's mother his own who had died five years earlier and whose loss hurts him as if it were the first day, as if orphanhood were a sorrow kept forever.

Don Patricio also has extended a hand in his own way. He has not made a gift of money so his employee can face Cuza's illness with some success, but he has paid him in advance for five working trips that Albertico agreed to make, and has sent food to cover two weeks, because he is convinced that the worst of all illnesses is hunger.

Antoine has returned from Haiti a few hours ago. The news has so upset him that he looks as if he himself were sick. He has brought back the books that Cuza asked him for in order to initiate Zero-One in the custom of reading. Providence gave her only one descendant, and that one neither speaks nor reads the language of his grandfather, Webert Durosier. That's why she asked Antoine to bring her the novels that her father read, but in Spanish translations, so as to give Albertico no excuse to leave them unread.

Antoine hands her a plastic bag containing the four books he could bring, then another package containing a yellow kerchief he bought her as a gift and finally a liter of *tafia,* knowing that

Cuza doesn't drink alcohol, but that this Haitian Creole rum might help her know the fine handicrafts from Miragoane and Jeremie. Cuza tries to laugh, though she has no strength to do so. She looks for something to say to thank Antoine for his visit and his courtesy for having brought her the books, but nothing occurs to her. She thinks that like all travelers, Antoine may want to talk about his trip, so she asks him a question to get his tongue going on the details, and closes her eyes to see if she, too, can travel with him.

"How did you find our people . . . was the return difficult . . . how was the border?"

She shuts her eyes, which are narrowing from the brilliance of the internal flame that is searing her reddened orbits. A light breeze cools the room and Antoine's words fall on Cuza's ears like a distant rain approaching slowly.

"Petion-Ville is the same. Old Gade doesn't have the workshop on Rue Liberte anymore: there's a cafeteria there instead. I asked about him and was told that cerebral thrombosis has atrophied his hands so he can no longer work wood. His older daughter, who lives in Port au Prince, took him home to live with her, and nobody knows what happened to the sculptures he had for sale. In my house they're all well, except for my brother-in-law, the painter. He disappeared two months ago and they've searched in all the hospitals and penitentiaries, but found no trace of him, as if the earth had swallowed him. My sister tells me that it's about a painting he was asked to paint, but he didn't finish it on time and the buyer, who has pals in the government, was angry and asked them to grab him. Others say that's only part of the truth, and that the owner of the painting— a high functionary of the Tonton Macoute, the Haitian police— forgave the delayed delivery of the painting, but couldn't stand seeing some photos of my brother-in-law marching at the head of a protest. From the look on my sister's face, I can tell she doesn't expect him to come back. Crossing the border was easy. Same as always. At the first stop, the guard took away two pairs of *soulyey,* shoes, and some belts I meant to sell. But they themselves hid me in the truck loaded with cases of whiskey, bolts of fabric and some disarmed and disguised pistols among the boxes of *bacalao.* I was traveling with seven women and two old men who had guaranteed jobs in Jimani. At the second post they took the rest of the merchandise I had brought. They left me only what I was wearing and a few *gourdes* that I had hidden in my shorts. I behaved very well. I let them rough me up a little and laugh at my mouth and my smell, until I was safe in the house of my cousin in Dajabon. I was itching to flatten the guard who called me 'stinky,' but you have to be quiet if you want to get back safely."

Cuza listened as if entranced, like a feather whirling in the wind stirred by Antoine's words. As she listened, she couldn't stop thinking that she couldn't return, that those streets he mentions, those places, they no longer exist. Those lost relatives, they never truly existed for her. They uprooted her from Haiti to bring her to this side, and like Albertico, she now belonged on neither side. She resists the idea, she clings to *Kompa Direk,* to traditional dishes, Resurrection celebrations, the maternal sounds of *creole,* but at heart it hurts her to know that she will never return to her birth country, and here, too, she is only passing through. She opens her eyes and looks for the right words to thank him for the visit and the gifts he brought, but her strength has abandoned her completely.

Antoine looks at her with profound sorrow. "Look, Cuza, *Mi compadre el general sol,* in Spanish, as you wanted it!"

He sets it aside and looks for some sign of pleasure in her, and adds enthusiasm. "I also brought you *Lords of the Dew,* the book written by your father's friend, who was imprisoned when Papa Doc was the chief of everything." He reflects on what he wants to say, in order to soften his bitterness a bit, and says to himself what he seems to be saying to Cuza: "Those who govern today are the same as the Duvaliers. They're black like us, but they think themselves European and owners of Haiti."

Chapter Fourteen
A Belated Letter

Cuza has not cooked the dishes that she habitually offers to passersby. She hasn't even risen from the little bed where she gathers strength to face the day that has already begun without her notice. The morning looks gorgeous. She was awake all night, submerged in an absolute silence. Albertico hears the creaking of the bed's legs when she turns her body looking for a position that will allow her to breathe with less effort. Only then does he realize that she is still awake, in a pretense of rest that is closer to death than to tranquility.

It hurts Zero-One to the bone to leave her in that condition. Maybe if he had more relatives in the capital things would work out differently. Antoine has promised to bring his cousin Sade, who lives in a small town called Palavé, so she can stay with Cuza for a few days until Cuza is better. He says she cooks as good as Cuza, which may avoid the loss of customers.

Meanwhile, the boy must keep the agreement made with Don Patricio a few days before. He must go pick up the load of plantains and bananas in Barahona, work to repay the pesos he has already received in advance and, in this way, leave the door open in case he needs another favor from his employer.

He tosses a dark shirt and a white shirt, a freshly washed pair of shorts and a toothbrush into the bundle he carries when he goes to the market. He heads for the door trying not to awaken his mother, but she sits up suddenly to give him her blessing and the item she has been preparing for several weeks. "Come here, son." She says it with a joyfulness that has no connection with her physical condition. As Albertico approaches, she draws another breath so he won't notice how difficult it is for her to breathe normally. "Let me embrace you before you leave for the market," she murmurs softly, her voice barely audible to the son who reaches for the refuge of Cuza's arms.

"Give me your blessing, Ma," he begs, as if praying. His words convey his desolation; he is afraid to embrace her. He fears that his embrace may do her more harm than good, as if she were as fragile as a newborn and about to break at any moment.

Cuza kisses him with the same tenderness she poured over him when she used to put him to sleep in cardboard boxes for lack of a cradle. She notices how much her child has grown, how adult he seems now, how clear the features of the absent father have become. She notes that all he has of her is the shape of his mouth, his laughter and some unconscious gestures he makes when he is angry.

"Take this, I want you to read it with full attention, as if it were a matter of life or death, as if everything we are depended on your understanding of what is written here."

He looks at her, astonished. Never had he heard her speak that way. He searches his memory to see if there's anything there related to her expression, but nothing in the past links him to the book she is bestowing on him with so much passion. He takes the volume from her and nods, to indicate that he will do as she asks.

Cuza kisses him again, now on the forehead, in his hair, on his cheeks, still clean and hairless. From the right pocket of her nightgown she draws a sealed envelope bearing the name of the recipient in cursive and no sender. She looks it over as if assuring herself that the envelope holds a part of her life. She speaks to Albertico in a tone suddenly full of energy.

"Please tell Don Patricio to leave you in front of the house of the Mendoza family. Once there, ask them to let you speak with Don Alberto. He is a white man, more or less as tall as you, with fine hair, but wild. Do not give this to anyone but him."

Albertico looks at the wrinkled envelope she hands him with hands that shake strangely. He takes it, slips it into his luggage and prepares to ask a question that Cuza guesses in his eyes.

"You will know if it's Albert himself who receives you. He has a round, black wart where the left cheek ends. I know he won't want to receive you. Make him listen to you and give it to him personally."

"But, Ma, you told me you didn't know anything about him. That you didn't even know where the man lived. That you had no way to communicate with my father."

Cuza cries quietly into the wall, a refuge. She swallows the tears, so her son won't know how much she suffers, and urges him to go.

"Before, it was not necessary for you to know. I didn't want your father to take away the little I've had in my life, as would have happened years ago. I never wanted this moment to come, when you would have to meet him, when you would go back into the past and ask about facts—events—that I've buried. But things have suddenly changed and I want you to go right away and tell him that you exist. Let him know that you're named after him, that life has treated us very harshly, but we're still on our feet, and we didn't need his help to survive."

"All right, Ma, I will look for him," says Albertico, sharing the same pain as Cuza. "But I can't guarantee that I'll tell him everything you've asked me to. I'll take him your message when I go to Barahona, but the moment and the hour will dictate what happens next."

Albertico leaves, Cuza watches him cross the street and turn at Daniel Henríquez, headed for the market. She sits on the edge of her bed, calmly reviewing the decision she made, wondering if she's done the right thing.

Outside the morning runs to nine a.m. Passing cars liven the atmosphere and the greengrocers cry out offers of their fresh goods in rhymed quatrains, trying to make their business more attractive with cheerful shouts:

> Run, neighbor! My dishes
> are all good to eat!
> My yucca's delicious,
> my ñame's a treat!

The day looks magnificent for celebrating life, but Cuza has lost all interest in leaning out the window in contemplation. She wants only to live long enough to see her son manage life for himself. That's the only thing that matters, although for her it has meant subduing her anger, silencing her pride and writing, as if bleeding, the text, the letter that now, despite her pride, is on its way.

Chapter Fifteen

THE GHOST OF BARAHONA

"The world can do nothing to a man who sings in his poverty."
Ernesto Sabato, 1911-2011

"Here, you drive! You wanted a turn. Here it is."

The commanding voice of Don Patricio would have been good news under other circumstances, but Albertico doesn't care to drive the delivery truck. If this order from his employer was happening at another time he would be happy. But his soul is hanging by a thread. He can't stop thinking about the mother he left alone. Her eyes have become as lightless as her hands are cadaverous. Don Patricio knows it and feels guilty. The lively boy who was his assistant has become a troubled young man without joy, whose soul has been emptied. That's why he regrets having asked the young man to drive. He withdraws the offer silently, taking back the keys and starting the engine, letting the boy stare at the rearview mirror, at the capital diminishing behind them.

He wants to say something that will liven him up. Talk about sports, maybe, or ask him if he's succeeded in entering into a romantic relationship with the girl who sells melons in booth number nineteen at the market. But he is absent from life; it seems to run on inexorably. Discreetly, he watches his beaten face and can't think of a subject that could be of use at this moment in life. The atmosphere in the cabin of the truck is very dense. Not even the air that comes in through the glassless window refreshes it. Don Patricio also feels uncomfortable. He takes off the tight shirt he's wearing and remains lightly covered by a worn flannel. He removes the gun he always carries when he travels to the center of the country and places it in the dilapidated glove compartment. It doesn't close all the way.

Albertico regards the gun as if it were a toy for adults. He's never fired a gun, but he's held one more than once. El Chino always had one on him. In conversation he would sometimes say, as if in a dare, "Touch it, don't be such a chicken. The gun doesn't bite." Then he would laugh uproariously until tears ran down his cheeks.

"Touch it," he would say and begin to laugh all over again. Then he would manipulate it slowly, apparently to teach Zero-One the mechanism of the weapon. He would remove the clip, with the left hand pull the barrel forward and with the right retract the butt with an even motion until both parts produced a compact sound.

Sometimes he would carry a .38. He would move the drum to the left and look at the six holes where the bullets would go. He would put his hand in his jacket pocket and extract the projectiles. He would insert them, one by one, into the hollows of the drum, which he would spin with great speed, and then slide that into the body of the revolver. At that moment he would repeat the order that Albertico obeyed with obvious fear.

"Hold it. Look, it doesn't weigh much," he'd say. Then he would begin the other part of his performance. "You never know when you're going to need a weapon. You may carry it for years without needing it. But sometimes, as soon as you put it away, some shithead shows up who thinks the world was made just for him, and then you have to pull it out. Remember, you must be ready to pull the trigger once it's out, because it's bad luck to show it and not shoot. If you show it and fail to shoot, they may even kill you with it."

Albertico looks at the revolver and laughs to himself remembering the talks with Martin, El Chino, the friend who sailed away with Lolo the captain of the yawl.

"Don Patricio, do you happen to know where the Mendoza family lives?" says Albertico, suddenly back from his trip to the past.

"The Mendoza family . . . of Barahona?" asks the other, surprised.

"Yes, boss, them," replies Albertico, and seeing Don Patricio's surprise, explains, "I have to take something to that house. I need to see a gentleman who lives there."

"Of course, my boy," answers Don Patricio enthusiastically, glad to know that the other knows the farm owners in the towns where he purchases the merchandise he sells. "It just happens that the order we're delivering today is a relative of theirs; those people have lands near one another. They're people who don't like to have strangers for neighbors and much less to have anyone interfering with their business."

When they arrived at the center of Barahona the sun was still refusing to sink into the west. The load they had in the truck was greater than many others they had delivered, but Albertico and the other peon figured out how to load the merchandise so symmetrically that those who noticed were amazed.

The truck stopped at the next-to-last block of Enriquillo Street. From there Albertico could see the monumental house that rose a hundred meters from the entrance and created the sensation that visitors had to be announced beforehand. A central hall, adorned with white stones on both sides, boasted a grand porch that surrounded the mansion. A pure-bred horse was stepping slowly in front of the house, tossing its mane with grace and confidence. Just at the foot of the staircase that preceded the entrance were two life-sized lions. They were so white that, at a distance, it was hard to distinguish what animal was depicted in plaster.

Farther on, half a dozen coconut workers were fanning the patio, reducing the heat of the season. On the right hand of the balcony, an adolescent black girl gently pushed a wheelchair, in which sat an elderly man who carried a newspaper and a pale blue hat on his lap.

"Is this the home of the Mendoza family?" asked Albertico, taking in with amazement the luxuriousness of that construction erected a few kilometers away from the poverty of Central Batey and the strings of miserable people who barely survived with less than was necessary.

"Yes, young man, it is. I came this far only to show it to you. First let's take care of something before the Agricultural Bank closes. You leave me in line to pay a loan and return here to do whatever you need to do. I'll be waiting for you in front of the bank."

They take the route in reverse toward the town center. Don Patricio puts on the shirt he had taken off on the way and climbs down from the truck with a pile of papers and a plastic bag containing money.

Albertico retraces the route with much timidity; he is not yet skillful at managing the truck. He steps on the pedal that precedes the change of force needed to start, and begins to feel more confidence observing how smoothly that iron giant moves along the battered streets. After a while he is back. He stops in front of the house he left behind minutes before, glad to see that the young girl and the man in the wheelchair are still on the broad balcony with its all-encompassing view. Before descending from the truck, he thinks of the advice from Martín, El Chino about being ready to shoot a gun.

The words of his friend enter his mind, searching for support for the action ahead. He feels for Don Patricio's gun in the glove compartment and secures it behind his waist, where his shirt will conceal it from all eyes.

"Greetings, *morena!*" he says with a certain dryness, but he offers a friendly smile to the young girl trying to make the old man in the wheelchair comfortable, where shade will protect him from the glare of the sun's setting splendor.

"Good afternoon!" she replies. "How may I serve the gentleman?"

Her words betray both politeness and fear. She addresses the visitor as if he were older, although it's obvious that they are of similar age.

"I would like a word with Mr. Alberto Mendoza," he says, patting his pockets instinctively to make sure he has Cuza's letter.

"Who are you?" she asks with a trace of fear. "I've never seen you here. What business do you have with the master of the house?"

Zero-One intuits that he must sweeten his request. He is a stranger, and the girl has no reason to trust him.

"My name is Alberto," he says gently. "It's been a long time since my last visit, but I'm an old friend of this house; my mother is a close friend of your employer."

He lied, but only by half: the last time he was in that house he was in his mother's womb.

"He is Master Mendoza," she replies, and signals the old man in the wheelchair with a hint of disgust.

Alberto regards him with rancor that is diminished with the sadness of seeing him in such circumstances. The sick man's hands tremble. His lightless gaze seems lost, and his hair and beard are ill-tended. His shirt reveals that he was fed recently:

there are bits of sweet potato puree near his collar and on the pocket that contains thick eyeglasses in a dark shell frame. Judging by his observations—and without much effort, Albertico rapidly concludes that heavy sporadic meals, the abuse of alcohol and a bohemian life finally charged their due of a young body lacerated by a disorder. His physical strength resisted the attacks of two strokes, but imprisoned him in a body left in the hands of the servants in his house, and whatever goodness resides there.

"Could you leave us alone for a moment?" Albertico pleads, adding, in order to be granted the favor, "I have something very personal to tell him. It's only for a moment."

"No, sir, I can't." And she adds, to justify the sharp denial, "I've been ordered not to leave him alone under any circumstances. I'm responsible for him when the family is away."

"One tiny minute can't get you into trouble," says Albertico. "The thing is, I must give him a very personal message from someone he has not seen in a long time. You can trust me." His request depends more on his gestures than on the words themselves. He appears to have convinced her to leave him alone with the old man. She no longer seems shy or belligerent.

"Only a few minutes," she says, returning to Zero-One the gesture made with his lips. And she adds, "The master has been forbidden visitors and the doctor who looks after him said he must avoid long conversations. Since he became sick, barely eats. He doesn't speak to anybody, not even his brothers or the friends who sometimes come to see him on Sunday afternoons. If you speak to him, he understands everything, but don't expect him to answer. I've been here more than a year now taking care of him, and he doesn't speak even to me; I know what I'm saying."

Albertico smiles again at the girl, who loses herself in the perfect snowy teeth he gallantly regales her with. He approaches a bit closer, takes control of the wheelchair and moves it to the extreme right end of the balcony. The adolescent is electrified by the gentle behavior of the visitor toward her. Alberto Mendoza, overtaken by illness, notices that something unusual is taking place. The girl never pushes his chair with such speed or violence. She knows the way to the balcony, and never stumbles getting there. It terrifies him to realize that the person wheeling him about now is crashing into all the furniture in the living room.

When they reach the veranda where the balcony's esplanade ends, Albertico places the sick man facing the street and stands behind the chair so as not to see him as he stitches together the words he has to say, born of the immediacy of the encounter that has just taken place.

"Mr. Mendoza, my name is Alberto Durosier. My friends call me Zero-One because I lost my left eye in a fight and the hollow in my face looks like that number. I've just earned my high school diploma at the Juan Pablo Duarte Lyceum, and if I have the chance, I may be a lawyer, although I also like engineering. I am the grandson of Madame Degá, who died in this house a long time ago, and my mother is Cuza Durosier. I won't tell you about her, I understand you know her well enough already. I'm not here to ask for anything, or even to reproach you for whatever may have occurred in the past. If you weren't in that chair I would perhaps beat you just as life has beaten my mother, but there are moments that one understands only when time clarifies them. I came to tell you that you don't deserve my forgiveness, but you have it. I have gotten where I am on my own, and whatever else I achieve I believe I can also manage on my own. Maybe it's your fault that I am not from there, from Haiti, nor from here either. I'm not sure. But I want you to know that my mother took me to a celebration where I discovered who I am and who I should aim to be. I will most likely not see you again, as this is my last trip to Barahona. If I have no future opportunity to return, I want you to know that my mother has brought me up right; that Cuza, my ma, has toughened through pain, poverty and anguish, but has never surrendered. And she has done me the honor of calling me her son. She always calls me Albertico, but I prefer to be called Zero-One, because that name was the result of a problem, but it belongs to me entirely. To her I owe my last name—Durosier; I have never needed yours."

Albertico thinks he hears a sob. He signals to the girl, who is dusting paintings that illustrate rural life, to come for the sick man under her care. Again he gives her a smile, as if with it he means to acknowledge the friendliness he has been shown. He takes out the book by Mona Guérin-Rouzier that Cuza gave him and finds a page he had marked because he liked the translation that Antoine made of the text. Clumsily, he reads the selected verses aloud, trying to let them speak for him:

When you want to deliver this diary
and unfold your gaze toward mine, which seeks you,
you will know that my heart, in love and faithful,
remained the same as the day it was conquered.

A blissful breeze fills the eyes of the girl, and the unexpected magic of the words keeps her from noticing that he has left without looking back.

He starts the engine and gets the truck on its way. As he drives toward the center of town to pick up Don Patricio, he weeps with opaque clamor and carelessly tosses out the window, piece by piece, the letter Cuza wrote, now in hundreds of tiny fragments. He extends his right hand to the back of his waist to find the revolver and place it back in the glove compartment.

He stops in front of the Agricultural Bank and waits a few minutes. When Don Patricio climbs into the truck, he looks at the boy and says, in a hoarse voice impregnated with the odor of the rum he's been imbibing, "Boy, what a frightened face you have! You look as if you've seen the dead. Or a ghost."

Chapter Sixteen

THE FINAL STRUGGLE

"At a certain point there is no returning . . ."

Franz Kafka, 1883-1924

On the return trip along the old southern highway, Don Patricio thinks of the young girl he's going to see when they arrive at the capital, how life is smiling at him after all and about the good money he's earned on this last trip to Barahona. Albertico, on the other hand, is wondering what his mother wrote in that letter he never delivered and destroyed without reading. But now there is no way to know.

While Zero-One calms his spirit by watching the landscape—the southern coast—pass by, Cuza is slipping into her final hours. She is going placidly into the labyrinth of a painful and early death.

She has already closed her eyes forever. She smiled remembering Albertico when he was not yet Zero-One, but a mischievous boy who made her scream like a madwoman as he descended, like a raindrop, from the tallest trees in the neighborhood of Villa Consuelo.

The neighborhood pursued its immutable course. Only for Zero-One did the city cease to be a refuge and become a monster of nostalgia that threatened to swallow him whole at any moment. He knew that his mother would die but he could not believe it would be so quickly. The work at the market and the plans that rumbled in his head did not let him prepare fully for this most crucial moment. Later he learned that one is never ready for the death of a mother.

As was to be expected, the funeral that led Cuza to her final home was as desolate as her nights of misfortune. Antoine was the faithful friend he had always been, forever linked to the Durosier family, to share the loss with them. Don Patricio was also capable of rising to the occasion. He could not attend the funeral because he had not returned from Tamayo yet, but he sent one of the workers from the market bearing enough money to cover the cost of the hearse, and the coffee and crackers that would be served to the few mourners and neighbors who would attend the funeral.

Cuza lay in a casket on the patio, with no ceremony other than silence and anguish. When Antoine told Sade what had happened, she didn't want to believe it. She ran out of the batey of Palavé like a soul in agony, sadness devouring her spirit, a knot in her stomach that finally remained imprisoned in her trachea. She neither spoke nor wept, only hummed a personal hymn to herself, by herself. She stopped only to find a garment that would be more solemn in the coffin. She would begin the singing again as she dressed the body.

Albertico looked as if he had aged all at once. He was wasting away, absent. He embraced the few people who approached him to offer their sympathy, but said not a word. His lips were sealed, as if he too were dying. Pupo refused to charge for the coffee, crackers and cheese that had been ordered from the grocery, and said only, "Tell the boy I'm very sorry."

Two neighbors who had never spoken with Cuza offered to prepare the body, but that was unnecessary, as Sade had already washed her and dressed her in a garment she had never worn and that was somewhat large for her build. Antoine, Albertico, Miguelón and another volunteer among those present lifted the coffin that had been resting on the seats of four guano chairs and crossed the alley, which was illuminated by an improvised trail of white candles. The car moved very slowly, but nothing suggested that it was headed for the cemetery, save for the dead body inside.

Only four cars followed the marchers. Some sorrowful faces, tormented by grief, contrasted with the drivers who spoke among themselves about sports and other trivialities.

When they arrived at the cemetery some ten friends of Antoine were gathered around the grave that had been dug by two young boys who spoke cheerfully, alien to the sadness of the mourners, because the little, last-minute job would leave them a few pesos to survive at least the first few days.

An improvised *gagá* saw her off as she would have liked, although she would not have said so during the illness that she suffered stoically. The wind instruments, the *yom* and the drums invoked a sad melody rather than the traditional joy that entranced the body. Some disposed of the handkerchiefs that adorned their waists, to make of them a final offering to one who always attended the traditional celebration of Lent. Very few of those gathered at the cemetery knew Cuza intimately, but the proof of friendship was for Antoine as much as for the dead neighbor. Eight calloused hands held the ropes that gently lowered the coffin as it descended to the bottom of the grave. Sade embraced Albertico. She kissed his brow, and for the first time he allowed a long-suppressed sob to escape. Antoine conveyed his gratitude to friends with a gesture of the hand, for he still found it impossible to speak. He gave some bills to the boys who had dug the grave and were now mixing sand and cement for an improvised headstone. Night was approaching and friends were beginning to scatter. Albertico knew he would not revisit the cemetery of Palavé. His mother was not there, he thought. Her body would at last unite itself to the earth, and her great spirit would return to *bondye.* He wanted to cry, but the tears would not come. In his heads, like the tolling of bells, the words of his mother came and went, full of their singular tenderness. He regretted not having had the opportunity to speak to his mother about his encounter with his father . . . how he was, what they spoke of; in short, he could only imagine the story he would have invented to tell her, so long as he could see her happy.

Antoine embraced him, urging him to go home. They were the only ones left, and soon darkness would swallow the way home. Albertico returned his embrace. It would cost him the world to articulate a single word, but he gathered the necessary strength to ask one more favor of Antoine: "Write something for my mother, now that the cement on the headstone is still fresh."

Antoine squatted on one side of the grave, and with a piece of a dried branch wrote a phrase, in precise letters, that seemed to have been preserved for that moment: "Cuza, *vanyan solda nan Petion-Ville.*"

Albertico extended a hand to Antoine to help him stand. He looked at him with affection and waited to be told what he had written. But Antoine did not react. He assumed that Albertico had read the message on the tomb.

"What did you write for Ma?" he said, overwhelmed by sorrow and the admission that he didn't know his mother's tongue. Antoine observed him for a few seconds. He was assaulted by the desire to confront him with the fact that it was his duty to know creole, but understood this was not the moment for another battle. So he embraced the boy like an older brother and told him softly, "It says what your mother was 'Cuza, the warrior of Petion-Ville.'"

The last lights that drain the color from the sunset fall imperceptibly on the evening. Two shadows intertwine while their bodies walk away, seeking the exit to the highway that links the batey to the communities of Manoguayabo, Cabayona and La Cuchilla. In the background, as if defying the inexorable climate, rises the little old mansion constructed in the sixteenth century by the initiators of the production of sugar. The ruin of bricks and metal remains upright in the middle of the wasteland where the old structure survives. The sugar mills mounted on crossbeams of *guayacán* and oak woods attest to the slave past that squeezed the bodies of young and old who arrived as cutters of the sweet grain and were never able to return. The silence is broken momentarily when a bus passes, taking local people to the capital. The cloud of dust left behind by each vehicle on the move hides the distance between them. Albertico looks back for one last glance at Cuza's tomb, but he can no longer distinguish one gravestone from another, and in the old cemetery of Palavé everything returns to silence.

Villa Consuelo, Santo Domingo, December 15, 2019

AURORITA

English translation by
Rhina P. Espaillat

Gimme the gourd for drinkin',
Marola, make it fast.
Gimme the gourd for drinkin', or else
this thirst gonna be my last.

Merengue: Dominican folklore

They, too, have my name

Chapter One

THE MIRROR

"She's still a child," he told it.

And then he proceeded to moisten the razor in the warm soapy water he had in the glass bowl that had been his mother's, and went on to settle the edge of the instrument in the strip of hide hanging from one side of the little table. He had a sparse beard, from a day and a half at most, that stood out in the barren territory of his face because he had no mustache and was going bald. A hint of black and white fuzz, barely visible, was all there was to shave, but he felt they threatened his old habit of going totally hairless.

He was half dressed at the outset of an August morning that promised to be hotter than usual for that time of year. The black trousers would lend him a sober dignity, and his white suspenders with their dark design would add that touch of good taste for Sunday Mass. The long-sleeved shirt of pure linen, still hanging in the closet, would complete the outfit he would wear, as he did every weekend. There was no trace of his hangover or even the recurrent stomach uneasiness, although he had drunk almost three fourths of the bottle of whiskey left in the house.

He had slept well almost all night, except for a coughing fit that shocked him out of sleep and forced him to drink some warm water with honey to clear his throat, which was dry because of his faulty breathing. When the roosters began their morning concert, he had already been awake a long time. First he heard Red singing, then Champ took up the song and immediately Belié joined in. He lay face up, with his hands clasped under the nape of his neck, which was beginning to sweat, waiting for the songs of the other fowl. When he failed to hear them, he thought the worst and leaped out of bed to look through the window toward the locked coop where the fighting cocks were kept. He counted them twice and, once sure that none were missing, he set himself to pee and then take the first pills of the day to control the sudden rise of his arterial blood pressure, caused by merely imagining the theft of his birds.

He felt fine, after all. One or another shade of some *mea culpa* dampened his good cheer, but nothing constituting an obstacle that the lifelong smarts of his old-fox wiles could not get around. Life still had certain joys in store for him that must not be put off any longer, or his vitality would desert him forever; he could not afford to come to terms with any scruple. He must end as a warrior, even if it meant leaving his soul behind on the field of battle. Nothing that could come between him and Aurorita would be great enough to keep him from working it out. He checked the clock on the wall and confirmed it with the watch on his left wrist, but he still doubted that the day had advanced to six o'clock.

He finished dressing without haste, following the ritual he had obeyed for over three decades, and began work on the daily crossword puzzle.

He opened the right-hand drawer of his desk and counted the cash he had on hand for bets at the cockfight. He looked over the titles to the parcels of land he owned, to assure that his debtors would pay for their misfortunes over gambling losses. He checked the cylinder of his gun to make sure that the chamber was fully loaded.

He hesitated before going out armed, because he knew it wasn't quite right to enter the house of God that way, but he convinced himself to overlook that detail and tucked his old .38 into the left side of his waist. After all, he reasoned, Mass only lasted an hour, but the visit to the cockpit could well occupy the whole afternoon, and their manliness has to be sustained by means of the toughest words, or sometimes just lead.

Luckily he had left his horse saddled the previous afternoon. He was in no mood to call over one of his peons to saddle his horse. Taking care of his own needs to this day, and beyond the trivialities of daily life, sent a clear enough message to the others as to his power and his place in the hierarchy. He was still the boss, landowner and lord over the lives of many who were dirt-poor. That must remain so, without any sign of weakness or frailty; he knew very well that wounded animals were finished off by hyenas. And he was lacerated as a man, in his self-esteem, but nobody must know it. He attached silver spurs to his riding boots and strode about a while in the living room, to hear the silvery sound of the rowels turning.

He felt pleased over the sensation of still being a horseman; that fulfilled him. He chose a hat to go with his boots, but nothing splendid, considering where the day would take him. When he was fully outfitted, he went to look at himself in the mirror again. He marveled at how impeccable he looked, although something in his face suggested sadness; he didn't look happy, though he had too much of everything in the world and wore the best that was sold. He caught his eyes in the mirror and once again said what he had before: "She's still a child."

He said it with reticent pain, as if every syllable were an immense stone and he had to push it uphill. It cost him a great deal to admit it; that's why his words sounded alien. But this time he toughened himself up, trudged over the moral recrimination, and once again buried himself in the memory of the eyes of Aurorita. He observed his other self—which, from the mirror, seemed an opponent like those he would encounter at the cockpit—and told it, with self-confidence, "Yes, she's still a child, but she has the look of a woman."

Chapter Two

THE CHURCH

When the tolling of the church bells of Our Lady of Carmen summoned the parishioners to Mass, Don Victoriano Zaldívar removed his hat of felt and leather to enter the holy place bareheaded. He had arrived half an hour before the Vicar appeared in the curial courtyard, followed by three altar boys still far from adolescence, dressed in white. The scene looked as if the priest was followed by three angels rather than three assistants.

The priest tried to avoid him. He contrived an excuse to look everywhere else in the stately court of the chapel just as he was passing Don Victoriano, but it was impossible in the narrow path; the encounter was unavoidable. He closed his eyes and fingered the next bead in the rosary in his hand. When they were almost face to face, the priest greeted him with a grudging gesture, expressing courtesy that passed from mistrust to pure and simple irritation. He couldn't even hide that hardly Christian way to observe Sunday morning.

Don Victoriano, too, found Father Jesús María Ordóñez not at all to his liking, but never said a word to acknowledge his utter rejection of the spiritual guide of that town, which sometimes seemed to have been forgotten by God. Both knew that each Sunday was to be a test of their patience and tolerance, of resistance and personal courage, if you will, so that each week began and ended a secret war between the two. One looked from the altar insistently, and the other returned the look at intervals, between glances directed at the families arriving for Mass and scrutinizing the movements of Jesús María Ordóñez.

The priest thought that Don Victoriano was far too libidinous for his age now that he was getting close to seventy. Victoriano, on the other hand, thought that Jesús María was too much of a man to be a priest. The secret quarrel between those two had begun long before the present. About a decade ago, the priest had refused to perform a religious wedding for the other. At that time Don Victoriano was doing all he could to become essential to the family of the little girl he wanted to take to the altar. He treated her parents with boundless affability. He was always prepared to help if they needed some medicine or furnishings for the house. He lent them money at no interest, provided the wherewithal for birthday parties, served as godfather to a nephew, gifted them with staples and fruit from the farm and bought school uniforms. If the girl was surrounded by relatives and friends, he called her strictly by her name, but when the coast was clear he would snuggle up close to whisper in her ear, "Gorgeous," "Queen," "Beautiful girl." Sometimes he would stare at her fixedly and issue a veiled threat: "You don't know how much I love you."

Of course, Jesús María Ordóñez was delighted when couples vowed eternal love before his altar, but the bride in question was a girl who could have been the would-be groom's daughter or granddaughter. She was barely fourteen years old, and Don Victoriano had just celebrated his sixtieth birthday.

That was a problem that could have been settled some other way, but what permitted no resolution was the fact that Victoriano's previous marriage had not been dissolved. His then-wife fled the house one morning like a soul fleeing the devil. Some said she ran off with the first man who showed her a sign of love: one of his best peons, who didn't even collect his pay, just took off with a mule, a machete and a woman on the horse's haunches. Others declare that she left to escape the physical mistreatment she was subjected to every time Don Victoriano came home drunk and made her pay for the defeat of some of his favorite fighting cocks.

"I won't perform his wedding in this church," the priest replied when one of the peons was sent to set a date for the wedding.

Don Victoriano, accustomed to overcoming every difficulty, never answered a word. He forgot about the business of pleasing the woman who insisted on marriage, as God ordained. He spent a great deal of time at the cockpit, waiting to counterattack with his best spurs. So when a parcel of land was needed to construct a cemetery and hospice for the parish, he looked the priest in the eye and said, with a scornful smile, "What I lack in faith I more than make up for in land. As far as I'm concerned, you can bury your dead in the parish square."

The priest changed his strategy and let the business lie for a while to see if he could find some weakness in the desires that needled the very life of Don Victoriano. He wanted to trap him in some moral failure, to have, once and for all, evidence that would facilitate the donation of the necessary land. At every Sunday Mass each found himself facing the same growing fury, the same aversion filling their bodies, but without giving ground or bowing to the other.

When some congregant revealed, during confession, that Victoriano had lent him money at very high interest and therefore he would lose his shack, the priest chose for that Sunday's sermon the biblical reference to usury and the corrupt souls of the Pharisees, who were not Christians, but tax collectors.

If he learned that Don Victoriano had bought land bordering on someone's farm, taking advantage of the extreme poverty of his tenants, then the preaching soared with passion and he could be heard shouting from the pulpit, "A camel will sooner pass through the eye of a needle than a rich man through the gates of heaven."

Don Victoriano listened unperturbed. He had returned to the dominion of the priest after a prolonged absence not because he had forgotten the refusal to grant him a religious wedding, but because once again he felt the desire to mate, to pursue new prey with his inquisitorial eye and feline nose. Once again his wits were troubled and had sent him to the edge of madness. What the victories of his favorite fighting cocks had not done to him, the coal-black eyes of Aurorita had accomplished, without willing it. And so he sat, every Sunday, in the pew at the end of row five, in the center of the church, in order to see everyone who went in and out of the old parish. He wanted to see her come in, holding her mother's hand, and watch her attentively without moving a muscle or even greeting her, avoiding any sudden motion that might reveal his obstinate watchfulness. In order to see Aurorita for a few minutes, he drank the bitter aloes of the barrage of hints hurled at him by Jesús María Ordóñez. He forgave the sarcastic tittering of the congregation, which knew that the sermons were aimed at him, and resigned himself to having to give the kiss of peace to beggars who asphyxiated him with their stink of dirt and local tobacco.

There was little that Don Victoriano could do to counter the systemic attacks of the priest's words. So he took advantage of the one moment that could afford him a measure of success. Those were scarce minutes, but every Sunday he enacted the performance with greater theatricality and efficacy. When the altar boy who collected the offering passed by him, he let the boy move on without putting in anything. The congregation was astonished to see that the town's richest citizen gave nothing at all, even to a divine cause. Then, when all were aware of his lack of generosity, he rose from his pew and walked toward the altar, making a rhythmic sound with his spurs. Once up at the altar and in sight of all, he took a roll of bills and deposited them slowly in the basket for offerings. When he had placed them all there, he tapped the pockets of his jacket and pulled out another fistful of bills he had prepared for the final act, and continued to put down this additional offering, bill by bill.

The priest was certain that with so large a gift Don Victoriano was flaunting the wealth that could buy any indulgence, but he was not in a position to refuse the money. Only then did Victoriano feel sure that he had won a small battle. He crossed himself with false gratitude and walked his way back to the last row of pews. He passed close to Aurorita, who was kneeling beside her mother, unaware of the details concerning the miracle that Don Victoriano was buying.

Chapter Three
ADALGISA AND EMILIANO

Aurorita is the first child of the loving union between Adalgisa Vásquez and Emiliano Reynoso. Before her birth, the parents were expecting a boy that the mother miscarried two months prior to the expected date of his birth. The doctor spoke for science, explaining that the loss was due to a tear in the womb of the first-time mother-to-be, complicated by the anemia caused by falciform cells, a gift inherited from some ancestors who suffered from the same condition.

"Adalgisa's blood doesn't have enough healthy red cells to carry oxygen throughout her body," said Dr. Reynaldo Henríquez calmly. And he added, in a sober tone and with a hint of danger, "She should avoid pregnancy during the next five years." He pronounced it as a warning, while writing out a prescription for some pills with an unintelligible name and a syrup to be bought at the pharmacy.

Before sending her home from the small E.R. where she had been treated, the doctor looked into Adalgisa's eyes, as if to tell her that the recommendation was for her, not for the man who would try to convince her otherwise: "Woman, like the earth, needs time to rest between harvests, or the crops she produces will be very weak."

Emiliano tried to protect his wife from the sword of Damocles suspended over their home. He remained in control when facing the bouts of desire that assaulted him as he slept close beside a young, beautiful woman. When his libido attacked him, he escaped it by thinking of something else, until the fatigue of a day's work brought him sleep, and the desire of the flesh was overcome.

Some three years after that medical recommendation, Adalgisa shocked him one afternoon, while he was downing a cup of black coffee, with the good news that she had not had a period for a month and a half. The words of the doctor circled their minds; one asking that the child be born, and the other asking that it be born healthy. Each prayed separately, and Aurorita came into the world as healthy and beautiful as they had begged of providence.

Emiliano wanted a boy to name him after himself, and she, who always knew that she would have a girl, wanted to name her Mercedes, after her maternal grandmother. A process of bargaining that lasted almost as long as the pregnancy ended with their naming her Aurorita, like the first light of morning.

They chose, as godmother for the baptism, old Carmela. And not only because she was related to them on Emiliano's side, but also because she had delivered almost all the children in the area. Of course, those most recently born came into the world in a provincial hospital, but that was possible only after the construction of the road that linked the municipality of Castillo with San Francisco de Macorís. All the others were born in the tiny room Carmela built in the back yard of her house, where a ramshackle cot served as the bed on which the birthing women were made to lie down. A dark-skinned adolescent girl heated water and set out clean towels so that the midwife would find everything she needed close at hand when the birth process began.

Carmela looked with troubled eyes at the prescription from the doctor and frowned, as if something unconscious seemed askew. Maybe there was some truth in what the man of science had said, she thought, but her many years of experience told her that the cause was something else. She was convinced, although she told neither of the two, that Adalgisa failed to retain the little boy in her womb because she had married very young, before her body was fully developed. Both had arrived at the correct truth, but by different routes. The doctor was partly correct, because Adalgisa's grandmother suffered, unknown to her, from a major anemia due to the defects of her cells; Carmela was also correct in her knowledge that Adalgisa had not even had her first period when she was sent to live with the man her mother had chosen for her.

Emiliano himself, once seeing her naked in the little shack they lived in, was struck by pity at the sight of that squalid little body, her chest devoid of breasts, without hips, her eyes full of fear, like a small animal trapped in a cage for the sacrifice. Adalgisa's father hardly spoke about the marriage; he simply knew that the union must lighten the economic burden that his daughter had become, and considered her departure a necessary evil. Her mother, on the other hand, simply let her go, with sorrow, as if it were one more link in a painful, endless chain of which she too was a part.

Unfortunately, Aurorita has very few similarities to her mother. Maybe something about the arch of her eyes and the two dimples that appear in their cheeks when they smile.

Now nine years old, already she has budding nipples that threaten to break through the flesh any minute, and the space between the thorax and the waist is curving in a way that foretells a body that her mother has never managed to acquire, even as an adult. She laughs with noisy cheer, as if a cascade pours from her red mouth, which hides a river of joyfulness behind very white teeth. Her hair is very straight, but when she bathes in the Nigua River it turns into a curly mound that frames the loveliness of her small face.

She still plays with rag dolls. She makes them dresses out of newspaper clippings like the outfits she dreams of for herself, which she would like to wear on her tenth birthday. She braids their hair and then unbraids it to create a bun instead, which she also undoes with enthusiasm; she jumps rope with an agility that makes the viewer dizzy, and she sings children's songs. Songs whose rhymed lyrics sometimes foretell terrible things. "*Estaba la pájara pinta*" was one of her favorites. And the game known as "*Convento sin flores*" was another. But neither Aurorita nor Adalgisa, much less Emiliano, suspected that a perverse man, when he watched her from afar, also sang a song for their child: "*Arroz con leche se quiere casar*," he hummed, his mouth full of teeth yellowed by tobacco and coffee, sparkling here and there with gold teeth that mark the joining of his lips, withered by the passage of time.

Chapter Four
DR. HUMBERTO

Dr. Humberto Céspedes leaned toward the glass that covered half the door of his consulting room to confirm what he already suspected. The quiet atmosphere of his workspace rarely became lively this way. The peace that should reign wherever a doctor is at work was altered by only two persons: Ordóñez the priest and Don Victoriano.

The priest hardly ever visited; he preferred to see the doctor in the confessional, where he could ask questions in more privacy and save himself the cost of a consultation. The very sporadic visits that he offered at the clinic were accompanied by a stream of beggars asking for all kinds of charity: sprinklings of holy water, which he tossed from meters away by shaking a sprig of mint leaves moistened with the liquid he brought with him in a little glass bottle. Others asked him to visit some relative in bed for the very end of his days, another to set a date for his wedding or to baptize a baby free of charge, or they begged him to intercede in court for some prisoner they declared innocent, and most of them waited for an opportune moment during which to whisper, "Man of God, give me a little something to get some food."

On the other hand, if the visit was from Don Victoriano things were very different. The clinic would suddenly fill up, but not with the same panhandlers who suffocated the priest. These were people with fewer pressing needs, well dressed and generally close to the visitor.

"Don Victoriano, it's good to see you. I've been meaning to ask you for a couple of weeks more, a grace period, and as soon as a certain matter is settled, I'll pay you what I owe you." More than one could be overheard apologizing for the delay in the payment of some debt. Some already advanced in age implored him to hire on the farm some down-on-his-luck relative. If by chance among those milling about Don Victoriano there was a fan of cockfighting, the conversation could drag on, because women and fighting cocks were the two passions that drove Don Victoriano mad.

"I owe my fortune to Red," he would say with boundless pride to the visitor in question. Then he would add, "That cock is more loyal than all my friends put together. With or without spurs, he's risked his life for me; I don't even have to touch him, he's ready to die wherever they toss him to fight."

Sometimes the visit would end without his having seen the doctor at all, he was so entertained by the hangers-on who gathered around him. And sometimes a lady would approach him surreptitiously and whisper something in his ear, after which he would consider the conversation and the visit to the doctor over.

The doctor is not pleased by the visit from Don Victoriano. He loathed hearing the tone of superiority in which all his words were couched. Every time Don Victoriano comes to the clinic, Humberto Céspedes must make a superhuman effort not to send him to hell. He breathes deeply and exercises the virtue of tolerance. He knows that he may even lose his professional practice if he commits some *faux pas* due to lack of tact. He recalls the saying of his mother: "A slip of the tongue must be dealt with quickly."

He fills the prescription for the lady who visits him monthly, an anti-inflammatory every eight hours and a liquid medication to stimulate her appetite. He knows that won't accomplish much for her, since her real problem is chronic loneliness and hypochondria. He is completely sure that she could be cured by a visit from some son or the laughter of a pair of grandchildren, but until that takes place, he wants to help relieve the pain in her knees. He sends her home knowing that the next month she will be back, a little older and with the same complaints.

The doctor shifts the order of the arrival of his patients in order to get rid of Don Victoriano as soon as possible. The other patients understand, and in fact approve. They feel pleased to give up their turns to the town's chief citizen, who crosses the small waiting room, with his hat in his left hand, while with his right hand he slips his gun into the customary side of his waist, where it won't trouble him either walking or sitting.

"To what do we owe such an illustrious visitor?" asks the doctor, trying to mask the disgust produced by said visit. While awaiting the reply, he occupies himself with the examination of an X-ray of a thorax backlit and then by writing something in a notebook. He does it to avoid looking Don Victoriano in the face, but they know each other very well and all subterfuge is useless. The doctor has no option but to receive him, and Victoriano knows that he is not welcome.

"I'm here to ask you a couple of questions, Doc," he blurts out with some irony, as if amused by the youth of the boy dressed in white. Don Victoriano takes out some bills and places them next to his hat on the little table where the doctor has his stethoscope and a blood pressure gauge. He wants to send the message that he is prepared to pay well for the replies, but that, far from placating the doctor's spirits, makes him even angrier than he was before.

"Ask away, Don Victoriano," he says dryly, and then softens his words, which strike him as too harsh. "I will tell you what science has to say."

"I also want to know what the man has to say," replies Don Victoriano.

"Well, that's more complicated, but at least I promise to be honest in my replies." The doctor regards Victoriano with a touch of contained pity. For the first time the visitor feels at a disadvantage.

"Let's get to the heart of it," Don Victoriano says, as if eager to escape from the impasse. And then he explodes: "Do you think your science can help me to have better outcomes as a man . . . let's say . . . some vitamins . . . some pill or other . . . or a cream . . . that could give me back the energy I had a few years ago?"

"And how old are you, Don Victoriano?"

"I'm going on seventy, son, but I'm still like an oak tree," Don Victoriano replies, boasting of a vigor he lacks.

"In that case, I'm going to tell you what science says."

The doctor searches the repertory of medicine's technical terms to see how to explain his reasoning without causing too much friction. But, not finding the adequate expression, he turns to the simplest words. "If you were forty years old, your problem could be resolved with mild exercises." He looks at the patient, trying to read his reaction, and continues. "If you were fifty, in addition to physical exercise, your problem would be alleviated with a proper diet. But at seventy, and considering how you have abused alcohol and tobacco, there's very little that can be done to bring back the energy that you've lost." Don Victoriano seems dazed before the clarity of the doctor' words. He doesn't understand why science can't do something for him. For him, who could pay for any medicine without worrying about the cost, or how far he'd have to send someone for it.

"And now the man, Doc. What does he advise?"

"In this instance, I will tell you what I would tell my father if he were still living." The doctor pauses briefly, looking for the way to say, in a straightforward manner, what the scientist could not say. "At seventy, with a previous infarct and a lifetime of abusing drink, the only thing you need is acceptance." He regards him with a measure of contempt and tells him, to end the recommendation, "Neither fighting cocks nor men can be expected to win every battle. I don't know who's the enemy you're fighting, but it looks as if the time has come to leave the cockpit of life."

Victoriano looks as if he has aged several years during a few minutes. Collapsing into the chair, he looks around the consulting room and finds something against which to unload his impotence. He stands up suddenly, as if he had forgotten something urgent to be done, jams his hat on with some violence and gestures with his hand to indicate that the visit is over.

"Don Victoriano," says the doctor, detaining a man obviously crushed, "You've left your money on the table."

"Yes, I know," the other replies in a fury. "Take what fees I owe you."

"The consultation costs only one peso, and you've left five," Dr. Céspedes replies.

"Then, I'm going to pay for all those who are out there waiting for you, Doc." And he adds haughtily, "Maybe a blessing from one of the poor can accomplish more than your damned science did."

Chapter Five

THE SCHOOL

As usual, the first reveille performed by the fowl in the coop found Don Victoriano already awake. He had a depressed look, as if a windstorm had tossed him around and left him beside the road, dispirited and beaten. His unshaved look after several days demonstrated his lack of concern for himself. He needed a visit to the barber urgently, given the fact that, as his hair grew, the gray in it became more evident, and the little hair he had left acquired a two-tone yellowish shade, like feathers tinged with ash.

He was half-dressed, wearing backless slippers with crossed straps that formed an X. His eternal suspenders kept his pants on his body without need of the belt, which strangled his stomach. The sleeveless flannel top subtracted somewhat from the dignity of his attire.

He had placed the rocking chair almost out on the sidewalk, to have full view of the street from north to south. On his lap rested the large glass bowl originally used to serve generous helpings of soup to several diners, but which he now used to mix, with remarkable patience, the feed for his Red, consisting of four hard-boiled eggs, two ripe plantains, boiled and a cup of honey. At a quarter to seven he roused himself to face the day. He shaved listlessly, looking into the mirror at his eyes, which returned his gaze with a haggard bag under each one. He put on freshly ironed clothes and returned to the rocking chair to prepare the bird while awaiting the hour when Aurorita would go by on her way to school.

The cock was already trimmed. He had removed his crest the preceding week, and there was little left to do to get him ready for his Sunday engagement in Pimentel's ring. He stopped polishing the bird's natural spurs for a moment when he saw a group of school children approaching. At that distance he couldn't tell who was present in the group, but felt sure that Aurorita would be with them as usual. The crowd passed by him singing a song popular just then, brightening the morning with a burst of joy. There were five girls and three boys, all wearing the obligatory uniform of the Olegario Tenares School. The boys wore their short-sleeved shirts half-buttoned and their pants rolled up, because it had rained a bit at dawn and the humid street still had small puddles of water mixed with clay.

For the girls that was no problem. Their skirts fell just below the knee but not as far as their ankles, and besides, they avoided the puddles so as not to wet their socks or the sides of their sandals. They passed near Victoriano, whose eyes went in search of the dark eyes of Aurorita, but she was not with them. He turned his attention to the grooming of the cock, waiting for other children to pass by.

He considered having the first whiskey of the day, but the words of Dr. Céspedes still echoed in his mind and he made do with just strong coffee, very sweet.

At seven-forty in the morning he decided to leave. He went over his accounts for debts to be collected that week. He made notes after each name to indicate who had paid the interest due that week, and crossed out the name of a woman who appeared on the list of debtors, but without specifying the amount of the debt contracted. At the end of the street, two groups of students who had fallen behind struggled to catch up so as not to be late. They knew that if they arrived during the singing of the National Anthem, not one of them would be allowed to enter without a valid excuse involving illness or some other serious cause. When they approached, Don Victoriano didn't even bother to search their faces. They were all boys. Sun-tanned, skinny but strong, wearing somewhat worn uniforms. They sang, all together, song lyrics rather inappropriate—almost obscene— and noting the near presence of Victoriano they fell silent all together, only to renew their singing and the lyrics farther on, away from the ears of grownups.

The last bunch of students headed for school was about two-hundred meters away. Don Victoriano reasoned that it was far enough to give him time to return the cock to its place in the coop of wood and wire where it would wait for its next combat. The animal had to be far from the cold, well fed and in total solitude; in that sense the man and the bird seemed related, as if they were two identical beings.

When the approaching crowd was less than ten meters away, a feeling of desolation overwhelmed Don Victoriano completely. She was not with them. He looked over the whole bunch several times, secretly hoping that his old eyes had simply failed to spot her the first time. But no, she was not with them, and that conclusion permanently spoiled the beginning of his day. He hastened to ask about her, as a last vestige of hope.

"Kids!" he called out cheerfully, trying to gain their confidence. And at once he asked, "What grade are you in now?"

"We're in fifth grade, but she's in fourth grade, because she got sick and had to repeat a grade and didn't come back to school," said one markedly proper little girl with round eyeglasses and long braids that framed her face. She pointed to another girl all the way over on the left.

"And my niece Aurorita, isn't she with you?" asked Don Victoriano with an innocent air, wielding the lie to mask his true interest. When no one answered, he asked, "Does anyone know if maybe she's sick?"

"No, sir," replied one boy energetically, apparently the oldest of the group. And he added, as one who knows the facts, "She's fine. The thing is today's her birthday. Her mother is doing her hair so she'll look pretty. When school is over we're all going to her house to sing happy birthday and see if she got any presents."

That information gave Don Victoriano back his peace of mind. *Wonderful that she's not sick*, he said to himself, finding comfort in the news that had just reached him.

Watching the crowd of kids move on, it occured to him that he had not been to a bakery in a long time, and he wondered what color Aurorita would like the cake to be that he was thinking of buying that very afternoon.

Chapter Six

THE INVASION OF LOS CAJUILITOS

Don Victoriano glanced at the watch on his left wrist. It was a unique object and extremely precise, as an expert had told him. He had acquired it as compensation in kind, when one of the other bettors lost to him and had no more cash on him with which to keep his word—and his honor—at the cockfight. He accepted it with disappointment, but when the watchmaker in the nation's capital offered to buy it, his ill humor dissipated, and he saw the incident as another lucky break life had saved for him. He looked at it often, as if by instinct, but during the recent few hours it seemed a nervous tic and not his old habit of managing his affairs on time.

The sudden arrival of his foreman drew him from the distracted state in which he found himself. Anselmo had been working for him for eight years, and he had never burst in upon him that way. He always knocked three times before saying that he wanted to speak to him, and spoke so softly that even just two feet away it was hard to hear what he had to say.

He was very young for the role of foreman in charge of supervising the other peons, and had a physical build that did not match his responsibilities on the farm. He had no school learning, but did exhibit certain etiquette envied by some who had finished secondary school. He always wore dark trousers and white shirts, even when at work. His hands were unusual to those who noticed them. He had not a single callus to testify to his skill with the axe, the hoe or the machete for clearing paths. He seemed never to be tired, nor to resent exhausting or dangerous work. Often fourteen hours of hard work did not keep him from going off in the dark of night to find a cow who had wandered off to a neighboring pasture with a newborn calf.

When Don Victoriano saw him come through the door that way into the little office where he tended to private matters, he thought the worst. Maybe someone had stolen one of his roosters, or set fire to the rice bin, or disappeared with his horse. Those were all alarming possibilities, but were not the reason for his arrival. With his hat half-rolled up between his sweaty hands, and his eyes fixed on the floor, Anselmo spilled the motive for his visit.

"Don Victoriano, excuse me for coming in this way, but I'm somewhat disturbed and forgot to knock first."

"It doesn't matter, man. What's happened?" Victoriano gave him no time to reply before rushing him with another question. "What the hell happened on the farm?"

Anselmo wiped the sweat dripping from his brow with part of his shirt sleeve and told him, with the same restraint as always, "Some men broke in last night armed with machetes and pickaxes in the plots and parcels of Los Cajuilitos. They claimed that they were taking back those fields because you had taken them by cheating the rightful owners, and that the titles you hold to them are as fake as the paper money printed by Lilís."

"Goddamn!" shouted Don Victoriano, bursting with fury. And without a pause, becoming angrier still, "Why the hell didn't you tell me this last night?"

Anselmo didn't reply at once; he paused, trying to keep the rush of blood from drowning his employer, and said gently, "I did come to tell you, but you weren't here. I didn't see your horse either, nor was there any light on in the house. I figured you were far away, so I took the liberty of trying to resolve the situation on my own."

Don Victoriano calms down and thinks, although he doesn't say it, he is proud to have a loyal man at his side. Others in his foreman's place would have even joined in with the invaders to take advantage of the situation, but Anselmo is a straight-up man. Proven under all circumstances.

"How many are they?" Don Victoriano asks, taking the revolver out of its drawer and placing it at his waist. His question hints at his underlying anger, and his apparent calm reveals the frustration that consumes him.

"They were nine or ten, boss," says Anselmo, as if to minimize the problem. "But I got rid of them, with help from another one of the boys." He takes a breath as if to recall what happened and offers the details. "When we got there, they were breaking the wires of the enclosure. They weren't even surprised by us showing up there in work clothes, thinking, maybe, that we were part of the gang. I got close to them quietly and as soon as I had one of them at arm's length, I gave him a good one—he seemed to be the leader—and the others just split. They probably thought that all the other peons were with us and not just two guys with a machete.

"When they realized that there were just two of us and they were almost a dozen, they tried to come at us again. That's when I told them something that wasn't true, but it helped. I told them, 'My boss Don Victoriano is coming with more guys, with shotguns; you want to wait for them, or shall we settle this ourselves, like men, until they get here?' The most scared ones ran first, and then two more, and the one who seemed to be the leader had no choice but to follow them."

Don Victoriano laughed lightly after hearing the account. Now it grew, his secret admiration for this man who defended his property so bravely. He returns his gun to the drawer from which he had taken it and extends his hand to Anselmo, with obvious satisfaction. "I made no mistake with you," he says. "You're a man cut from fine wood." He squeezes his hand forcefully and loudly says, "You handled this on your own."

"No, boss, it's not solved yet," replies Anselmo, and adds, with concern, "The guy I smacked with the machete is supposed to be the brother of some army captain who is posted in Macorís."

Victoriano observes his worker, who seems nervous, and tries to reassure him by sharing his own sense of security. "Don't worry, son, I have enough to buy an anti-tetanus medication for that machete sore."

He takes five pesos from his pocket and hands them to Anselmo, as thanks for the job he's done, and asks him to do one last thing for the day. "I left a cake all paid for at Carmina's. Take it to Emiliano's house. Just tell them that it's for Aurorita's birthday."

"Right away, Don Victoriano," he says as he leaves, an Anselmo liberated from the responsibility of having beaten up the leader of the invaders of Los Cajuilitos.

Don Victoriano watches him leave with the same speed that brought him. He pours himself another whiskey. Breathing in the penetrating aroma of the distilled malt, he thinks again of the dark eyes of the birthday girl.

Chapter Seven
THE LAND CHANGES HANDS

———

Emiliano was afoot before the usual hour. He was turning inside himself like a waterwheel, in the old bed that creaked with every move he made as if it were coming apart. It was more an uneasiness of the soul than of the body, so it would have been no use to get up and smooth the bed; it had nothing to do with bedbugs or the steaminess of the weather that made him so uncomfortable. Adalgisa watched him, between sleep and waking. They were a few meters apart and covered by darkness, but she sensed him rising, walking around and returning to bed beside her. She didn't open her eyes, but she felt her husband was in a bad state of mind, with no interest in conversation and ill at ease for lack of sleep.

She has never seen him in such a state of discomfort. She thinks that maybe he's had some problem at work with one of the rice growers. They're people with big mouths and her husband doesn't get along well with people who talk a lot. Whatever it is that's nagging at Emiliano, she's not going to ask about it at the crack of dawn. The following day will have its own fussing to do, she reasons with a kind of common sense, and tries to get back to the sleep that her husband keeps disturbing with the tossing he's doing in the bedroom.

By the time Adalgisa got up to make coffee so her husband could begin the day, he had been up for hours, seated in a palm fiber chair, watching the first morning light. While she prepares coffee and stirs some coal embers to boil a few green bananas, Emiliano settles his axe in place to cut a branch that will serve as a hook with which to clear scrub out of the field he has to prepare for the new plantings.

He knows that hard times are coming. The poor have never lived easily, but this time things seem much more complicated than usual. It hasn't rained in four months, and what little he's managed to save from the harvest was finished after a week. Nobody is offering steady work; all he's earned in a week is a dribble for loading a truck and two-days' worth of weeding, for which he was paid a little less than charity. And now there's the other trouble. "The naked get everything but clothes," he says to himself, analyzing the situation he will surely have to face.

The parcel where he was allowed to build his little house was bought by Don Victoriano recently, and although the new owner hasn't said anything, the most likely thing is that he will want to clear out of his land all those who used to work for the former owner.

He downs a cup of very strong coffee, and bitter too, as there's no more sugar or honey with which to sweeten it. He regards the horizon of distant clouds, which promise no rain, and goes over his recent past. The old owner of the land treated him like family. The man allowed him to build his shack in the middle of the property, when he learned that Adalgisa was pregnant and would soon give birth.

"Keep the farm clean and don't let any squatters in," he said, and then added, by way of payment, "Put up some poles and roof the structure with palm leaves or sheets of zinc so you can live right here. Plant staples and garden vegetables so the family can eat, and after the harvest I'll give you some money."

The only thing Emiliano has in his life is about to vanish. All he has accomplished with hard work is suddenly tied to the will of a man who thinks only about fighting cocks and the money he piles up between crooked loans and doing business with people selling their belongings under economic stress.

"Are you going to leave without telling me what was the matter with you last night?"

She waited until the last minute to see if Emiliano will talk about it of his own accord. She knows that her husband doesn't like questions, and will do anything to avoid answering anything, but he's already hung his machete on his belt, his hat is in his hand, the bottle containing his coffee for later is in the knapsack in which he also carries the bananas that constitute his midday meal. So she risks asking him, knowing that this, too, will increase the hopelessness of the night before. Adalgisa has no choice but to question him directly. If Emiliano leaves for the farm without telling her what's wrong, she too will have a bad day.

But Emiliano asks his own question: "Why did you accept the cake that Don Victoriano sent to Aurorita?" The question doesn't surprise the woman. She knew beforehand that Emiliano would ask it, but she reacts as if she had not expected it.

"I didn't know it was Don Victoriano who had sent it," she says, a bit nervously, which she conceals by looking everywhere except into Emiliano's eyes. She knows her husband's temperament. She tries to evade the burden of responsibility facing her, and adds, in her own defense, "The man who brought it didn't say who sent the cake."

"The peon who came is one of his trusted men. I know him. His name is Anselmo, and he is not only his peon but also his bodyguard," Emiliano recriminates her with some severity. "And besides, who in this town is going to make a gift of a birthday cake, as if it were nothing, just for the fun of it?"

Without even changing his facial expression over this displeasure, he unties the rope that secures the mule that he uses for transportation, climbs onto the animal's back with one leap and heads for the trail that leads to the road. Before leaving the shortcut he remembers something he should have told the woman and pulls violently on the left strap that muzzles the mule's mouth and turns back to the house.

"Adalgisa! Come outside for a moment," he shouts from the gate where the fence begins, without dismounting, and waits for the woman to appear in the door.

"What is it, *viejo?*" she says, trying to tame the wild animal who lives inside the husband when he is angry over something. Emiliano looks at her for a few seconds, trying to tell her what he thinks without letting his words become undeservedly harsh.

Once he's found the words to speak to her without injuring her, he says dryly, "If Don Victoriano's peon comes back, don't accept anything he gives you. You know very well that when the donation is very large even the virgin is suspicious."

"And what if it's Don Victoriano who comes, what shall I tell him?"

"If he comes, don't let him in the house. Tell him I'm clearing a field and I'll see him later."

When the woman went back into the house, Emiliano spurred the mule on, and told the animal, as if both were companions in misfortune, "Pray God Don Victoriano doesn't force me to kill him."

Put the gourd this way by me,
not there on the road to town,
'cause you wouldn't want to see
some poor little birdie drown.

Luis "The Terror" Días
[1952-2009]

Chapter Eight

EDUVIGES, THE TEACHER

The school year is ending, but Aurorita is not happy over that. She gets bored during vacations, because she has nobody to talk to, no siblings to play with, no little friends to sing with or play hopscotch. During those first days without school she enjoys her free time, but by the end of the week she wishes classes were starting again at Olegario Tenares School. It's true that occasionally you could hear her fussing over having to get up. She thinks rainy days are great for staying home and not getting up at six in the morning, just when the rain falling on the roof makes that sound she likes so much, as it puts the body to sleep with the steady sound of raindrops.

If there's a heavy rainstorm, she likes to pretend she's sick, to get up later and get her hair a little wet, because when it's wet it acquires a shiny look from the clean water falling on it. The last time she did that it didn't end well. She said she had a bit of a headache and Adalgisa took pity on her and let her stay in bed. But after half an hour she put on a pair of shorts to play in the rain and her mother pulled her into the house by her ear, helped her to get dressed in a few seconds and immediately took her to school.

Aurorita has never been to the capital. One time she went to San Francisco de Macorís when she had to be vaccinated against tetanus and tuberculosis, but that's not really a trip, so she says that she's never been outside of La Gina, where she was born and has lived until now.

Eduviges, the teacher, has no favorites among her pupils, but clearly enjoys the company of Aurorita. She taught her in second grade and now is her teacher again, but in fifth grade. Aurorita never calls her by her full name. The other children are amazed when she speaks to her familiarly or addresses her as "*tú*." Some see that as lack of respect, but she has always called her "Teacher Edu" as a sign of affection.

Eduviges also is very fond of Aurorita. Sometimes she pretends to be angry with her and calls her Aurora, but that's only to see the child's shocked face. Seconds after addressing her that way, everything becomes a funny game, as the teacher can't keep from laughing when her play-acting makes Aurorita blush, and she, too, laughs out loud and gets the whole class laughing.

The teacher is happy with her, but also regards her with some concern, maybe even a touch of pity. During her fifteen years of teaching she has seen scores of girls disappear from the classroom and then from the town, before they've even reached puberty. The teacher then learns that they've left for Nagua, or Guayubín, into a state of cohabitation that not only goes against the condition of their bodies, but also condemns them to a life of separation and poverty.

Upon the arrival of each new school year, Ms. Eduviges stands at the school gate looking at each child to see how many girls have returned. She greets them with great joy, sustained by the certainty that she still has a few months to transform, to some degree, the lives of her students. If all her female students return, she looks up and thanks the creator that no crazy man took one of her baby chicks. If one of the girls is missing, she falls into depression for a little while, but by the fifth day she must accept the fact that she has to set on the right track those who are still in the classroom and beg providence to protect those who are missing.

When she has the time, she gathers a group of girls to sit with her under the almond tree that casts a shade over the entire yard. When they're all together, she makes sure there are no boys nearby and tells them about the nature of girls' bodies when they are almost adolescents. She reminds them of how they must keep clean, tells them about the arrival of menstruation and insists emphatically that they must not let anyone touch them.

"Nobody should kiss you: not your uncle, or your grandfather, or your father's *compadre,* or the cousins who sometimes come to your house to visit."

The youngest listen without understanding and remain in a kind of limbo. The older ones look at each other as if they have already heard this many times before, and then burst out laughing as one, and Eduviges joins them jubilantly, feeling like a girl again.

If the school held meetings for parents, the work would be much simpler. But adults are too busy with their own problems, and the daily effort to earn a living, the daily struggle to survive, and so they trust that their children are safe as a group as long as they remain in school. But Eduviges knows that's not so. On more than one occasion she's noticed men who pass by the school precisely when the girls are out for recess.

They stand outside the chain-link fence that circles the perimeter and offer lollipops, candy and pastries to those they've selected as new victims. Don Victoriano is one of those perverts. He still has not been able to approach Aurorita because the teacher stays with her from the bell that announces recess to the second bell that invites students back to class. Maybe it isn't Aurorita he's there to stare at lasciviously, but it's all the same to the teacher.

That devil is not going to get what he's after, she tells herself when the nimble horse paces close to the fence. She watches as he turns away, then turns back again after going two hundred or so meters, passes by again and then leaves. When she is certain that the girls are not in danger, she tells them, as if she were their mother or older sister, "Go straight home . . . no stopping to talk to anybody . . . remember what I told you in the yard . . . see you tomorrow." When the last little girl has left, she releases the repressed anger that is almost drowning her. "Dirty old man!" she exclaims, containing her anger over what she has seen; in reality she would like to spew out language to match the ignominy involved. Then she adds, as if to free herself, "I hope he falls off his horse, the nervy louse!"

Chapter Nine

The Relapse

Don Victoriano sent one of the youngest peons for Anselmo: an adolescent just out of the shell, extremely skinny, bare-faced, with a wide, innocent smile. He has hands frail as a corpse at the ends of arms not yet developed enough for farm work. He came to the farm a few months ago, when Victoriano promised the mother of the youngster he would make a sensible man out of him and protect him from hunger and laziness. He keeps him as the farm errand boy until he fills out enough to do farm work.

The boy rarely rides horseback. His youth permits him to walk long distances in a short time, going quickly at an even pace. He's been sent to find the foreman and give him an urgent message from Don Victoriano. That seems like a simple task, but Anselmo is a whirlwind, hard to find on workdays. He seems less a human being than an arrow that checks on the milking of the dairy cows and the delivery of the milk before sunrise. He checks the lock, counts the fighting cocks and makes sure that the coops are clean. He moves the cattle to the pasture where the grass is good, or buys sorghum and corn to feed the herd. He looks over the cacao and the field of plantains, even takes a look at the most distant spreads, to make sure no squatters are starting small farm plots or building shacks. No sooner does he finish all that than he moves on to the pigsties to see if there's enough feed there to fatten the hogs, and then straightens the fence posts that need it, as well as mends the barbed wire.

The youngster is diligent; in a matter of minutes he's discovered Anselmo's whereabouts. He returns as speedily as he started out, to tell Don Victoriano that the message has been delivered, but there's no need for that. Anselmo passes him by at such a vertiginous rate of speed that he doesn't seem to be riding the mule bareback.

He knocks three times, as usual, and waits for permission to enter. He hears no voice on the other side of the door. He wonders if he should leave to see if his boss is somewhere else in the house or try another round of knocks. He hears a light clearing of a throat inside the room, almost imperceptible, but Anselmo has a sense of hearing developed by life on a farm, where smells and sounds are fully appreciated. He waits a few seconds and, hearing nothing, knocks again, but a little louder.

"Come on in, man, I'm waiting for you," orders the distorted voice of Don Victoriano from the other side of the door.

Anselmo is frozen in place. He hasn't even voiced a greeting with his usual reverence, because he can't believe his eyes. The all-powerful—his boss—the imposing figure who goes to Mass every Sunday impeccably attired, with a solemn presence and fearful expression, lies before him in a state of inability that inspires both scorn and pity.

It's the first time he's seen his boss without his boots and silver spurs. He's half-dressed, but Anselmo can't quite tell whether he is going to bed or has just risen from it. Worn underwear barely covers his privates, and the white undershirt is worn with use. His thin hair is unkempt, his beard untended and his lightless eyes are buried at the bottom of two holes darkened by deep bags. It's difficult that a man in such condition is the master over the lives of so many others. Anselmo regards him and tends to pity the man who has summoned him.

"How can I be of use to you, boss?" he says, with some delay caused by the look of orphanhood that has made such a powerful impression on him. He looks all around and notes, everywhere, disorder and the traces of chaos. The half-empty bottle of liquor is witness to the bender that possibly took place the night before. The table that functions as a desk is of a piece with the disorder that reigns everywhere in the room. Only the vial of the pills he takes daily to control his blood pressure suggests that it may not have been one more of Don Victoriano's binges.

"I want you to run two errands for me immediately," orders his employer, in a very low tone of voice and with interrupted breathing. He has not even moved from the chair where he is not so much sitting as seeming to try to lay down, but tilted to one side.

"Whatever you wish, boss," says Anselmo, now with renewed energy, no longer dazed by his first impression. Don Victoriano stretches out a hand holding a roll of bills. It takes him a world of effort to switch position to reach the fingers of the foreman.

"Take this to Doctor Humberto," he says, as if counting the words. "Make sure nobody else is in the consulting room when you give him the money and deliver my message. If there are many people waiting for him, wait outside a while, and when he's completely alone, go in. Don't come back until you've seen him face to face. Tell him to come as soon as possible. If he asks if it's an emergency, tell him all my conditions are immediate. As if it were your own idea, tell him I have chest pains and terrible fatigue. Let him think that you noticed it and not that I told you."

"Whatever you say, Don Victoriano. I'll do just as you say. And what's the other errand for me to do?"

Don Victoriano gets up as if to give a preamble about what he's about to order his worker to do. He weighs whether he should entrust his right-hand man with information about what is disordering his mind and drilling into his chest. A man is master only of what he has not said, and he doesn't want to grant anybody the confession of a secret or the admission of a weakness.

"Go to Emiliano's place and tell him to come by tomorrow— early, so we can have a little talk." He weighs whether he can reveal more without exposing himself too much, and then adds, in a threatening tone, "If he tries to get out of coming tell him that his continuing to live on my property depends on it. I don't want to throw him out by force."

Anselmo puts on his hat and touches the brim as if he were giving a military salute. He leaves to fulfill the orders he's been given, trying to get them done with enough time left to complete the day's work. He rejoices in the vain satisfaction of knowing that, despite his poverty, he needs very little to live. His chest doesn't hurt, he's not exhausted, he doesn't like the taste of whiskey and, if it were up to him, every rooster would end up in a pot of *locrio,* with fried ripe plantains and two slices of avocado.

So many pretty little girls
look so flowery,
and to this day don't know
what love may be.

Domingo G. "Tatico" Henríquez
[1943-1976]

Chapter Ten

THE LITTLE GIRL IS GONE

Ms. Eduviges is standing silently at the gate of the school, although five minutes have passed since the bell rang summoning students back to class. She makes believe she's waiting for Don José Polanco, the principal, but when he arrives and passes by her on his way to his small office, she has no further excuse to explain her being there, so she accepts the idea that Aurorita is not coming to class this Tuesday.

Odd that she didn't come on Monday. She hadn't given it much importance, because it had rained the whole night before, and the morning was relatively chilly. She contemplated the idea that she is asthmatic and maybe her mother didn't want to risk her catching a cold and then having to miss more class time. But Tuesday was sunny, and she wasn't back in school.

She's asked the other children if those who live farther away have seen her when they passed her house, but nobody knows anything. Not even her best friends who joke with her have any news of her. Eduviges doesn't want to think the worst. She tries to stay calm so as not to alarm the teachers and avoid having Aurorita's friends become aware of the fear that has seized her.

The previous year, about a week before the Christmas holidays, the disappearance involved a child named César Augusto. The boy was absent for several days, and she went from instant worry to subsequent forgetfulness. When she learned what had happened, the event was nearly a tragedy for the whole community. On leaving school, César Augusto had stopped on the way home with some children his age at the home of his grandparents. He bet them he could climb a coconut palm that his grandfather had planted at the far end of their parcel and shake down a bunch of fruit, cutting it with a small knife. The poor boy managed to reach the top of the tree with no difficulty, but an enormous nest of wasps surprised him halfway through the cutting and in his haste to defend himself from the insects, he lost his balance and fell from over seven meters. The other children were so frightened over that fall that they ran away to avoid the blame for what happened. When some neighbors of the family found him some hours later, he was having convulsions caused by the severe trauma of a fall from such a height.

Eduviges doesn't want her inaction to join with the grief of the past, repeating what happened to César Augusto. She prefers to get ahead of misfortunes and become aware in time of what has happened to her young friend. She's reached the house of Adalgisa and Emiliano by trial and error, asking for directions on the way. She has never visited Aurorita, since their affectionate relationship begins on Monday and is interrupted on Friday, to be resumed the following Monday morning. Emiliano has not yet returned from the fields he tends to, and Adalgisa is seated on a stump that serves as a chair, shucking *gandules* she takes from a bowl-shaped gourd.

"Good day, Doña Adalgisa, I was passing by here and came to see the child." In her greeting there's no trace of the motive of her visit. If there's any problem, she wants to hear of it from her mother's lips rather than seem to be poking in other people's affairs. She extends her hand and says, with a familiar gesture, "How is everything here?"

Adalgisa stands up as a sign of respect. Her grandfather used to do the same, and her father when he came to visit. She has not abandoned the custom they inculcated in her.

"Well, thank God." She sighs briefly and adds to the reply: "Doing well some ways and poorly in others."

The teacher peruses the sky that promises early rain. She's searching for a way to avoid seeming nosey but doesn't want to leave without learning how the child is. "How is Aurorita? I haven't seen her for two days and since I was passing near you I wanted to know if she's well."

Adalgisa allows a silence as if to avoid explanations. While she evades the teacher's eyes, she thinks that since this woman is more than a teacher, a friend of her little girl, maybe she ought to know what's happening.

"Come inside and see," she says, pointing to the curtain that separates the living room from the small bedroom. And she adds, "She's indisposed, but she's going back to school tomorrow." Aurorita is lying face up with her hands clasped over her abdomen. She still has colic and headaches, and her eyes seem sunken in her gaunt little face. Adalgisa had not foreseen what was happening to her little girl. Along with the housework, seeing to it that Emiliano didn't leave for his toil without eating first, and doing other people's laundry for a few cents, she somewhat neglected Aurorita.

The teacher touches the child's forehead lightly to see if she has a fever. No, there's no fever, but she looks like a little battered animal, without the spirit to laugh over the visit of her beloved teacher.

The child's body gave several signals of what was taking place, but no one became aware. Neither the teacher with her obligations, who must watch over two dozen small tornadoes dressed up as children, nor the mother harassed by daily problems, and she least of all, who at the age of ten recently attained still does not know her own little body. The first hint occurred a year ago, but the mother thought nothing of it. The two little dots on either side of her thorax began to redden and grow, looking something like insect bites. The second message from the body appeared in her groin. Suddenly the lower part of her abdomen began to darken. Adalgisa scolded her for not washing her panties well enough, but the small grayish white secretions on her underwear announced the imminent arrival of her first period.

"She killed the goat on sunday night," she told the teacher, wishing to lighten the uneasiness she notices with the common expression used by Dominicans to indicate that she has started menstruating. She tries to comfort her, adding: "I prepared some protection for her from an old towel and made her a soup." Eduviges doesn't know whether to laugh for the child who is leaving or weep for the young woman who is starting. She wants to embrace her as if she were her mother.

"Give me a little water," Eduviges says to Adalgisa, who is embarrassed because she has nothing to offer the unexpected guest. It seems like a request, but it's really an excuse to be alone with her young friend while the mother leaves to get the water asked of her.

"My child!" cries the teacher, repressing her tears. "I would have liked to be with you on Sunday, but I didn't imagine that this would happen so soon. You must take even better care of yourself now. Remember all we've discussed in the yard when we all get together during recess . . . Now you're in greater danger because men will begin to look at you in a new way."

Aurorita looks at her as if to understand what the great danger hovering over her is. She gathers all the strength remaining in her small body and asks, innocently, "The way Don Victoriano looks at me, Teacher Edu?"

Eduviges hugs Aurorita and says, sorrowfully, "Yes, my little girl, just that way."

Chapter Eleven

THE PRICE OF EARTH

Anselmo led Emiliano to the door of Don Victoriano's house. They traveled the whole route in silence, from the property's entrance to the golden ring where the boss ties his horse. They've known each other for years, but no relationship links them, either hostile or friendly: one simply works with the team and the other at whatever work he finds. Anselmo regards him with some doubt, and Emiliano responds with disdain. Anselmo is unarmed. Emiliano never parts with his machete, which is the instrument he works with; he has never used it against anyone. He is silent by nature, not given to much speech, and no one has ever seen him become violent.

"Wait here. I'm going to let Don Victoriano know you've arrived," says the foreman dryly.

Emiliano says not a word. He looks the other in the eye and nods to indicate his approval.

Anselmo returns with the same speed with which he left. Since the hours of the day are not enough for the day's chores, he uses every second and wastes no time on trivia. "Go in, Emiliano. Don Victoriano is waiting for you."

The foreman remains at a certain distance, as if anticipating something. If there is some disagreement and Emiliano gets out of hand, he will of course act in accordance with justice first and then in the interests of his boss.

The conversation doesn't sound heated, and since his boss did not order him to stay, Anselmo decides to get back to the work before him. The host has received him in work clothes, not in his usual outfit. The small office looks orderly, as if a dutiful hand has organized everything with care. The revolver is on the table, but near the edge, where the glass top touches Don Victoriano's enormous stomach. He lets it show to impose submission, but far from the hands of the visitor, to prevent a sudden altercation.

"Tell me, Don Victoriano, how may I be of service to you?"

Emiliano knows why he's been sent for, but decides to ask, in case he's mistaken. It may be that the farm needs more hands to function, and they know him as a hard worker. Maybe they need somebody to prepare the soil, repair the fallen fences and watch over the animals. Nothing indicates that he hasn't been summoned to fulfill some necessity of the landowners.

"I guess you know that I've bought the acreage on which you're living with your family."

The phrase, pronounced in a chilly tone by Don Victoriano, is preparation for the assault to come. He serves himself a glass of liquor and drinks it down at one gulp. He observes slowly the motions of Emiliano's hands to detect what is going on in the mind of that man who knows he's beaten but has not lost his composure at all.

"Yes, Don Victoriano, that's the way it is," Emiliano assents firmly. Then he goes on, somewhat saddened. "The previous owner made me aware of that when he left. He said that since I'm a hard-working man, I could go and live in a small plot he has near Dajabón, but I calculate that's too far from where I was born and I'd rather stay."

Emiliano wants to make Don Victoriano understand his situation, knowing, however, that it's going to be hard. In fact, what he really wants is to spit out three strong words and walk out, but he has no other option. A hungry man can't be proud, much less show such pride with bare feet. So he controls himself. He steels himself and even manages to lower his head, appeal to his charity or at least get a reasonable extension of time to pay the rent on the small parcel of land he lives on. He thinks of his family and rejects, with sorrow, what he would do in other circumstances.

"Don Victoriano, I don't have the money to pay rent on your land, but my body is capable of whatever work may need doing. I can pay with my work for the corner I live in and the little strip of *conuco* I've worked to avoid going hungry. It doesn't matter what kind of work you need me for, just point it out and I'm here to serve you. It's a bit of earth where I built my shack . . . I don't imagine you need it . . . I swear by the Virgin Mary that I will look for a place to go as soon as I can."

Don Victoriano gives no sign of his delight, but joy is squirming inside him over the thought of an early celebration, persuaded that he's halfway to victory in the struggle toward his true objective. The despair of the farmer before him clears the way toward his weakness. When a man is afraid, he can be bent, and Emiliano has proven his fear of rendering his wife and child homeless.

"Since things are very clear, there's nothing more to be said," says the landowner with an air of resolve. He regards the other with a degree of contempt and faces him with some mordant phrases. "I give you ten days to look for a place, Emiliano, my friend. I want that parcel cleared and free of occupants by the beginning of the month. I'm going to cede that parcel to sharecroppers, some tobacco growers who will pay very well for the use of that land."

Emiliano knows he has no more time to beg and must now begin the struggle to survive. He puts on his hat quietly as if it were a ritual to calm himself. With a gesture of his right hand, he indicates that he's leaving, and with four words resumes his silent retreat.

"Good afternoon, Don Victoriano."

He hasn't reached the door when Victoriano stops him. The old landowner knows that Emiliano is wounded, but not yet defeated. "I could rent you, too, a piece of land, as I did with the tobacco growers," he says with sarcasm.

"You know very well that I don't have that kind of money; if I did, I would have made a deal with you, instead of looking for your generosity."

Don Victoriano smiles arrogantly, as Emiliano sets off down a tunnel of despair from which only the eyes of Aurorita can save him. The blow is already prepared, but it's essential to let the bull bleed enough to guarantee the final thrust. He raises his glass as if to make a toast, and says sarcastically, "No matter how poor a man may be, he always has something with which to pay a debt . . . don't worry, my friend, Emiliano, we'll find some way for you to manage to pay the rent."

Chapter Twelve
TELL HIM THERE'S NO REMEDY

Anselmo tied the mule about one hundred meters away before getting to the rural clinic. He's been told to be discreet about this special errand, and riding up might attract attention, among nosey people. He's not wearing work clothes. It's hard to recognize him without the rubber boots he always wears to cross channels and irrigation canals. He was wearing his hat, but removed it when he approached the entrance. Without the hat that was always part of his outfit, it was almost impossible to recognize him. He was combed front to back, pomaded, with a few silver strands of hair announcing that he would go prematurely gray. He patted his front pocket to be sure he had not left behind the money that Don Victoriano had given him for Dr. Humberto.

He enters and says hello with a hand gesture. There are no empty chairs, as a dozen of the usual patients are waiting to see the doctor.

He'd been ordered to be as discreet as possible, so he won't let the doctor know he's here. He will wait until the doctor has seen all the others first and then give him the money. He will comment on his boss' state of health as if it ocurred to him.

Two hours have passed since his arrival at the doctor's office, and there are still three patients left: a lady who coughs into a dark handkerchief, apologizing each time for the dry sound that chokes her up so badly that her pale green eyes begin to water. Next to her, a younger woman who nevertheless looks sicker discusses the illness that is taking her life. She lifts her floor-length skirt to show the wounds covering her legs, evidence of badly tended diabetes.

The last patient waiting is a very old man who Anselmo has seen outside his boss' house asking for spare change in order to survive. His hands tremble constantly. The handkerchief he keeps dropping due to the involuntary motions of his fingers has been handed back to him time and time again. A child who may be his grandson brought him and then went off to play, planning to return after the doctor has seen the old man. Anselmo has offered to take him home if necessary.

After the two women left and the child came back for the old man, Anselmo reviewed in silence what he had been told to discuss with Dr. Humberto.

"Next!" the doctor calls out in a clear voice. Anselmo slowly approaches the door of the exam room. It's been a very long time since he visited the dispensary of a clinic. He notes the human skeleton hanging from a wire in a corner of the room. He spells out silently the letters in different sizes and colors in a rectangle in another corner and looks curiously at the certificate that gives the doctor the right to practice medicine.

"Good afternoon, doctor," says the foreman and tries to speak more about what pleases him. He looks into the eyes of the professional and extends a hand bearing the envelope containing the money. He adds, gently, "My boss, Don Victoriano, sends you this."

The doctor takes the money and slips it into a big book with thick blue covers and black letters that say, *Treatise on Human Anatomy,* by Henri Rouviere. He observes the foreman, scrutinizing him as if looking for something suspicious, and tells him in an energetic tone, "Tell Don Victoriano that this was not necessary. He knows I'm simply doing my duty as a doctor, and I need no further payment for my work."

Anselmo doesn't know what kind of treatment has been agreed upon by Dr. Humberto and his boss. He is only a messenger who's been given a job to do, and he limits himself to doing exactly what he was assigned. He doesn't want to imagine anything more. He thinks knowing too little is bad and knowing too much is worse, so he turns to the second part of his errand.

"Doc, just between us . . . Don Victoriano doesn't look too good to me. He doesn't have his old strength. Look, last Sunday he didn't go to the cockfight and even decided to have an old friend handle two cock fights with roosters he had prepared for." Anselmo pauses and goes over in his mind the message he had been given. "And sometimes, he looks tired and even has trouble putting on his boots."

Dr. Humberto doubts that it's a good idea to diagnose Don Victoriano—when he's not present—of something he's already aware of. But the foreman has shared his confidence, so he plays along and remarks, not as a scientist but as one sharing a personal observation, "Your boss is on shaky ground. His body is demanding payment for all that he's done wrong for many years, and if that is not taken care of in time, the heart can't withstand the damage. That's the problem," the doctor says, as if describing the source of the illness bothering Anselmo's employer.

"I'm a simple guy," says Don Victoriano's foreman with candor. And as if to prepare and clear the ground where he's about to lay out his opinion, he soberly adds, "But, as I see it, the boss doesn't believe in your science." For a moment he regrets what he's said and tries to phrase it differently so as not to offend the doctor. "Pardon me if what I've just said offended you. But just yesterday Don Victoriano had a bottle of some stuff made up for him—supposedly to clean his blood—and the woman who brewed it said she made the mix with some *anamu* twigs, a little star anise, some basil leaves, a few sticks of cinnamon, sweet cloves, some *pegapalo* vine and sea-turtle meat. Don Victoriano first filled the bottle with Paloviejo rum, and when it dried out he filled it again, but this time with the whiskey he drinks all the time. Even if I were nuts I wouldn't drink that stuff, but the boss has a dose of that garbage every half hour."

The doctor looks at him and struggles to keep from laughing out loud. Under other circumstances he would have explained to the peon the risks his boss is taking. If his recommendations were not enough to dissuade him in the previous visit, the opinion of a simple employee would also not be of any use either.

"The stupidity of people!" says Dr. Humberto, beside himself. Then he calms down, recalling that such a phrase is not what's expected from the lips of a medical professional. He tries to erase the look that his outburst has left behind in Anselmo's eyes, and says, with restraint, "It seems that it is in the nature of man not to be prepared for the final moment of the pleasures of the body."

"The boss also told me to ask if you got the medicine, the stuff he asked you for," says Anselmo, breaking in, hoping for the right moment to leave. He waits for a reply from the doctor, who seems at a loss. When Humberto shakes off his inarticulate silence, he says, in the same resolute tone with which he first began, "Tell your employer he knows very well that wild animals cure themselves with herbs and their own spit."

Anselmo regards him without understanding the string of words that sounds like a litany to him. He decides to investigate for his own enlightenment and also to be prepared to explain it to his boss, should he have to.

"Explain it in simpler terms, doctor. What is it that I have to say?"

"Forget what I said, Anselmo. Just tell your employer that when he finishes that bottle, he should have another prepared for him, because science has not yet found a cure for his sickness."

Five minutes after the foreman left, the doctor opened the anatomy text and counted the money Victoriano had sent him with more discouragement than curiosity.

Chapter Thirteen

THE MASTER'S CHAIR

Don Victoriano makes a superhuman effort to create the impression that he is still the same fearsome man who oversees a dozen peons in his service. Only Anselmo has seen him complaining, crumpling into the rocking chair with a defenselessness that draws forth pity from the worst of Christians. At cockcrow he gathers the forces necessary to stand up again.

He hides his pain from the eyes of his day laborers. He can't afford the luxury of showing signs of weakness, that would endanger the obedience and loyalty of his workers. Although his nights almost always lead to a calvary of dry coughing and chronic fatigue, he rises every morning like the touch-sensitive mimosa—the *morivivi* plant—with a newly recovered capacity to find and order done whatever task has been neglected by the foreman.

The previous day had been a quiet one for Don Victoriano. He didn't even have the energy to attend Mass, although the priest had summoned the congregation. He wanted to conserve what strength he had to face Monday's challenges. The boy he was training as a peon obeys the order to place himself at the boss' disposal at six in the morning. At his age he eats very little; he barely tastes the black coffee, which peons use to prepare for the start of their daily tasks.

From the horse stable, he has brought the pure-blood mount that Don Victoriano rides when he has an important visit to make. He was told to have the horse ready by eight in the morning, but since the boss was breaking in a new saddle, he chose to arrive with plenty of time so as not to get there at the required hour without having finished saddling the animal.

The saddle had to have cost a fortune. Someone said it had been ordered from some saddle-makers in Montecristi, but finished in Loma de Cabrera. It's a first-class work of art, a perfect work of unbeatable craftsmanship whose every detail has been seen to with care.

The framework is made of woven *guano* and jute fibers, so perfectly symmetrical that seen from above it looks like a vertical smile on the horse's back. The rider's seat is padded with stitched quilting to avoid irritating the back of the mount. The saddle-skirts are made of virgin hide that has not been worked, and under the tanned leather there are crossed ribbons that keep the rider's legs from rubbing against the belly of the horse and secure the girth to the harness. They've left the stirrups open, so that when he dismounts, he will not encounter a tangle and perhaps risk a fall. The saddle-cloth—both front and back—are made of a different, darker leather and the riding whip has a tip made of small strips intended to move the animal without injury.

Don Victoriano examines with joy the work of the boy who aspires to the role of foreman. He's well pleased to see the effort he pours into achieving perfection in all he is asked to do. As he watches him caress the horse, he imagines that the boy is dreaming of owning such an example of perfection. When he is handed the reins, Victoriano smiles, puts his hand in his pocket and takes out twenty cents to offer the boy, who is slow to accept the money, although he needs it.

The time is now just about seven-thirty and Victoriano thinks he may not have enough time to finish all he has to do.

Today he plans to turn up suddenly, unexpectedly, at Los Ca-juilitos to personally take care of the invaders who have once again occupied his land. Anselmo did what he could with those squatters, but apparently it's true that, as the saying goes, "the eye of the master fattens the horse."

He must also meet with the lawyer who is settling the titles of his properties; he wants to be sure that those who lose their bets sign before a notary. When it comes to counting on any-body's word, he knows the only ones he trusts are the *galleros*.

He interrupts the overview of his agenda because, in the distance, he sees that the students of Ms. Eduviges are approaching. The first group consists of the boys, the troublemakers who button up their shirts only meters from the school entrance. They pass him singing unfamiliar songs, full of a joy that over-flows, as if the world were an endless party.

The second group has only five students, but he doesn't recognize a single one, so he once more examines the recently purchased saddle and is filled with satisfaction over this new acquisition. The third group approaching disrupts his blood circulation. They are six, but he recognizes only one of the girls.

He hides the fact that he's been waiting and alert by caressing the horse, which is impressive with the new saddle. Aurorita scrambles to the far-right of the crowd, hoping to slip by unnoticed. He follows her with attentive eyes, but with no other motion that might reveal that he's been waiting for her. He sees her cross a few meters from where he is breathing quickly.

He can almost smell her and feel the silk of the hair that Adalgisa has combed, and although he now sees only her back, he is still not over the few thrilling seconds he experienced when she looked into his eyes with a blend of fear and shame.

When the silhouettes in the distance can no longer be distinguished, he rises with difficulty from the saddle, which still does not have his shape and is therefore beautiful, although somewhat uncomfortable. He dismisses his previous plans— places he had to stop at—and feels enthused by the visit he has decided to make to the little house of Emiliano and Adalgisa. The date he gave them stands as the time due for their departure from his parcel of land, but just in case, he has planned another offer that will make it possible for them to pay him rent.

He begins to ride slowly, and the rhythm of the spurs suggests the tune of "Dolorita," a *merengue* by José Lazaro Sosa that he's always liked, but that for over a year now he's taken to singing with different words. He sings it in silence when others are present, and out loud when he's alone.

He whips the horse's haunches vigorously. He wants to be on time to the first appointment of the day and, like the children who passed him earlier, sings the secret song with guilty pleasure:

Aurorita, if my eyes fill you with pity,
Aurorita, I will pull them out, you'll see.
Aurorita, when you look at those deep sockets,
Aurorita, how much sorrier you'll be.

Chapter Fourteen
THE OFFER

Adalgisa is becoming impatient as she searches the horizon from the yard of the shack. It's past midday, and the child will be back from school at any moment. The visit from Don Victoriano makes her so anxious that her nerves won't let her serve the coffee that's already been requested by the guest.

She walks away, takes down some washed clothing she set out to dry in the sun and replaces those with three freshly washed sheets to dry before nightfall. She goes to fetch the eggs newly laid by the hens and then goes near the fence to gather some green fava beans for the next day's midday meal. She tries to collect her disordered hair in a gray kerchief to serve as protection and at the same time provide her with a *babonuco* on which to balance the water she must fetch from the stream.

She goes and returns, vacillating and feeling lost. She agonizes over last-minute chores, wasting time on details to avoid the small living room where the two men are in a rather heated discussion. She understands it's a conversation between men, but listens with sharper hearing because she thinks she hears Aurorita's name, and that falls outside their purview and into hers.

"Doña Adalgisa, our teacher Eduviges sent you this," says a small song-like voice, as if glad to be fulfilling an obligation by handing her a note entrusted to him for delivery.

"Aurorita stayed with the teacher, but she's not being punished," adds another small messenger, without even imagining how that innocuously spoken phrase has given some peace of mind to one who needs it badly.

Adalgisa hands them a bunch of ripe bananas as both gift and thanks for the service rendered. Watching them devour the unexpected treat from her, she turns her eager eyes to the note she rushes to open.

> Good morning, Doña Adalgisa. I'm writing to tell you
> not to worry about Aurorita. She'll be home later. I will
> take her myself so she doesn't have to walk alone.
> She needs an older person to give her some advice,
> as sometimes little girls listen more attentively to their
> friends than to their mothers. I'm her teacher, but also her
> best friend, and your daughter loves me very much. I'll see
> you later.
>
> Edu, the teacher

Adalgisa looks up at the sky, grateful for the note Aurorita's friends have brought her. She breathes deeply; her soul has come back to her body, and she turns her attention to salvaging the rest of the day. Inside, the men still have not settled their affairs. She catches only bits of words that reveal nothing to her imagination. And she doesn't recall Emiliano speaking with anybody for such a long time, not even with her when in bed, looking up at the ceiling, when they talk through their insomnia until sleep finally comes over them.

"Excuse me, Don Victoriano," Adalgisa rushes to say, interrupting a dialogue that is rising in volume, and that she is trying to understand. The speakers are silenced by the abrupt new presence. "I'm going to get water to fill the pitcher. I'll be back right away."

The men return to the discussion, but somewhat calmer now that the entrance of Adalgisa has softened the rigidity of their talk. "I'm going to allow you to remain on my property without paying rent for another year," says Don Victoriano, with some reticence, and adds, as part of the proposition, "but I want you to pay me what that costs with three days of work every week."

Emiliano thinks he has seen the light at the end of the tunnel of his despair over finding some place to live. He has no idea how far the debt will grow that now has a tinge of ignominy.

"Just tell me where you need me and what I need to do, and you have my word that I won't cheat you, Don Victoriano."

In the twisted eyes of the landowner gleams a diabolical light whose meaning Emiliano has not yet grasped. He has been pushed to the edge of the ravine, led by the nose, step by step, to the trap, and now it's only a matter of hastening the fall; the whole plan set in motion on Aurorita's birthday will be accomplished. Now he must know enough to wait until the fruit ripens, and then climb the tree and pluck it, because it never falls on its own.

"The work is not for you, Emiliano. Look, I don't have anybody to do the chores around the house that need to be done in order to keep the place from falling on me. The last woman I hired to do that ran off with one of the peons, and they stole some gold jewelry and a little money I had in the house. So I prefer doing it differently this time. There's not too much to do but sweep the place thoroughly, dust the furniture, make the bed, wash a few dishes and, from time to time, straighten out the clothes when they get out of order." Don Victoriano talks around the issue, masking his true motives. He hopes to deceive Emiliano's reasoning, which must be clouded by the time they get to his family's obligatory departure.

Don Victoriano prepares the ambush and says, in a calm tone, "Aurorita can do that. It's obvious she's a bright, hardworking girl. And it won't interfere with school, because she would only go from Friday to Sunday, and she will return home at about five on the afternoon each day."

He pauses, as if to let the blow land in Emiliano's consciousness, and gets ready to leave. "Talk it over with her mother, Emiliano, my friend, and let me know by Monday."

Emiliano watches him leave, untie the horse's reins and rise without haste into the saddle he had ridden for the first time that very morning. When Adalgisa returns with the water, she realizes, without a word from her husband, that the visit has not ended well. Emiliano has a sad, lean look. He appears to be a different person, different than the one she left only minutes before. She's afraid to ask why, because she knows that anger reverberates in the blood of her husband whose face is already deformed by rage.

"And what did you and Victoriano agree on?" Adalgisa asks, to see if speaking for a few minutes will allow Emiliano to rid himself of the fury that is only too obvious to see. He looks at her and replies with the usual silent stare.

"On nothing, woman, but we have to find a place to move to tomorrow." He takes the hat hanging on a corner of the guano chair he has been sitting in and starts out to find some other air to breathe.

"But you didn't arrive at any agreement?" she asks, without any hope of a reply. She knows that after he leaves it will be a long time before Emiliano chooses to bring up the issue again.

"That shameless old man wants Aurorita to go to his house as a servant, three days a week, supposedly to help with household chores."

"But she can do that," Adalgisa hastens to answer and explains why. "She knows a lot about how to take care of a house, because she's seen how I do things. If she doesn't have to do it during school hours, I don't see any problem with her going."

Emiliano hastens the recently oiled machete to his belt, takes his sack and the *garabato* and decides to go back to his parcel. When he's near to the fence that surrounds the small house, he stops and reprimands the woman with repressed hurt because he realizes she does not understand what is happening.

"And as for you, when are you going to give up being a damned fool?"

He swallows the curse he was about to spit out, and says, as if resuming the conversation he had with Don Victoriano, "It's not true that he needs a servant. That's a big fat lie. That bastard wants to have our little girl."

Chapter Fifteen

THE DECISION

"No, Mommy, I don't want to go to that old man's house."
Aurorita shakes her head, expressing refusal. She is begging.
Adalgisa's plea has left her with no interest in her food, something she normally enjoys a lot. She came home from school
thirty minutes ago and still has not even tasted the bit of
spaghetti with rice that awaited her for lunch.

In between sporadic tears and broken sighs, she has removed her uniform, folded it well before hanging it up and
taken off her shoes to replace them with slippers to relieve her
wet feet.

Now she's seated at the edge of the bed, tying up her hair
with a red woollen bow while choosing a pair of shorts to wear
while helping her mother finish the housework not yet done.

Her mother watches her with both joy and nostalgia. It was
not too long ago that she used to carry that child in the crook of
her narrow waist while cooking on the stove or taking Emiliano
his food so he wouldn't have to waste time coming home from
his parcel. *She was a child not too long ago*, thinks Adalgisa,
suddenly frightened now that men will see her as a woman and
she herself will learn to flirt in response to their flattery as they
compliment her eyes, hair and full lips.

"But, my child, nothing will happen to you."

Her mother wants to calm her down, but she herself is not clear as to what she needs protection from. Emiliano says she'll be in danger in Don Victoriano's house, but she considers that to be the fear of a jealous, overprotective father. "Look, silly girl . . . you go on Friday after school, Saturday all day and on Sunday you'll be home again by about twelve o'clock. And besides, your father will be close by in case you need him."

Adalgisa doesn't know if she's done the right thing asking Aurorita to help them avoid having to move from Don Victoriano's land. When the plan was proposed to her the day before, the child didn't seem to give it much importance, but now it seemed she wasn't going to cooperate of her own free will by agreeing to the sacrifice her mother asked of her.

Watching her come to the table with no appetite, her mother troubles herself with the thoughts that pierce her mind. *Maybe,* she thinks, *Ms. Eduviges has had something to do with Aurorita's change of attitude. She claims to be my child's best friend and advises her as if she were her mother or older sister. Maybe she's told her that she's too young to work and that, if she begins, she'll end by quitting school. It may be that she doesn't like housework and does it to help me because she feels obligated toward me, but doesn't want to do it for anybody else.*

Adalgisa shakes her head violently, trying, to no avail, to stop thinking of the child's motives and to stave off the fear that has begun to assail her.

Emiliano is due home any minute and it would be terrible if he found them in the middle of that conversation. She must persuade her to go and clean the house, make the boss' bed, wash his dishes in the kitchen and organize the clothes that are in disorder. She must win her over, before Emiliano arrives, because he is determined to leave the parcel rather than bow down to Don Victoriano.

"Did you discuss this with Ms. Eduviges?" she asks. She wants it not to sound like an interrogation, and decides to go about this in another way. "Don't tell me you blabbed and told the friends you walk home with about this."

The sound of the mule puts an end to the conversation. She places a finger on her lips to insist on silence, and says, softly, "Start eating, we'll finish talking when your father leaves."

Emiliano sits down to eat without a word. He hasn't removed his hat or undone the belt that supports his machete in its sheath. He looks at the little girl for a little while and silently attempts a faint smile that dies in the corners of his lips, then turns his eyes to his wife, so that she can find in them the fury that has not left him.

Rather than eat, he chokes. It seems something in his throat doesn't allow passage to any food and he leaves the table without finishing half of the portion they've saved for him. He goes to the water pitcher, serves himself a jar and sweetens the rest of the coffee left over from breakfast; then he goes to the yard and brings in the whetstone to sharpen his machete and takes to the road the same way he came in.

He said not a word, barely touched his food, did not stroke his daughter's hair as he always did when he came home; he only stared into Adalgisa's eyes with a mute and furious look of reproach. He knows that a war has begun for him and doesn't want to fight on two fronts at once. First he must conquer the heartless Don Victoriano, and later he will come to terms with his wife, if he survives the ambush life has placed before him.

Adalgisa wants to resolve the impasse, but doesn't know where to begin. She runs out to see if she can catch up to Emiliano, perhaps to tell him some sweet word that may mitigate what is tormenting him, but her husband is already a shadow moving away, disfigured by distance.

It would be so easy if only Don Victoriano would allow her, rather than the child, to do his housework. In that case there would be no problem with Emiliano. He's never been jealous or mistrustful. She was even gone for ten days when she went to Nagua to her grandmother's funeral and spent the whole time there until the vigil of the final night.

Adalgisa goes back into the house and finds the child has calmed down. She finished her food and is nodding off seated in a chair that's leaning against the wall where the living room ends.

"Now that we're alone, tell me, my child, will you go to work at the house of Don Victoriano?"

Aurorita looks at her, and holds back the tears that want to fill her eyes. "Yes, Mommy, I'll go. I'll go for you, but I don't want to be in that house."

"But, why not, my child?" says her mother, adding, "From what I know, he hasn't done anything to you."

Aurorita gathers her courage and allows her fear to come through. "Every time I go to school, Victoriano is standing in front of the house. He looks at me a long time. I pretend I don't notice, I turn my face, but I feel him looking at me. When I come out of school he's still standing there, waiting for me to pass by. The kids tease me a lot. They say, 'The old man is waiting for you,' and then they all start to laugh. It's true that he hasn't done anything to me, as you say. But when I pass his house, I think about how he has damp clay in his eyes, because he has a look that makes me feel dirty."

Adalgisa interrupts her with a close embrace, kisses her hair and her forehead, moves away slightly to look into her eyes and hugs her again in a live knot that lasts and lasts until the tears of both mother and daughter join in a single grief.

Chapter Sixteen
THE MOVE

Emiliano jumped off the mule in one vertiginous move that took him back to his best youthful days, and Adalgisa was surprised at the good spirit he was in. He walked in with his face illuminated by an internal excitement that transformed his usual opaque appearance into a new face. He had left the parcel earlier than was his custom and gone into town to speak with the former owner of the lands he still lived on, and he had been given the news that brought him this joy.

"Start packing our things, because we're leaving early on Monday," he called out from the fence where he was tying up the animal that provided him transportation, and in two long strides he was inside. He took off his hat, unburdened himself of his machete and approached the table. He didn't even glance at the plate where they had saved him a bit of white rice and a fried egg. He unbuttoned his shirt, which was soaked with a viscous sweat, and told her more calmly, "I was hired as assistant foreman at a farm they just bought. God doesn't abandon anybody, and especially not good people like us."

He settled down to eat, but his enthusiasm didn't give him any rest. He looked at the food but again covered it with a plate to keep the flies away.

Adalgisa never questioned any decision made by her husband. But to move so far away was not to her liking at all. Of course a wife had to accompany her husband wherever he had to go, but what about Aurorita's school? She had nobody to leave her with until the end of the school term. Not even her teacher could take on such a sacrifice, and since she had no family nearby, there were no intimate friends. She had no other solution than to abandon everything and start over somewhere else.

"Emiliano, why don't we wait until Aurorita is in the next grade?" She says it more to herself than to the husband, who will not listen. Adalgisa knows that proposition is useless. She knows, as no one else does, the soul of her husband, that he will put off saying something for days and weeks, but once the words are out of his mouth, they never go back in. Really, she doesn't want to move. She hates going from here to there and from there to here, running around without settling down in the place where she truly belongs. Poor and landless in Pimentel is the same as poor and landless in Dajabón and Monte Cristi. But she is aware that contradicting Emiliano means months of quarrels, so she resigns herself and begins to throw their few belongings into a couple of flour sacks and a few cardboard boxes.

"I've already told you we have to leave," he replies immutably.

Leaving the town is not escaping, much less a defeat to Emiliano. It's a strategic retreat before returning. He loves the place where he was born and has been all his life. It's only a matter of a change of air, working hard as he has done from boyhood, putting together some savings and buying a piece of land of his own. A place where he can grow what he likes to eat, where he can celebrate the rain as if each drop were a gold coin. A piece of land for all that life would send him, to love Adalgisa, have other children, grow old without any distress, look after his grandchildren when they arrive and be buried under some oak or caoba tree, so that his bones could return as branches, where the mockingbird may sing and fireflies light up the night.

But to achieve that, he has to leave. Leave his parcel to the landowner before he strips him of it.

Emiliano accepted, though grudgingly, the fact that the child would go to work three days in the house of Don Victoriano. He would stay close to her, close to the house, be there if any threat were to put her in danger. He thinks that Aurorita too has faced a degree of heartache because the family is forced to leave their home. Her willingness to work as a servant has given him the strength to hope for what was previously considered impossible. Now he has somewhere to go, to take his wife and daughter and start over, with renewed faith in himself.

For her part, Aurorita did well on her first day at work. She told them on Friday afternoon after coming home that she had washed a mountain of glasses and dirty dishes, emptied a chamber pot full of urine, made a big bed and another smaller one in one of the rooms at the back of the house. Cleaned the glass over photos hanging in the living room, hung up clothing that somebody had washed and swept the roosters' coops because the peons had the day off and the cock shit stank like the devil.

She would return the following day. It was Saturday; there was no school, and surely she would finish much earlier and would get home with enough time to play with the other children, even bathe in the river and work on a composition that the teacher had assigned.

Emiliano also had extra work to do. When he finished his usual tasks, he would return to clear the parcel they occupied, leaving it better than when he took it over; he would pick the lima beans and gandules that he knew were ready to eat, cut the ripe eggplants and okra, knock down the remaining bunches of green bananas and tie up all the laying hens in order to restart the brood in the new place.

Emiliano figures that with good luck he'll be at his new job on Monday at six in the morning. He would leave on Saturday afternoon to put up the shack in the new parcel, put a few things in place before the women arrived and on Monday morning, he would go to the foreman for his orders. Aurorita and Adalgisa would arrive Monday afternoon. They would find a school where the child could be enrolled and keep learning, speak to some grocer willing to sell food on credit to the farmworkers and work from sun to sun until they could afford their own land.

Victoriano still doesn't know that Aurorita is leaving the next Monday. It's a beautiful Saturday, sunny, but with a temperature that hardly feels tropical. He's planning to have drinks with some friends who have opened a new bower for dancing beside the Nagua River. He examines the clothes he left in total disarray but that were now organized and hanging up neatly.

He says to himself, "She's almost my wife, that little girl."

Chapter Seventeen

THE MERENGUE

Don Victoriano left with plenty of time, so as not to miss the details of the celebration. He was to be the baptismal god-father of the firstborn of his friend Rigoberto, a man given to drink and interminable binges, a lover of billiards and the game of Pintintín and, like Victoriano himself, a hardened fanatic when it came to betting and rearing fighting roosters.

He went to the celebration on horseback, rejecting the offer of a vehicle. He wanted to prove to himself that he could still ride for several hours, dance all night, knock back several whiskeys and get back home with no young people to guide him or peons to hold the reins.

It was more than a year since he had last been to the place, and he had a hard time recognizing it from afar, until he heard the music from the speakers. The bower that preceeded the bar was full of young girls who were enjoying their beers in the company of older sisters, or perhaps an aunt, or, in the case of the emancipated ones, a sentimental companion. The party had not yet really begun. A group of musicians were entertaining those enjoying the light early snacks, singing old songs such as "El picoteao" by Trío Reynoso. In their voices, they seemed to be irreverent reincarnations of the true performers of those melodies:

Come here, black girl with flowing hair,
Come be with me right now;
I need a pretty girl like you
To dance this *picoteao!*

The clear voices of the musical ensemble rivaled the nocturnal atmosphere of the bar, The Three Roses. Before the establishment acquired that name, it was called Candilejas, and then became Rigoberto's Bar, until the owner became the father of triplets and celebrated the achievement by renaming the place after that birth.

The accordion player was from Mata Bonita de Nagua, the drummer from a place in the community of Arenoso, the *güiro* performer and the singer from Pimentel and the marimba player from Azua, but he went to live in El Cibao at a very young age. They had strict orders not to play any new *merengues*, or those that were popular with their own generation. They were told to stick to the emblematic pieces from the era of the *perico ripiao* that were sung by those who initiated the style. They were to perform anything in the *merengue* classics from Toño Abreu to Bartolo Alvarado.

The young musicians complied begrudgingly, and only to stick to the agreement. The owner of the bar had his reasons. It made no business sense at all to hire young outfits that would play music for people of their own generation, because those would not drink three pesos' worth all night. At most, they would have one or two beers, maybe a jug of Brugal rum to be shared by two couples, and this was not making anyone any profit.

That's why they had to insist that the band perform the *merengues* of yesteryear. The pieces that had formed the musical life of "real men," the "hairy-chested" types who respected the tradition of a family name and the strength of character that would have helped them to face tough times. Music to suit the taste of the region's tobacco growers, the large-scale cultivators of coffee and cacao, those who had made a fortune in the shade cast by the regime of Rafael Leonidas Trujillo or the government of Joaquín Balaguer, the owners of honors and fortunes, those who had no difficulty advertising their magnanimity by ordering drinks for the whole house and spending money with both hands.

Rigoberto had a good eye for business and therefore set out to test his luck with the bar. He knew from personal experience that music has a prodigious ability to return to an old landowner his love of life, the pleasure of squeezing the waist of the girl seated on his lap, pulling her closer to their obese abdomen and their libidinous intimacy, thereby marking her as their property, just as they marked their newly purchased herds.

Alcohol too produced the touch of magic that might be missing from the night. Each libation broke the hinges imposed by moderation and sense, and hard liquor made it possible to pretend that they were still men with the ability to cover a young body with boundless ardor. The owner of that bar built on the riverside knew all that very well, so he repeated, at the end of every set of *merengues*, "Play only what those old men applaud." He would give the order with authority, and then he would go to check the cashbox to see how sales were going.

Don Victoriano refused the amiable offer of the table that had been reserved for him by his *compadre* Rigoberto, and chose, instead, one where he would feel safer. He selected a medium-sized table not suitable for more than four people. He positioned it at a forty-five-degree angle to allow him to face the street, the singers and the adolescent girl who worked as cashier.

He ordered two bottles of the same brand and four glasses. One bottle was for Rigoberto and his wife, should they choose to sit with him, and the other was for his own use. The fourth glass was for serving doubles, sometimes straight, sometimes with tonic, to be sent from time to time to the cashier with the young man who served as waiter and to whom he gave generous tips for his work.

The band singers understood the orders and were pleased with the results. The older men applauded madly, sending beers to them, offering contracts for future events and dancing the slow *pambiches* that did not overwhelm their heartbeat. In the voices of those boys the legend of the best performers of *perico ripiao* lives again. They're kids just learning the music, but with respect. The old men close their eyes to enjoy the tunes. As they listen, they each return to their memories, to the Poza de Bojolo, Matancita de Nagua, to bohemian nights with friends of the Los Juglares Trío serenades, to all the places where they were happy, to those memories of pleasure and aroma that lead to the nights in the past.

They are three young men, not even yet thirty, but the dancers don't see them—they're transparent—translucid spirits that bring back to life Francisco Esquea, Pedro and Domingo Reynoso. They all sing, a fiery chorus, a potpourri of the old guard:

> Saint Anthony says
> I'm the boss—that's so—
> The one patron saint
> of *guaraganó* . . .

> Other people's women
> ain't my cup of tea,
> 'cause they taste like eggplant—
> not a treat for me.

> If you're gonna love me
> don't make me feel bad;
> I don't got nobody
> and it makes me sad . . .

Joy surrounds the table, but in the soul of Victoriano one complaint burns hot. He wants to sing like them, out loud, but he can neither sing nor dance to the *merengue* that he hears in his mind, distant but clear, because every letter of the lyrics hurts him. When the music stops momentarily, he has another mouthful of liquor and furiously hums:

What a good spearman I was before!
Even my voice now won't rise no more . . .

Chapter Eighteen

THE LAST BET

Victoriano returned to the big house at dawn on Sunday. His *compadre* Rigoberto kept him company from the route out of Pimentel to the crossing with Arenoso and from there on watched him go on, still singing loudly the *merengues* he had danced with the cashier of the Tres Rosas Bar. They begged him to stay overnight at their house, but he refused all offers they made to avoid his having to ride alone at that hour.

"Men are born one day to die another," he preached angrily and filled his glass again to toss back the final elixir. He handed a bill to the waiter and after a quick signal the boy returned with the horse from the stable behind the establishment.

In other days he would have complied with the wishes of his friend. He would have stayed to finish the drinking party in safety and comfort, awakened by the aroma of a border style *sancocho* and, once he was over the headache that follows a binge, would have taken the trail to town. But he wanted to end his days as he had begun, without softie nonsense or timidity, heading into every risk head first, building the wall of his good name brick by brick. The day before he had sent away all his hired men and day workers, leaving only Anselmo, who said that he was off to San Francisco de Macorís and would be back the next day without fail.

That's why he chose not to stay in Rigoberto's house. He calculated that he would get home at about four in the morning, sleep some four or five hours and wake up to discover Aurorita sweeping the house, straightening up the kitchen and maybe attending to his clothes. As he rode, he whistled the old *merengues* to the beat of the rhythmic motion of the mount he was riding. Sometimes he stopped whistling to go over his accounts and sums to be collected from those who owed him money; he thought of his cocks and his occupied parcels of land, his cows ready to be milked and the parcels that needed immediate attention. Then he turned his eyes to the road so as not to go astray, and he remembered Aurorita and sang once again "Juana Mecho" the last *merengue* he had asked the musicians to perform:

> I love and adore her:
> Who'll steal her? She's mine!
> She's been private property
> since she was nine.

Adalgisa has already packed all the household things for when Emiliano arrives. She's put together only those things that are essential, to keep the trip and the moving in as bearable as possible. The most painful aspect of packing was folding up the little girl's clothes, wrapping up in newspapers the two dolls that Eduviges gave her and disposing of the blouses and shorts that have become too tight on her and not suitable anymore, given the changes that have taken place in her body.

Emiliano has less to carry. He will never dispose of his machete or the whetstone or his work boots, so it's simply a matter of tossing into a bag the hat that she gave him, which he has not yet worn, the photo of his parents, the scapular depicting the virgin of El Carmen, a pair of khaki pants he seldom wears and a pair of shoes he never wears because they're uncomfortable, precisely because he never wears them.

Aurorita has not thought about the details of this sudden move. She's only sad over leaving the house, being far from her teacher Edu, never seeing again the children with whom she goes to and from school and leaving the life of freedom she has lived in the middle of that wooded area where her father built their little house.

"And what if there's no river where we're moving to?" she asks, as if all her happiness depended on swimming in fresh water, dunking her body in it entirely, as the *cayman* does, and splashing hard to wet her mother, who doesn't like to be splashed wet.

The move also offers her another joy. She imagines that the new town may be more beautiful and the house doesn't have to be lit with an oil lamp. Maybe the hospital is nearby and when she graduates as a nurse, she will be able to walk to work. She imagines dressing with a tiny hat placed on her hair gracefully, and a long, beautiful gown with her name embroidered on it in blue letters on her chest. What she really wants to be is a veterinarian, ever since the time she had to help her father assist a cow that was giving birth. Watching her father's devotion as he saw to the animal moved her so much that she's dreamed, ever since, of easing the lives of others, including the animals she loves so much. Maybe the school she will attend is enormous and has a place for doing exercises, and, above all, there will be no eye full of damp clay waiting for her when school lets out.

Aurorita notes with resentment that the boss' horse is tied to the gilded ring at the entrance. She had hope he wouldn't be home, so she could finish her chores quickly and run off before his arrival. She turns the doorknob carefully, enters without a sound, walks gingerly toward the kitchen, avoiding along the way a disorderly pile of shoes, a bottle, a strap and a belt with a silver revolver.

Victoriano snores at a halting rhythm that ends with the sound of a sweet flute. Aurorita hurries to gain time. She washes the dishes with extreme care. Not even allowing the glasses and plates to touch, she rises gently so not even the water can disturb the peace she needs, as she wants to hurry without noise, sweep the living room a bit and then run hurriedly toward her house.

She focuses her hearing, because she thinks she's heard a grunt. She doesn't move a muscle; in total silence she sniffs in the direction of the contiguous wall, behind to where the don is sleeping. She recovers from the momentary scare. She's already almost done with washing the dishes and organizing things; all that's left now is the sweeping, and she'll be all done. But fear seizes her again: She thinks she's heard something, but this time louder.

"Aurorita, please bring me a little water." It's the voice of Don Victoriano, but at first, she doesn't recognize it. She thinks maybe he's still drunk. His voice is distorted and it's hard to understand what he says from a distance. "Come, child . . . hurry up, girl!"

A spasm of terror runs through the soul of Aurorita. She knows it's an order, but fear stiffens her, and no part of her body wants to obey. The bedroom is closed, but she imagines that behind the wall he's half-dressed, seated on the bed, waiting for her to come in, so he can look at her with those eyes that are always dirty. Like a little cloud, the mockery of her classmates crosses her mind: "The old man is waiting for you."

In the room somebody seems to be getting up; he approaches the threshold, and suddenly there's a thump, as if something large has fallen to the floor. Aurorita trembles, dazed, waiting for the tears that she feels rushing to her eyes; looking around her she is overwhelmed by despair over being alone in the middle of that house, without the touch of Adalgisa or Emiliano.

Anselmo comes in to place himself at the orders of his employer and this puts Aurorita at ease again. "Little girl, is Don Victoriano awake?" Aurorita is still afraid and finds it hard to answer at once.

"I'm asking you if the boss is awake," Anselmo repeats; he needs to know before leaving for the farm.

Aurorita recovers, looks at him with secret gratitude for his presence and says, faintly, "Aha, he's awake. He called me, asking for some water, but then I didn't hear anything else. I heard the noise of something falling, but he hasn't called me again. I'm almost ready to go, I'm all finished."

Anselmo is concerned over what the little girl has told him. He goes near the transom, sets his ear to a crack in the old wood but hears nothing on the other side.

"Don Victoriano, it's Anselmo. I'm back."

There's no sign of life to be heard from the main room of the big house. Anselmo repeats the phrase, raising his voice a little in case his employer is fast asleep. "Don Victoriano, if you don't want anything else done, I'm going to Los Cajuilitos." Anselmo pushes the door gently to ascertain if he's asleep, but without violating the privacy of his boss.

"Aurorita, come here!" shouts Anselmo, beside himself, and before she can react, he gives her an order. "Run! Go to the dispensary and find Doctor Humberto. Tell him Don Victoriano needs him urgently."

Anselmo wonders whether to stand him up or let him lie on the floor just as he's found him. Victoriano is lying on the floor, with his right hand crossed over his chest at the level of his ribs, his eyes rolled upward and his mouth half-closed. Anselmo continues to talk to his boss to see if he can reanimate him until Doctor Humberto arrives. "Boss," he says, "I know you don't believe in the doctor's word or in his science, but maybe there's some sense to it. If I were you, I'd stop the drinking and leave the partying to the young guys. I'm a man like you and I understand there are things you hate to leave for good, but sometimes there's no place to hold on to and life tells you that's enough. Forgive me for saying so, but that's what friends are for."

When the doctor arrived Victoriano had been dead for ten minutes. He left the world one Sunday morning, and his friends must have waited in vain for him to arrive for the cockfight riding his pure blood horse and tending his invincible birds.

Anselmo went to inform the police, and on the way got the peons together and prepared for the news.

Dr. Humberto regarded Aurorita, under the false suspicion that she had been the cause of that massive infarct. He looked at her with pity, as if she were just awakening to life with a sinister mark that she would have to remove from her memory. He stroked her hair with a touch of tenderness. "Go home, little girl, it looks as if everything is over."

EAST OF HAITI

English translation by
Mark Cutler

Chapter 1
OLD JEAN MORISSEAU

" . . . In what split second were our lives snatched from us,
what place, what twist in the trail?
Along which of our journeys did love
pull up to bid farewell?"
Jacques Viau Renaud

Old Jean Morisseau has just turned seventy years old and
still works the land as if he were a boy. His arms are very thin,
but still look like branches of a ceiba tree. Although he looks
gaunt, his chest muscles give the impression that in the past he
was a great athlete. He has a circumspect but rhythmic gait. He
almost does not look at the ground when walking. He moves as
if he were a cane stalk, protected under a reed hat which he
rarely removes. His big round eyes stand out over his thin lips,
which upon opening show two rows of sparkling teeth. He
watches the horizon as if waiting for a sign from nature. The
neighbors are accustomed to that elusive figure in the shadows,
which sometimes wanders through the narrow streets of the old
Haitian town of Miragoâne.

On his right wrist, he wears a woven leather bracelet,
adorned with a fuzzy effigy of some indistinguishable deity. On

his other arm, between the elbow and the wrist, he has a tattoo in red and blue ink. Someone tried to draw the national flag for him when he was young, but it did not go well; that is why, perhaps, old man Jean hardly ever shows it. Below there is a phrase in printed letters that says: *L 'Union Fait La Force*, unity makes us strong.

He has just returned from the small farm where he spent his day shift. He has not had a steady job for a long time. If he arrives early at the square, he is hired by the trucks that depart toward the capital. At other times, he is merely employed as a rustic bricklayer in the buildings being erected on the outskirts of Miragoâne, where the village borders Petionville.

If he's lucky, he may get a job as a gardener at one of the houses of the rich people, near the village, or as a tour guide for the few foreigners who come to visit this rural part of Haiti. Guiding tours is what he enjoys the most because he likes to walk visitors through the alleys and places from his childhood. He proudly tells them, "In that square, Toussaint avenged the affront of the French who questioned his authority as leader of independence . . . There is the new market of Les Cayes. It used to be a market for trafficking the slaves that the Europeans brought in ships. Here," he is sad to say, "is where my ancestors brought from northern Nigeria were sold. Now it is a handicraft market. This large house, this ramshackle house is what remains of the great Hotel La Boheme, where the best artists from Europe exhibited their works."

With more time, and if he does not suffer too much from the pain in his bones, he leads tourists through the old quarter to see the workshop of his friend Gadel, the best wood carver in the country.

Old Jean takes off the hat that protects him from the blazing sun. The day's heat has not given him a minute of truce. He looks up and considers the passing clouds that stud the sky. He knows that it will not rain, but still hopes for a small downpour. The dust lifted by the passing cars thickens the sweat that the afternoon has deposited on his face. He squints, as if the dust did not exist and plunges back into the stage of his life when he was the same age as his grandson Christopher.

For a moment, in the tangle of his memories, he recalls the smell of ripe guavas piled up in a wicker basket on the kitchen table. Childhood floats around in his head like soap bubbles. He looks toward his youth and feels a thin drizzle that attempts to spoil the happy evening that he has set aside for playing soccer. Yes, memory has the power to revive everything, to turn the wheel of time in the opposite direction so that nothing remains in the past.

A car passes in front of the hut and drops another layer of dust on the vaguely pleased face of the elderly man. Old Jean returns to the present. He does so suddenly, as if shaken by an unexpected blow, with the weight of so many memories squeezed together in his head. He takes off his thick eyeglasses. He looks younger. His marked cheekbones and elusive forehead give him the look of a man descended from warriors. He cleans his glasses mechanically and in the same way puts them on again without great effort. The two grooves on the top of his ears slide the glasses into place. Although he has already cleaned them, still looking over the round glasses, he does so again out of habit.

In the distance, a row of cramped huts extends to the village of Petionville, equally poor but bigger than Miragoâne. From that distance, they are almost imperceptible. Old Jean looks at them without seeing them. What his dull eyes seek is the silhouette of a robust young man, dressed in khaki pants and sneakers. His eyes scrutinize the distance, looking for that strong, tall man, whose silhouette evokes the ancient Yoruba warriors of northern Nigeria. Perhaps that man will appear with other clothes, a new hairstyle, a wider face or sharper features, but he remains in the old man's memory as he last saw him ten years ago. Despite any superficial change in the man, his fatherly heart will warn him unequivocally when his son, Claude Morisseau, makes his entrance to Miragoâne.

Chapter 2

MRS. TURTLE AND MRS. DOVE

"Grown-ups never understand anything by themselves,
and it's very tiresome for children to be always
and forever explaining things to them."
Antoine de Saint-Exupéry

The sun has gone off imperceptibly, blurring the landscape while dyeing everything gray. The natural light languishes and bulbs lit in the distance seem to increase in size. During the day, the sun of Miragoâne is a large, radiant gold coin. Fortunately, at nightfall, it changes the direction of moist winds, brings them on land from the coast and surrounds the roofs, cooling the stiflingly hot day. It is a blessing to live here and not anywhere else in Haiti.

Miragoâne has no more than two hundred huts, but as a crossroad toward other towns and regions, it looks like a village that is more active than the others. The traffic in the streets, incessant during the day, decreases at sunset. Narrow alleys separate the houses. The women wash their garments there and hang them on improvised clotheslines. In the same space, they cook the few meals they get. The children play among the drying clothes. When the work of the day ends, men bring chairs made of thick palm leaves to take advantage of the shade along thin walls and rest there. Late at night, you can hear the muffled voices of marital arguments and the whisper of lovers. Without electricity it is not possible to watch television, and the battery-powered radios do not support loud music. Only the chirping of the crickets and the grasshoppers' chants are heard. The village seems to fall into a deep sleep, but in reality, it remains half-awake with the movement of trucks and the heat inside homes.

A thunderous music breaks the silence. A car passes. The driver moves to the contagious rhythm of a song by Quatuor Septentrional. The driver's partner seconds him, moving to the rhythm of the music and singing the chorus in Creole, the native tongue of the village. The lyrics are in French, a colonial legacy of past slavery. Suddenly a truck crosses, weighed down with a load of bananas. Old Jean sees them pass, and the seconds-long glance is enough to cause him to dream of another world and another life that he knows takes place outside of Miragoâne.

Young Christopher tries to finish dinner. He is eleven but speaks as if he were older, the result of hardships suffered in his short life. When his father left town, he was not yet two years old, and Christopher does not even remember his face. The little he knows of him comes from the spoken portrait created by his grandfather, Jean, but in all the descriptions something of the real person is lost. He remembers less of his mother; she left before his father and has never returned. These absences have matured the child. He and his grandfather have become two partners united by blood and misfortune.

Christopher hates yams and *malanga*, but he has long known that many hours will pass before the next meal comes. So, he tries and pushes the food into his mouth, mixed with a salami whose taste and smell cheat the palate. He cuts the one slice into bits to extend the enjoyment of the food and pretend there is more of it.

"Grandpa," Christopher says as he finishes his modest lunch, "tell me again the fable of the turtle and the dove."

Old Jean does not answer. It is hard to move from one memory to another.

"Grandpa!" the boy repeats, raising his voice. "Tell me the story you told my dad about the dove and the turtle that went on a trip."

"Why do you want to hear it again? I have told it to you many times."

"It's just that I really like the stories of when you were little."

"Life was simpler then," Old Jean observes to himself. "The world was simpler."

"Come on, Grandpa, tell me that story again."

"Okay, just this one time," his grandfather says and puts on his glasses and hat, as if preparing to enter into the story along with his grandson.

"Long ago, in a distant time, our land had many flowers in its fields and many birds in its sky. Not like now, when only the falcon-like *mafini* and the owl fly, and in the savannah only a few poisonous *javillas* and thorny *guasábaras* still grow. At that time, the birds flew from Port-de-Paix to the North, to a city even farther called New York.

"All the birds went back and forth, and on their return, they described how beautiful that place was. But the turtle could not leave because she was born without wings. As the doves are kind, like some people, one of them felt sorry for the turtle and said, 'Mrs. Turtle, I will take you with me to the North. This is what we are going to do. I will carry in my beak one end of a branch of the mahogany tree, and you will cling tightly to the other end. But you must not say a single word during the long trip. No matter what happens, don't say anything. Do not release the branch or you'll fall into the water.'

"Mrs. Dove grabbed one end of the mahogany branch and Mrs. Turtle the other. She moved her wings strongly and began to rise, reaching ever higher in the sky. Mrs. Turtle clenched the branch with her jaws, and little by little they were gone from the village. When they reached the sea, Mrs. Turtle and Mrs. Dove looked down at all the animals that had gathered at the shore to say goodbye to their pigeon friends who were leaving for the North, as usual.

"The animals were shocked to see Mrs. Turtle also flying and said gleefully, 'Look who's going up there! Look, look, friends! Mrs. Turtle is going to New York!' They shouted all at once: 'Mrs. Turtle is flying to New York!'

"Mrs. Turtle was so excited flying through the air that she forgot the advice of Mrs. Dove. So, to prove that she was ready to live in the North, she said in English the words she had learned: 'Bye, bye, my friends!'

"When she opened her mouth, she let go of the mahogany branch and fell into the sea. And so, dear Christopher, there are many doves in New York City's parks, but the turtles are still in Haiti. . . . "

Old Jean looks sideways at his grandson to make sure he has fallen asleep. He can't help thinking that, if the child's mother were with them, she would take care of him; things would be easier. But like many others, the woman crossed the border into the neighboring country, and nobody knows when she will return. He repeats the ancient fable that he has told himself. His father told it to him at night, and before that, his grandfather told it to his father. He would have liked his son to be Mrs. Turtle and stay next to him, not like Mrs. Dove, who flew away and still has not returned.

It is Sunday in Miragoâne. Christopher plays in front of the house, under the distracted gaze of his grandfather, who is leaning against the window of the house. He has drawn a hopscotch with crooked lines and jumps over the numbered boxes. Although he is the smallest of the group, he does not fail to skip the lines and count.

"*Yonn, de, twa!*" he exclaims, while resting in the third box. The other children look at him incredulously. They do not understand how he can jump so high with such short legs. Christopher catches his breath and returns to play again.

"*Kat, senk, sis!*" He reaches the sixth box, and his face shines because he is very close to winning the round again.

The other kids applaud him. Despite his short legs, he somehow behaves more maturely than his peers, helping his grandfather as none of the others do with their families. Before going to school, Christopher passes by Mr. Antoine's house to collect the bucket of leftover food that helps him to fatten his grandfather's only pig, as he is responsible for feeding it. Then he goes to Martine Labatte's grocery store to get some chocolate and bread or oatmeal to eat for breakfast on the way to the École Président Toussaint. It is just shy of seven o'clock in the morning, and he is ready for school. He stands to one side of the road in case a passing driver wants to give him a lift to school. If he does not get a ride, he walks as fast as he can down the narrow, dirt side street the four kilometers to school.

"*Sèt, uit, nèf, dis!*" Christopher shouts, while jumping like an antelope or a frightened rabbit. Now he laughs, and his childish laughter flies, mocking the hot afternoon air.

From the hut, his grandfather makes a gesture of victory. Christopher raises his arm and claps hands with Jacob, which means that he accepts the challenge and will try to beat Christopher at hopscotch.

Darkness has covered the horizon, and mothers call their children urgently: "Jacob!" "Paul!" "Stephen! . . . *vini nan kay la, li nan jwèt ni!* Come inside, no more playing."

Chapter 3

The Escape of the Warrior

"The departure of Mackandal was also the departure
of the whole world evoked by his stories."
Alejo Carpentier

Christopher returned from school two hours ago. He is
sleepy and tired. He spent most of the night spying on his grandfather who, as usual, rummaged among the things he kept inside
his old trunk. He never opens it during the day. Although small
and of common wood, it seems to have been a very elegant
piece, with big black hinges and leather corners. Every night
the old man pulls out some papers and reads and rereads them,
as if they are very important. Sometimes he takes out some yellowish postcards that he carefully examines for a long time. He
looks nostalgically at the diary Claude was writing before leaving. He ends up by reading faded newspaper clippings about
political events that are already part of Haiti's history. Then, as
if overcome by a stampede of memories, he gets angry with
something or someone and tosses the papers out the window.
Then he regrets it and goes to the backyard to pick up what he's
thrown out and returns it carefully to the trunk. If he's very tired,
he doesn't open it, but rather just sits on it and caresses the faded
wooden lid as if making sure the past is still there. His grand-

son has always wanted to know what the papers say, but the old man hides them like a treasure, preferring to wait until his grandson has learned to read them alone without having to ask permission. That moment has arrived.

The boy still does not come to the table to see what his grandfather has made to eat. Nor has he taken off his sweaty school uniform. He has rolled up the hem of his trousers past his ankles because a light drizzle turned the dust of Miragoâne's main street into mud. His shirt has lost its blue color from so much washing.

Old Jean sees him from afar and thinks his grandson is sick, he who, although hating *malanga*, sits quietly eating the dish on the table. Jean approaches slowly and touches his grandson's forehead to see if he has a fever. No, his temperature is normal. If the child is sick, it may be his stomach. But it's not that either, because the boy has not complained or held his belly.

"Come on, boy, eat. I cooked you a delicious meal of eggplant and white rice."

Christopher does not answer, but looks at his grandfather standing a few steps away and launches a tirade of unanswered questions into the air.

"Grandpa, what is my father like? All the children at school talk about their dads and moms, but I can't. I can only talk about you. . . ."

Christopher's question seems matter of fact, but Old Jean is concerned. To answer his grandson is to once again walk barefoot on the hot coals, to relive the painful absence of his son.

"Well . . . ," his grandfather says, wondering where to start, "when your father was born, I was the happiest man alive. I saw his smile and I didn't mind that there was little work for me in the market, or that your grandmother had died in childbirth, leaving me the baby, a small and fragile little thing. I felt strong and capable of taking care of him.

"I struggled to lift Claude out of the poverty we were in, so that he would not suffer. Everything I earned was for his food and his school, so that he would not lack anything. Your father grew up with a healthy mind and a strong body. God rewarded me with a good son, one who always behaved. No one ever complained about him to me. He was no friend of taverns or gambling. He did not drink, just a small glass of *clerén* on Sundays, and he hated cockfights, things that I liked a lot. I won the lottery with my son, because he was always an upright man. But then he fell in love, and everything went to hell."

"How?" Christopher interrupts.

Holding back his hurt and missing his son, Old Jean answers, "Well, that was when a woman from Dominiken came to town. Your father told me later that she had been a very important person in her country. He said she had studied at a law school. I remember she spoke with such authority that no one contradicted her. Your father told me she was not a bad person, but she fought to defend the workers, and this had brought her many problems with the authorities there. So, she had to leave her country and go abroad to avoid trouble. Then she decided to return no matter what happened, even though the waters had gone down. Your father liked to say that she returned because she loved her country. To me, she seemed like a nice, intelligent person, but I did not want her for your father. I did not want anyone from the other side for your father. When she came to this town, I thought something serious had happened to her that caused her to leave her life and come to Miragoâne, this forgotten town where no one comes for pleasure.

"Yes, my grandson, she suddenly appeared and changed your father's life. She came with some Americans who wanted to make a documentary about the customs of the villages that had been enslaved during the colonies. She served as a guide, and could travel here without problems, speaking Creole with us and

English and some French with foreigners. The children went crazy when they saw the cameras and microphones. They were always in the middle of everything. The vendors offered them everything wherever they went.

"Your father was the only one who stayed away. She was the one who sought him out . . . I do not know why. They met somewhere. The woman was explaining to foreigners how Petionville had been founded and was wrong about some of her information. Your father corrected her calmly and had the courtesy to do it in Creole, so the others did not realize that she was wrong. She was very grateful; that's how they met and continued interacting.

"At that time, neither your father nor I had work. The little we got at occasional jobs was just enough to eat. So, when she offered to pay him to guide the research team, he accepted immediately. It was not much, but they would give him food, and if the project was extended, some money would be left for the rest of the month.

"In the morning she would pick him up to take them to places they wanted to see. At first the people looked at them with suspicion and refused to answer the questions they asked. But little by little the people softened and agreed to be photographed and tell their stories. Your father showed them the markets and the wood craftsmen. At night, they went to see religious ceremonies and voodoo rites in Gonaïves, and he would explain their meaning so that they did not say wrong things about our culture.

"That work did not last long. One day, they told him that the money had run out. They had to leave, but would come back later to complete their research. Your father was paid a few dollars with the promise that they would look for him on their return to finish the interviews with the village elders and visit other places of interest. My son did not believe the story, but they returned shortly afterwards; there were two men, a fat one with a camera and another one with glasses. They remembered the names of people from the village, and that impressed me. The woman came with them, and Claude was glad to see her again. He became one of the group. They brought him a T-shirt just like the ones they wore and a cap with the logo of the organization. The woman came to bring the gifts and, at least in front of me, she was very nice and friendly with Claude. I think that bewitched him.

"This time, they stayed longer. They convinced your father to stay with them, offering to increase the payment to take them to other villages in the central part of Haiti. Although they would give us more money, I objected because I knew your father well. I knew that if he got involved with them, it would keep him away from home forever. But he did not listen to me. He was seduced by curiosity, by the novelty, by the woman and by being part of such an important mission.

"Early one morning, the woman came alone to look for him so they could leave together. He said goodbye to me in few words. It was a cold goodbye because we did not agree on this decision. They first went to Jimaní to meet someone. When he returned, he seemed like another person. Your father lived through something that made him change his way of thinking. I saw in his eyes that he was determined to leave this land. Although he hugged me with his usual affection, his spirit had seen other horizons and his heart now belonged to two places. He, loving this land as he loved it, only spoke of moving to Petionville, to better himself by doing something else, to save money and settle down with this woman but to continue to travel the whole country.

"She turned your dad into another man . . . that's what women do. He began to read books on Haitian writers who died long ago. She convinced him that he was a talented storyteller, that if he wanted, he could write about his life, like in a diary. Surely, someone would be interested in it, she convinced him. Your father started writing and was very happy. He did not let anyone see what he was writing, not even the woman he was in love with. When he did not return home, I started to look among the things he left behind and found the diary in the bottom of a box, among many other books I had never seen."

Christopher is mesmerized by the words falling from his grandfather's thin lips. Jean does not even look into his grandson's eyes when he speaks, only out into the distance, toward the road out of Miragoâne. Like his grandfather, Christopher dreams of the return of this man he has yet to know, whom the grandfather describes as a Yoruba warrior, brave, strong, daring. With his childlike imagination, he pictures a mulatto giant with tense muscles, a spear in his hand instead of a book or a pencil.

"Grandfather, can I see my dad's diary?"

Old Jean pauses and considers quietly whether the boy should know that part of his father's life. "Why do you want to see someone else's diary?" he asks, feigning a certain harshness in his voice.

"I know how to read, Grandfather, and I would like to know what my father was like."

The old man thinks for a while. He does not want to violate his son's privacy, but deep down he knows that Christopher has the right to know everything about his father's past.

"I promise to dig it up and let you read it. I'll do it Saturday afternoon or Sunday, when we get back from church."

Christopher's face suddenly lights up as if a sunbeam has shined on him through a door that is slightly ajar.

Every Sunday, Jean takes Christopher to hear the wise words of the old minister in charge of the congregation. Christopher does not like to attend the early service at the ancient hall on Liberté Street. He has never liked the musty smell of the decaying, peeling walls. He prefers to enter almost at the end of the ceremony, to take the candies offered to the audience and enjoy the religious songs adapted to popular music. Christopher knows that these songs are sacred to the elders, but he likes to move to the joyful and contagious rhythm of the Sunday praises, and many others also dance celebrating the deity Ogun, the incarnation of the warrior with eyes of fire, machete in hand and holding the keys to the kingdom. He is violent and shows no mercy to his enemies. *Will his father be like that?* He doesn't think so. His grandfather has told him that Claude got along with everyone and gave him no problems.

Other worshippers dance and profess their devotion to Eleguá, the deity of the roads who opens and closes the road of life. When foreigners, eager to observe this ritual celebration ask what saints these divinities correspond to, the answer is that the first of them is the very same Saint Michael the Archangel and the second is like Saint Anthony of Padua or the Holy Child of Atocha.

After church, Old Jean rummages through the papers kept in the worn trunk. Christopher's heart races as he imagines finally being able to read his father's diary. His grandfather takes out a notebook with a thick brown cover and solemnly steps closer to deliver it to his grandson. Christopher cannot wait.

"Is this my dad's diary?"

"Yes, boy. I'll let you read some pages, but be careful not to damage them. I have worked hard to keep it in good condition all these years."

Christopher's whole body shows his delight as he examines the cover and repeatedly reads the word in golden letters: *DIARY*. He runs his hand slowly over the surface to show his grandfather that he'll be very careful. Then he slowly opens the newly discovered treasure. The pages do not have printed numbers. At the foot of each sheet, his father drew a small circle and, in clear handwriting, numbered every page himself. Christopher thumbs through it quickly, just to see if his father followed the ascending order of the numbers, and then returns to the first page to start reading.

The first sentence gives him pause: "Claude Morisseau's diary." At his age Christopher does not know what a diary is, but his grandfather says it's about someone's life. Then he realizes that somewhere in those pages he will find his father's handwritten explanation of why he left, like Mrs. Dove, rather than return to his natural home, like Mrs. Turtle had done when she let go of the mahogany branch.

Chapter 4

THE DIARY OF CLAUDE MORISSEAU

———————

" . . . Mercy, Lord, mercy for my poor nation, where my
poor people will die of nothing . . . "
Luis Palés Matos

Although Christopher understands the story that his father
tells in his diary, the boy stumbles on words he does not understand. He has had to guess the meaning of many odd words, but
keeps moving forward and thinks he might ask his teacher what
some of those words mean. Or maybe he can ask his grandfather, another day. He has heard similar words in the news his
grandfather listens to on the radio, but still they do not have concrete meanings for him. What his father wrote perhaps is unre-
lated to his small world. Christopher has never read the word
"game" nor the word "ice cream" nor "cookie." That's why he
always ends up agreeing with his grandfather when he says,
"Before, the world was easier for all. . . ." Yes, that must be it,
Christopher concludes. The world of his father is very different
from the one that he has had to live in. He thought it would be
easier, of course.

Christopher spends the weekend reading, moving slowly.
He has read fluently up to the page his father marked with the

number thirty, then backs off to try to understand what is happening. In those pages his father covered October to December, but did not indicate the year he began to write.

October 10
    Mercedes gave me as a gift this notebook with stripes. It is a standard notebook except that the cover is a bit thicker. She bought it for herself but gave it to me. She says that my way of telling things has really pleased her, that I have a certain ease of speech, and she wants me to write the same things that I tell her when we are together. She jokes that if I write in the same way that I speak, Haiti has one more poet and one worker less. She says that a poet lives inside me, and sadness is not letting him leave. This is another of her exaggerations. She wants me to start writing about my life because it is what I know best.

    When she lends me a book by those writers she likes, I understand why they are poets and I a mere construction worker and any other job I may find. They have the gift of saying things better than anyone else. They speak about pain and life, freedom, anguish, nature and feelings, in the most beautiful way. They add music to their words. They are real poets, even though hunger surrounded them and closed their doors. That is why they can talk about blurred faces, like this Jacques Roumain in his poem "Filthy Blacks."

    I'm not as confident as her. There are days when I am at a loss for words and I cannot find a way to put down on paper what I am thinking. The path from the mind of a man who is suffering to the hand of one who wants to write a story is a convoluted one.

October 21
    Mercedes came to visit me today. She came as fresh as a cayenne with newly opened petals. I wanted to ask her about a

new book she's reading, but something stopped me. I have not told her yet, but every time she laughs so lavishly, the world stops and I notice her plump, well-delineated lips and her white teeth. I've only kissed her once and I feel that with that one kiss I've known her forever. Sometimes I want to ask her to give me her mouth, so that I may keep it and kiss her endlessly. And it will not matter to me if she later becomes a bird, a dragonfly or a firefly. I know well that through that mouth I can love her in all forms. Whatever she decides to be after our love runs out will make my fears evaporate and my grief disappear into her body. She has only kissed me once, and I do not care if she flies or crawls, if she lives on the other side of my delirium or if she's the queen of my inner demons.

Sometimes we look like two suns in the same sky, eclipsed in unison, like a phenomenon without compare. Me in Miragoâne and she in one of those placid corners of her country to the east. But she also hinted that, if the difficult situation that exists there because of her collaboration with the workers is not resolved in her country, she will have to go abroad, to Europe, where her cousins live. She says that she can find a project and save some money. On the contrary, I believe that we must continue fighting here. Every time I look down and see the earth cracking due to lack of water, every time I see the bleak landscape of Miragoâne, I think this land is sick, as are its people.

November 2

Last night I agreed to take Mercedes and her team to the All Souls Day party. I walked ahead so they would feel safe at all times. She was near me, two steps behind. I noticed she was either worried or nervous. Following behind us was Jimmy, the chubby photographer, with protruding eyes like a frog and an angel face. He repeats every word he hears in order to remember it. He's an economist, but in his free time he works as a photographer. Mercedes says he has a chronicler's eye and the sensitivity of an artist. Eduard, a middle-aged sociologist, takes notes and writes. He doesn't speak much but observes a lot. He becomes another person when he interviews people in the villages—the musicians, the spiritual intermediaries and their officiants, the artisans and the keepers of legends and traditions. His eyes sparkle, as if a volcano had erupted in his pupils, and immediately he asks lots of questions and records his conversations in the notebook that he always carries with him.

The rumble of a drum in the distance served as a guide, a beacon to illuminate my route along a dangerous coast. I remember as a child I walked the same path following my grandfather. I felt the drums call me. I felt them in my blood. My grandfather would look at me from time to time to make sure I was not far behind. Many people went to these celebrations. The town was left empty, soulless. The voice of the drums boomed closer, breaking through the darkness and silence.

When we arrived at the Gonaïves cemetery it was about midnight. There were scattered groups, almost all belonging to the brotherhood that organized the ritual. Some formed a circle around the musicians, giving instructions. A large bonfire cast flickering light and shadow. Another group cleaned an imposing marble tomb, throwing scented water and local liquor on it. The women placed different-colored flowers and candles all around it. A goat soon-to-be sacrificed to the gods had been tied to a dry, leafless tree.

Dressed in red and black and holding white handkerchiefs, an old woman and a young girl danced barefoot, shaking their bodies with their eyes closed. The two women belonged to the brotherhood, and the younger one seemed possessed by a spirit. Jimmy moved around and shot photos nonstop. A skinny man, almost all skin and bones, crawled among the feet of the people like a snake. Jimmy caught him with his camera and then turned to capture the moment when a woman drained the blood of a black rooster over the grave to the right of the entrance. It's the first to be dug and dedicated to the Lord of the Cemetery.

They gave us cups with clerén liquor which we accepted without hesitation. It was not the time, nor was it wise to reject it; we had to do like everyone else.

Jimmy headed toward the musicians beating the kettledrum; they were adorned with red, green and yellow handkerchiefs. He took several shots without the performers realizing it, they were so absorbed in their drumming and their rhythmic, monotonous songs. Meanwhile, Eduard asked questions and took notes about each group. Mercedes translated and explained, struggling to be heard above the deafening drumbeats.

My new friends wanted to meet the supreme official of the Feast of All Souls. His real name was Emmanuel, but many people in Gonaïves call him "Papá," and others who are less close call him "El Viejo." My friends asked if what they heard about the old man's powers was true . . . that he could pronounce an invocation and become a snake or a bird; if he could go through walls, walk without leaving tracks or on burning coals, or if he levitated. Has he been seen in Port-au-Prince and in Jérémie at the same time and on the same day? Had I seen him eating broken glass without cutting himself?

Papá Emmanuel was sitting behind the musicians. One hand stroked an unmoving black dog with narrow ears and the other held a walking stick. His beard, splattered with gray hair, hung long and thick. To speak with him, it was necessary to get permission from his junior officiant, a huge mulatto woman with dark, frizzy hair. She was dressed in a long, green tunic. Every once in a while, she rang a bell and took off a handkerchief from the many that she wore around her waist to throw it into the fire.

We asked her if we could speak with the old man and she let us approach.

I went up and asked the old man to bless us. Mercedes was very interested in meeting him, but to my surprise she did not say or ask for anything. Jimmy did not even attempt to lift his camera, perhaps impressed by the aura of majesty and seriousness that emanated from this figure. Eduard, always in control of his emotions, was startled by the penetrating gaze of Papá Emmanuel. The old man, venerated by the people of Miragoâne as master and lord of the rain, capable of selling your soul to the mysteries he embodied and leaving you like one of the living dead, filled the air with astonishing stories of his powers.

He stopped petting the dog and slowly rubbed his beard. I looked closer and noticed wasps flying in and out of a hive they had built in that scrubby, tangle of hair. The junior officiant explained to us with great conviction that the wasps were the souls of the spirits Papá Emmanuel served. Amazed and incredulous, we moved on in silence and went to sit down on a gravestone, where we could calm our pounding hearts and continue watching the ceremony. Mercedes did not speak a word. I went to get glasses of clerén.

December 16

Mercedes was very distant today. Maybe she was upset because I told her that she was giving more importance to going away than to our plans to do something for the dispossessed in Haiti. She did not mention anything about our short affair. I think I understand her. She is in transit and has no roots in this sick land, as do my father and me and these men who are aging prematurely. But it's also not right for me to say that; if I count the days she has spent here, I hardly get to a few weeks or months. I cannot leave the life I have made here. The world that she paints for me beyond Miragoâne is very beautiful, but I also hear many stories of those who left and have not been able to return. We should not have to choose between the things we love. I know she will ask me to accompany her to the other side. My heart is divided and fears that it is time to make a decision.

December 24

A week ago, Mercedes went to the Dominiken. During the walk from the guest house where she stayed to the bus stop of Petionville, she just answered yes or no to the questions I asked to make conversation. She looked at the landscape and the houses as if she wanted to keep every detail in her memory. She was leaving, and we did not know when we would meet again. She did make vague promises. Maybe she has learned to love these streets and the little boys who run around without big dreams. She returned the greeting to someone we met and then retreated into her silence, which to me seemed sad, over-whelming.

Mercedes has promised to return to Miragoâne as soon as she finishes a job that is awaiting her and she can save some money. Sometimes, she talks about living together in another country, not her country, perhaps in Puerto Rico or Central America, where the sun and the sea are similar to ours. I like this plan a lot, even if it's only a dream. She has broadened my horizons so much.

In reality, I do not know if any of that will be possible. I believe in her words, or, rather I dream of her words, but it's her silence that tells me she will not return. Maybe we have not been together long enough for her to have a reason to stay with me. Bondye, jan mwen ta renmen genyen zèl! *My God, I wish I had wings!*

December 31

The table is ready to ring in the New Year. All of Miragoâne celebrates the festivities of the end of the year, a time to forget the hardships. The boys dress in clean shirts in keeping with the party atmosphere. My heart does not feel like celebrating. I went through Madame Du Pre's grocery to buy some griot *with white rice and beans to encourage Dad to forget that Mom is not present. Although many years have passed, he feels nostalgic during these times. He did not want to have more children, and now we are alone. Madame Du Pre's* tassot *looked appetizing, although it was too spicy for my taste. It's a shame that not even Haitian food is the same.*

The radio is playing a collection of songs by Charles Aznavour. Each of the themes reminds me of Mercedes. That's why I prefer to read the book she gave me for my birthday, because it also reminds me of her but in another way: I feel her closer to me. The book is by a Cuban writer named Alejo Carpentier. He knows better than I the reality of these wastelands—I am amazed. The name of the book is The Kingdom of this World*. He describes a popular celebration like the one that takes place at the end of the year in Hinche and around Ouanaminthe. The author refers to two kingdoms, one in which men can choose their destinies and another where the Yoruban gods have everything decided from the beginning. He describes the Yoruban kingdom with such certainty that sometimes I believe him, but I do not see that kingdom in which each person is free to determine his own fate. . . .*

The jubilation and hollering that have exploded outside mean that the New Year has arrived. I step out for a moment to mingle with the crowd, to extend my greetings and rejoice a little, although I must force myself to smile. In the distance I see fireworks. I cannot hear them, I can only see the eruptions of golden light. In four or five hours the morning will begin. It is a new year, but nothing has changed.

January 1

We have forgotten what January means in the life of this town. Nobody remembers what we are because they are too involved in partying and drinking. I remember that when I was a child January was a month mainly to celebrate our freedom and honor the earth, to renew faith in the future of our nation. At the school in Jérémie, the teacher, Anne-Marie, would line us up in front of the visiting authorities on Independence Day and instruct us, in her deep and serious voice, "Now, children, we are going to sing La Dessalinienne *for our visitors." Some would sing the national anthem with love for that beautiful song, but many of us did it to earn the extra points that she promised us for our performance. I remember the time she lined up four or five of us children in front of the visitors and, without warning, told us, "Claude, Saule, Phillips and Josephine, please explain among the four of you the biography of Toussaint." I trembled, being very shy, until emboldened by the courage of the others. Saule recounted the hero's childhood. Phillips commented on his awareness of the need to fight for the liberation of the slaves. Josephine narrated how he succeeded in proclaiming independence. My task was to describe how he died in France. I never liked that part. I would have preferred to explain how a slave was freed from the stock and chains and achieved glory. Or Phillips' part. Josephine's part would have been better, because I could have explained the incredible feat the blacks achieved in their struggle for freedom. To me, they were like an army of fireflies that went through that historical night, giant trees with ebony skin and the heart of Ogun that won the Haitians the pride of being free and making a name for themselves.*

No one remembers that in January anymore, except in the schools. Outside, however, January is a time to party, to set off fireworks, drink clerén, *listen to loud music and enjoy the hustle and bustle of the festivities.*

January 3

The hangover of the New Year's festivities has passed, and we return to the same old thing: the daily struggle that overwhelms the senses and dulls the mind. I look in all directions, and people languish little by little, along with their houses. A distant cloud means that perhaps it will rain in another town, but not here. Here, the earth begins to show the scars of intense use, of a predation that only brings hunger. I am reading Masters of the Dew, *and Jacques Roumain's verses about us do not leave my mind. It would seem that they are eternal.*

"But working the land is a battle day by day, a battle without rest: clearing, sowing, weeding, watering until the harvest is done, and then you see your mature field, lying before you, under the dew, every morning and you say . . . 'Me, just another guy, master of the dew,' and pride fills your heart. I speak the truth: it is not God who forsakes man, it is man who leaves the land and receives his punishment: drought, misery and desolation. . . ."

His words resemble the truth, and the truth is not always useful for the speaker. But there should be another way. Somewhere in this country, from the cradle to the grave, there must be some key to reversing what happens. Mercedes is convinced that organizing is essential, that so is understanding what happens to us and why, and then agreeing on what we can do. On the way, we must protect each other so we each can take a breath, feel some relief, find consolation. However, this strategy has only given her problems. Organizing migrant workers in the eastern part of the Dominiken has been a matter of bringing justice, but the landowners will never approve, and the colonists here are not fond of my closeness to her. Had she stayed calm, remained invisible to the eyes that scrutinize the movements of others, she could have survived without taking so many risks. But it's too late for her and me.

Knowing the truth somehow forces you to live the consequences of that certitude. Knowing Mercedes and reading the books of Roumain, Alexis, Carpentier . . . has made me a different man.

It probably changed her to see the poverty of the cane workers and witness the onset of death at every bunkhouse crammed with migrant workers. It has changed me to know her and understand that the misery there and the misery here have the same roots. But the sun rises again, and it is a clear message that Haiti still breathes.

Since he begin reading his father's diary, Christopher has not been playing hopscotch on weekends. He has realized that the adult world described in the diary does not belong to him at the age of eleven. Despite this, he will not give up the opportunity to enter his father's life and observe the difficulties of the poor people, like his grandfather. He already feels a little bit older.

His playmates think he's being punished for something and they hang around the door to his hut, hoping for him to appear. Jacob, the oldest, asks his grandfather what has happened to Christopher, why he doesn't come out to play. Old Jean replies with a certain air of pride, "He's is reading a very important book."

Jacob looks in to find out what book can possibly make his friend miss a game of hopscotch, at which he beats them all. Jacob spots him sitting at the table, head hung over the pages. He's too far away to read the title. *It must be a great book for Christopher not to come out and play with us as usual*, he thinks, as he moves away slowly.

Chapter 5

THE MIRAGOÂNE SCHOOL

"There can be no keener revelation of a society's soul
than the way in which it treats its children."
Nelson Mandela

It's the beginning of a new school week, but Christopher is
not feeling up for school. He lies on his bed, staring vacantly,
avoiding his grandfather's inquisitive eyes. On the table, his oatmeal cookie and his cup of chocolate await him for breakfast.
Christopher is enveloped by the sweet smell rising from the hot
pitcher, and his body slowly begins to react. Old Jean, at his
side, thinks about the absent son and then calls the boy to hurry
up and get ready for school.

"Ti gason ale, jwenn ke li nan tan!" the old man says, without any reaction from Christopher. "Come on, boy, it's getting
late!" he repeats in Creole.

Christopher rolls off the cot, rubbing his eyes. His grandfather picks up the small backpack with the few school supplies,
but not before removing the diary from one of its pockets.

"On Friday after school you can continue reading," he says
softly.

Christopher's face takes on a strange mixture of obedience
and anger. After all, it was his father who wrote the diary, and

if there is anyone with a right to read it, it is he. His grandfather pretends to be busy, afraid to face the boy's eyes because he once faced the same firm look in other eyes.

An old friend of his father offers to take Christopher to school in the van along with the day workers he transports. This wealthy-looking man sometimes visits his grandfather. Today, he honks for Christopher to climb aboard, but the boy rejects the offer, shaking his head, "*Non, di ou mèsi anpil. Mèsi anpil, mesye.* No, thank you, sir." The man smiles. It is good to know that there are still boys with good manners.

At school, Christopher takes a seat toward the middle of the classroom where he always sits—never in front, near the teachers. The rule is to sit alphabetically by last name, and his starts with the letter *m*.

The teacher's name is Edith, but almost everyone calls her "madame" or just "teacher." Christopher is the only one who uses the teacher's first and last name correctly. She likes that. She is tall, very thin, distinguished and has a harmonious voice. Her uniform always looks neat and impeccably ironed. The blue color combines well with her black skin. As she walks, her hips swing rhythmically. In the whole school, only she moves like this, much to the distraction of the boys as she walks down the desk rows.

Edith was born in Port-au-Prince and grew up in a southern suburb of Paris, where her father served as ambassador for many years and where she had studied to be a teacher. When she returned to Miragoâne to meet her grandmother and saw that children grew up without learning to read, she decided to stay. Illiteracy was unacceptable to her. There was no better place to exercise her vocation but to help the children of the area. Then she fell in love with her native country. Christopher loves her very much, and she loves him too. He feels quite comfortable addressing her directly.

"Teacher Edith, what is a diary?"

Edith smiles, somewhat surprised and curious. "A diary is a notebook used to write important information about the life of the person writing, even small everyday things, thoughts, observations, feelings . . . what you like or what you don't."

"Do you have one, teacher?"

"No, Christopher, I do not have a diary, but I know many people who do. There are famous diaries, such as Anne Frank's, a Jewish girl who had to hide with her family from the Nazis during World War II. There is also the diary of Admiral Christopher Columbus, the discoverer of America, where he wrote down everything he saw on his travels to new lands. He speaks of how beautiful this island was to him, of the peaceful Indians and the greed of the men who came with him.

"Why do you ask? Are you writing a diary?"

Christopher hesitates while his thoughts take flight, but after a few moments he comes back to reality and says to the teacher, "I don't have a diary, but I'm reading one. Maybe I'll write mine when I grow up."

Edith nods, pleased, while thinking to herself that at Christopher's age she would have rather played than read a diary. It seems an achievement that one of her students feels such an unusual interest in writing about his life.

Edith then asks Christopher to come to her desk and announces firmly to the class, "Look, children, take out your geography books. Look for a map of the West Indies on page twenty-four. You will read and complete the questions on the next unit."

The children open their books. The sun enters through the windows of the old building that houses the school. The windows reach the ceiling from halfway up the wall and do not allow anyone to look in or for the students to be distracted by looking outside. It's the last class of the day.

Edith feels like she is living in three countries at the same time: the Haiti of unpaved streets unrelentingly crossed by cars, drivers, donkeys and retailers of produce and coal; the Haiti that she is trying to build, educating a group of restless, distracted, rowdy children; and the France she left behind to come to Haiti with her grandmother. She misses France, and especially Paris, the city of light: exquisite cultural evenings, memorable museums, afternoons on the boulevards and in charming cafés.

The bell announces the end of class. A river of sweaty boys, dressed in khaki and blue, floods the corridors, rushes down the stairs to stampede through the narrow doors, crosses the yard and the soccer field covered by weeds and into the street. The oldest children reach the sidewalk first and disperse. The little ones wait for someone to come and pick them up.

Christopher, distracted, takes a new route back home, mentally reviewing the landscape and following the route his father described in the diary. The boy sweats as he walks along, the shirt sticking to his back, the road burning the soles of his feet. The sun reigns in a dazzling sky, cloudless. He keeps thinking about the diary, but then gets a whiff of hot *tassot* and white rice with goat's meat emanating from the roadside food stands, and hunger strikes. Christopher envisions eating his favorite dish today: pork with okra and white rice. Just as quickly that vision dissolves. His grandfather will have prepared the usual lunch of taros, sweet potatoes and fried salami.

Chapter 6

THE FOREST OF WORDS

"In Latin America, marvelous reality is around every corner, in the chaos, in the picturesque of our cities . . . in our nature . . . And also in our history."

Alejo Carpentier

It's Saturday, and Old Jean keeps his promise to let Christopher continue reading the diary. He has forgotten how angry he was last week when his grandson tore out a blank page to draw a hopscotch grid with blue boxes and numbers in red letters. Although he was very upset, Jean could not resist the boy's smile for having just earned a ten in history class. Sometimes his grandfather disciplines the child too harshly and, deep in his heart, something tells himself not to be so strict. After all, Christopher is just a child. But then, Jean looks around and crashes into the reality of Miragoâne. He does not want his grandson to have to endure the misfortunes of being poor, like most of the boys of the town and of Haiti.

In nearby villages he has seen children half-dead at roadsides, out of school, begging for handouts. He has seen children turned prematurely into men and women who survive by selling things or taking the few occasional jobs available. He has seen many others who, as soon as they have a little strength, go to the Dominiken to cut cane for a few miserable pesos. He has also heard of those who get into the holds of merchant ships to try to reach the United States. He does not want that future for Christopher; he wants him to go further in life. That's what Claude would want, too.

That's why he wakes Christopher up early and assigns him small tasks, so that he gets accustomed to work and responsibility. He demands and strives to ensure that the boy behaves well, in and out of school, and fulfills his duties. He also gives him free time to play with other kids in the neighborhood, to build kites with colored paper and ride his friend Paul's bike. And Old Jean tells stories about their ancestors that Christopher enjoys listening to. *Loosen and tighten the rope* was the method he used with Claude, his father with him and his grandfather with his father, and each time it produced good results.

Christopher continues reading the diary more peacefully than when he started. . . . He has overcome the excitement of the first pages, now that his father is a known figure. He knows what his father did and thought, what he read and whom he loved. However, he wants to hurry to the end to see if his father has said anything about returning to the village. He always puts a piece of ribbon between the pages to mark where he left off reading, just like his teacher Edith does.

January 16

Today I received a letter from Mercedes. She says she still cannot return to the village because they just finished the documentary and have not been paid for their work. Her life is like a puzzle she has yet to finish assembling. In a photo she sent me, she's wading waist-deep in a river, smiling in her light blue bathing suit, a bikini showing off her beautiful mulatto body and great figure, surrounded by fish. It reminded me of my father's stories about going after fin fish, horse mackerel, shad and barracuda on the coast. He said that on stormy nights thousands of crabs would come out of the caves toward the town of Gonaïves to die, crushed under the wheels of cars. The neighbors would leave their back doors open so the army of blue and black crabs with hairy claws would come into the houses, ready to be placed in the cauldrons, where they'd open and close their pincers, fighting to get out. Or they'd climb the curtains that separate the rooms in a futile attempt to escape. They ended up as succulent food for hungry tables.

January 28
Often my father speaks of the Haiti that he knew when he was young, where people dressed in garish colors and celebrated festivities by dancing and playing to gagá *and* kompa *rhythms, when harvests were plentiful and women sang along the roadside and men would throw pebbles to express their interest. He saves a lot of old newspaper clippings that, if neglected, will only serve to line cockroach nests.*

There is little left of that Haiti. Mean Haitians govern us, condeming millions of their brothers to misery, victimhood and fear. The brilliant path laid out by the ancestors has been obscured by the ambition of a single family and its entourage. This nation of drums and rainbows has succumbed to neglect, to the arid land without water or trees. French tourists take home the Haiti shown in paintings, with curvy black women and excessively ornate scenes of boats and street vendors. But we have had to live in a country in black and white, the Haiti of dust and desolation; thirst, escape and weeping.

February 5
In my wanderings with the research project, I have seen a very sad reality up close: men and women living precariously on the edge who will never know the joy of having a good roof over

their heads, food on the table, crops to sow or good schools to send their children to. Traveling around my country has done me more harm than good. From part of southwestern Haiti that is almost unknown to us, from the beauty of the coast to the hill of Cul de Sac and the plain that stretches into the Dominiken, I thought, this land deserves better luck. Do I regret having left?

Yesterday I was in Gonaïves for the feast in honor of Erzulie. It seems that only popular music can bring people together who are immersed in pain and the exhausting struggle to get something to eat. Haitians were born to dance, despite everything, although they do not have many reasons to celebrate. They go or come from doing their chores with an inner strength. They carry the music inside, whether kompa *or* merengue—*it's all the same. Pain unites them when a misfortune occurs; together, shoulder to shoulder, they cry the same collective cry. When the drum or bamboo sounds or the horn rumbles, like a call of the ancestors, all respond and dance as one being. Women, men and children forget the lack of food, lack of work, the lack of play. . . . I think they dream of one good day when the fields will bloom and there will be legumes and food for all. Maybe I am the one.*

February 13th

I do not tell my father the things I wrote last time. I do not want to give him any more cause for sadness. He makes his living in these streets, among the shabby huts, in the half-fallen church where every Sunday he prays to the Yoruba gods for the souls that have already left and those that will soon leave. I do not talk to him of life outside this town. He will never see that and I hope my children do not see it either, that's why I cannot stay in Miragoâne.

And because I do not talk about what lies elsewhere, neither does my father know that due to my relationship with Mercedes and her friends, I am now frowned upon by certain members of the country's security forces. For the government, it does not look good that someone asks questions and has meetings with the representatives of sugar cane workers, merchants, churches and migrants.

It must be the same everywhere when someone talks about what is wrong, especially if he is a foreigner; alarms are triggered and all are put on notice to remove the inconvenience, as if we should not fight against injustice and defend our principles. I do not want my father to get into difficulties with the authorities and the police because of me. My relationship with Mercedes is moving along and is stable, which brings other more serious implications. I've become an accomplice and mediator of her inquiries. This can put our lives at risk.

Christopher moves his improvised bookmark forward. He has been writing all the unfamiliar words down in his notebook. The list is long, but he has already crossed out those that his grandfather or teacher Edith have explained. He still does not know some words. He looks at them again and again, waiting for the right time to find out their meaning. Christopher reads the word *ancestors*, continues with *ruse*, and although he has heard it at school, still does not understand the meaning well. There is another very long and difficult one: *precariously*. It sounds to him like *serious*, but he is sure it is not the same.

He looks again at the words *brotherhood* and *desolation* and has the feeling that they are in the song his grandfather sings when he wakes up in a good mood. The last of the list is *feat*, which he associates with slaves and independence. He is sure of that, because teacher Edith has explained the story several times. Those are the strangest ones he has found so far. Still, there are others he has heard in adult conversations, although his grandfather does not want him near the conversations of grown-ups, and he catches them on the fly when they arouse his interest. *Maybe the teacher will lend me her dictionary so I can keep looking for the words in the diary,* he thinks.

From now on, a whirlwind of words float in the air around Christopher through his mind. He grows with each new word he discovers and with the sounds that correspond to the syllables that he reads slowly. They are strange strings of words that little by little will sink in until he knows them all.

And something even more unusual is happening while he reads the diary. He feels his heart is divided into two. One feels the tenderness and protection of his grandfather. The other hears the words of his father, which are like an invitation to leave the town, to know the places that his father mentions and the woman he fell in love with. On his father's side, things happen that he does not even imagine, but on his grandfather's, there are small, concrete things: find food for the pig, go to school with his faded uniform and listen to the discussions of his grandfather's friends. What he does not like is that his grandfather never laughs, or at least he does not remember the relaxed sound of his laughter; nor does he admire his grandfather's hands, cracked from so much work or from the horrible taro of their meals. And his father? He does not know yet if he has read his wishes. Although in his gut, he begins to believe that there may be a way out of Miragoâne waiting for him. . . .

Chapter 7

EDITH, THE TEACHER

"Truth is on the side of the oppressed."
Malcolm X

Christopher has finished the errands his grandfather has requested earlier than usual, except that he has forgotten to pick up the bucket full of food scraps to feed the pig. It does not matter, because the man who saves the scraps for him is in the hospital, and Christopher doubts that he has eaten at home. His grandfather did not have to wake him up or rush him to get ready for school. The boy has been so focused and quick in doing his tasks that it has surprised Old Jean. Perhaps the boy has started to mature early. Since Christopher began reading the diary, he is quieter than usual, concentrating on the diary and rarely going out to play with his friends.

When Christopher arrives in the classroom and sits down in his assigned seat, he picks up a worn but sharp-pointed pencil and takes out his notebook. None of his friends have arrived. The school looks very different before eight: no sound of the morning bustle, no excited voices of the older boys, no fights between children vying for the same seat. He knows that teacher Edith will soon enter the classroom. He hears her rhythmic footsteps as she approaches. He associates her sound with her smile and kindness, and with the graceful swing of her hips. Some-times he thinks of her and fantasizes, "If I grew up suddenly and in two days I became a big, handsome man, I would surely ask her to become my girlfriend. . . ."

No one has ever kissed Christopher. He wishes she would at least kiss him on the cheek, but he cannot imagine how that would happen. He rejects such an unreasonable thought for someone his age. And besides, she has generously given him her affection and guidance. It's not good to imagine her other-wise. "The time will come for me to meet girls, when I grow up." Then he remembers other nice things that are within his reach, such as soccer and the food that awaits him at home.

Teacher Edith sits down and rearranges the papers on her desk that a breeze has displaced in her absence. Her desk is small but each object is in its rightful place. Unlike others, Edith's classroom is adorned with several posters on the walls and has a table with maps. On one side, there are pictures of he-roes of the homeland; on the opposite wall, there are others with famous literary characters and historical figures she has read about and admires. Here and there hang some photographs of monuments and landscapes of the country. On a wobbly table lie rolled maps of the geography of Haiti and the current political and administrative divisions of the country; another shows the island of Hispaniola and a world map, with countries drawn in different colors.

Christopher often looks at the faces in the photographs. He does not have to read the names that his teacher has written below them. Because she has repeated them so often, he already knows who they are and what deeds have brought them there. The first face he sees is that of a great writer and politician, Jacques Stephen Alexis. It is followed by the photo of another writer and politician who fought for the poor, named Jacques Roumain. On the back wall, she has hung a poster of a famous general, Simón Bolívar, a great hero of the independence of South America who is called "The Liberator." The teacher repeats this word, "Liberator." At the end are other Caribbean writers; one is Cuban and she calls him by his surname Guillén, and the other, he is almost certain, is called Cabral. He turns his gaze to the desk where the teacher has a photo of herself when she was a few years old. In the photo she has the same smile as now, and she is wearing a tiered skirt. Christopher approaches with some shyness, worried that he will disturb her.

"Teacher, can I ask you a favor?"

"Whatever you want, my dear," says Edith, putting aside the papers and extending a hand as a welcoming gesture. "What can I do for you?"

"I want you to let me use your dictionary during recess. I promise to take good care of it." Christopher tries to justify his request and adds, "It's just that I'm reading a diary and there are many words I don't know."

The teacher looks at him, surprised, and waits a few seconds before asking who this diary belongs to, although, she decides, any reading will help. She hands him the dictionary. The boy almost drops it. It is a very large and heavy book to carry. It is entitled, *Petit Dictionnaire Larousse Français*.

Recess ends with the bell calling the children back to the classroom. The children hurry up, pushing and smacking each other. Christopher always comes in on time. He knows that the teacher does not like delays after recess, and she gets upset. Also, when a child is late three times, she calls in the father or the mother and has the child promise in front of a parent not to do it again.

Christopher has been wondering how much a dictionary like the teacher's might cost. Maybe not much. For a moment, he entertains the idea of owning a book with all the adult words, the good and the bad ones as well as others that even adults don't know or can't pronounce. Whoever knows them all, he thinks, must be very important. There's probably no such person in the world. Perhaps his father knew many of those words, and that's why he used them in his diary. If he really concentrates, Christopher thinks, he'll be able to master the contents of that giant book. Or, at the very least half. He also thinks it would be fun to talk to people without them understanding what he says, using difficult words, which happens to him as he reads the diary. But adults understand each other. And he does not always understand their words.

"Thanks for allowing me to use the dictionary, Ms. Edith," he says. "I don't think I can learn those words, there are too many."

She smiles and assures him that he can do it little by little, memorizing two or three words every day and using them.

He nods. It seems like a great idea, and he decides that he will begin the next day when he returns to school. He places the book on the table and returns to his desk. Then he smiles: if he doesn't learn all the words, then at least he can memorize a good many of them.

As soon as Christopher gets home, he begins looking up the meanings of the unfamiliar words he has been underlining with his pencil, unseen by his grandfather. He reads slowly, re-reads, feeling he's making progress while pausing here and there. For example, he sees no relationship between his father and the word *desolation*, and more than once he has reviewed the definitions of *brotherhood* and *precariousness,* but feels more confused than before looking them up. The only definition in the dictionary for *desolation* projects an image in his mind of the fields near the village, where the land is dry and arid, without a drop of water, where yams, corn and beans no longer grow.

Chapter 8

THE ILLNESS

"The strong scent of earth rises up her divine beast-like
body. Her breath is like the wind of the Cosmic cyclone
(the ritual inebriates her much more than the rum)."
Manuel del Cabral

Christopher has spent three days in bed with an illness that
came on suddenly. Old Jean prepared a tea with leaves of sour-
sop, cinnamon and lemongrass. He also tried in vain to make
him drink white onion juice with sunflower oil. His grandfather
has been unable to get him up from the cot where he lies.

Ms. Edith has sent a note inquiring about his health, along
with some homework for history and mathematics, to help him
keep up with his class assignments.

Christopher is happy to receive his teacher's message. He
looks at her writing and recognizes her way of making the letter "s" and how she crosses the line from the inside out in the
"q." Behind the letters, he finds her eyes and remembers her
smile. He closes his eyes and hears her heels approaching the
classroom and imagines her dancing on clouds.

Christopher was probably more sick from the absence of a
father's protection and a mother's tenderness than from the
poorly nourished state of his body. In his fevered mind, objects

in the shadows were transformed into horrifying monsters. His sudden illness, maybe not easily diagnosed, perhaps was brought on by his memories. Sometimes the desire to be with someone sickens the body, and a person ceases to be whole and becomes fractured into many pieces that refuse to get back together and up from the sick bed.

After school, a bunch of neighborhood kids, his playmates, come to visit him. They laugh and joke around, telling him he's lazy and faking it just to stay at home. But Old Jean knows that something serious keeps his grandson in bed. There is nothing else that would prevent him from going to his beloved classroom, neither April rains, nor August suns, nor December winds. Three days have passed already. The illness has also taken his appetite. He barely chews a spoonful of rice and then turns on the cot to face the cardboard wall that separates his little room from his grandfather's.

Old Jean is vigilant, fearing for the child's life. A witch doctor has blessed him on his belly and said a prayer for the *orishas* to restore the child's health. It is not working yet, or perhaps the gods have not heard the request for their intervention. Old Jean is terrified, worrying selfishly that he will lose his grandson to illness; Christopher is the only company he has in his old age. Hoping to cheer him up, he pampers the boy more than usual, but Christopher does not react, nothing seems to interest him. Old Jean then suggests the boy continue reading his father's diary. Maybe if he keeps reading, his condition will improve, even while he is not attending school. Christopher takes the diary, reluctantly, and his interest is immediately aroused. After a few minutes, he realizes that he has skipped some pages without realizing it and begins to turn the pages, going backward. He does not want to miss a single detail of his father's life. He returns to where he left off and continues reading.

April 7
    I do not know why I am so bothered by the simple joy of peo-ple. Today is a day when we must think about the past, listen with pride to La Dessalinienne *and meditate on the future. In the streets, however, people are being disappeared by authorities. The neighbor next to me raises the volume of the radio to a level so high that it nauseates me, not because of the music, because I also like the* kompa *and* merengue *he plays, but why do they im-pose on others their musical tastes? No one remembers that on April 7, today, Toussaint died. Today is a bad day for Haiti and also for me. Perhaps the death of the warrior has shifted the fate of these people. Today is April 7, and I have not heard anything from Mercedes in a long time. Maybe she also has altered my destiny. . . .*

    Christopher writes down the word "destiny" in his note-book. He looks again at the diary and compares it with what he wrote to make sure that none of the letters are missing. Then he returns to a place in the diary in which only torn pieces of pages remain. He is sure that his grandfather will not blame him for the damage. Perhaps it was his own grandfather who removed them, because his father wrote something improper. Maybe someone else read the book before him and ripped out those pages, or it could be his own father who removed that part of the story. So, he is resigned to remain ignorant about what happened between June and November.

    Every time he reads the diary he experiences the same happy feeling, learning of the unknown history of his father. He is overwhelmed and fascinated, inspired to continue discover-ing in the writing details of Claude's life. Reading the diary has reanimated him with a well-being he has not had for a while. His grandfather attributes much of his recovery to his prayers, but Christopher is not so sure. His father's emotional tale, even when sad, gives him a sense of belonging and fills him with an overflowing energy. His symptoms vanish.

December 8
  Finally, I receive news from Mercedes. She says she's fine and misses me. She has openly stated she wants to have a child, because although I have her and Christopher, she only has me, and if something happens and we separate, she will be very lonely. She tells me that a childhood friend has promised to get me a job if I can cross the border. Her friend works as a country or security guard at a sugar factory in a town called Barahona. That is what's available, and that it will help me to get another, less challenging job where I do not have to sacrifice my habit of reading, maybe in the capital. . . . I'm not sure that I want to go. I don't want to leave my father with the burden of caring for and educating Christopher. Although on the other side there may be another life, for them and for me. . . .
  Why does it hurt so much to leave this dying town? Mercedes says we will be fine. I just have to be careful and not get noticed, mix with the others and speak only when necessary. She says that all blacks are equal in the eyes of the pursuer, that I should go unnoticed among the vendors, the merchants and the hustlers crowded in the markets. "Be invisible to the eyes that look for the dividing line between Haiti and the other country." She gives me the address where she lives now, warning me that if I take too long to get there, I may not find her and will have to look for her around the village. It torments me leaving Christopher with Dad. He's only a year old and so tiny; he needs his mother, and she is not there either.

Chapter 9

THE TRIP IN THE FORD

" . . . I, too, sing America.
I am the darker brother.
They send me to eat in the kitchen
When company comes,
But I laugh,
And eat well,
And grow strong."
Langston Hughes

It is Saturday morning, and Old Jean receives an important visit. His old friend Emmanuel has come to make himself available, in case the old man wants something from Dominiken. Emmanuel was lucky and acquired the skills to get ahead. He speaks French well, is fluent in English, and handles the Spanish language well. These skills have brought him success in business. He started a decade ago with an old pickup truck that had to be pushed in the morning in order to start up. With the old clunker, he was able to connect Miragoâne with Jimaní, Ouanaminthe, Cap Haitien, Pedernales and even Barahona. Every Friday at dawn he stuffed the truck with things to sell to the Haitians who stayed on the other side: shiny rubber shoes, imitation leather purses, cheap lingerie, oval mirrors to hang in bathrooms, plaster copies of African gods for rituals and paintings bought for pennies at the markets of Petionville. From time to time, he also carried Chinese and Cuban immigrants that arrived from Port-au-Prince, desperate to cross to the eastern part of the island and continue on their route to other beaches. With a little Haitian currency, he buys the blindness of the border guards and silences the customs tax collectors. He knows it is illegal but does not stop going in and out. Later on, Don Emmanuel buys a new Ford F-150 pickup, with an impressive engine that roars like a wild animal. Emmanuel calls it "Caroline," after his first wife, but the people from the village call it "The Frigate" because it was once almost stuck in the middle of an overflow of the Artibonite River.

On the floor of the truck, under his seat, he packs the highly prized Barbancourt five-star rum that sells at an inflated price in the bars of the small towns where the two countries meet. He also carries creole *clerén* for hawking on the streets and for his own consumption. On the return trip, Don Emmanuel brings the products sought after in Miragoâne: sardines and peanut oil, ground coffee and condensed milk, dried cod and herring in wooden boxes, eggs in plastic containers and cardboard cartons. Sometimes he also brings fighting cocks and small goats for peasants who do the impossible to acquire one.

Old Jean is grateful for the offer, saying that he has no money for orders. He really needs many provisions and wants a toy for Christopher—fortunately, Three Kings Day is still very distant.

"Thank you, dear friend, I do not need anything now. Ah, but I have a favor to ask. If you go through Barahona, ask around if anyone knows someone called Claude." At this time, the old man would be satisfied with knowing something about his son, even if he is not alive.

"In fact, I will arrive on Monday at Barahona," Emmanuel answers. "I'm going to take a girl to work in the house of a landowner, and on the way, I have to buy a saddle I was asked to pick up some time ago. I'll ask about your son in the neighborhoods where Haitians live."

Christopher widens his eyes in the darkness of the small room and focuses his listening to hear what his grandfather's friend says. For sure, he mentioned Barahona, the same town named in his father's diary. That must be the place where his dad lives. As his grandfather says, "Everything has a reason for being." Suddenly his heartbeat quickens.

Monday dawns fresh with a sweet, cool breeze that does not resemble the usual weather. Christopher's grandfather gives the usual instructions: "Don't stop on the way until you get to the École Président Toussaint."

While the boy tucks his poorly buttoned shirt into his pants, his grandfather continues: "Do not talk to strangers on the way, and behave like the big kid you already are. Do not make me look bad in front of Ms. Edith."

Christopher does not pay attention. Every day, his grandfather repeats the same rules, and the boy answers in the same way: "Yes, Grandfather, I'll be a good boy."

The street toward Petionville looks like a whirlwind of blue and khaki colors, the same as his school uniform. In the middle of the hubbub, the children walk in a disorderly row along the edge of the sidewalk. Christopher remains hopeful that Don Emmanuel will offer to drop him off, as he has before, close to the school. He checks his bag again to make sure he has not left out anything; today he does it more than ever to calm his jittery nerves. At the bottom of his bag is some overly toasted bread with a drop of oil, which his grandfather prepares for his recess snack. Along with the three-rule booklets, he has placed his father's diary in the bag. He has marked a page and read it over and over again, with the name of the town where his father may have stayed. He wants to have it close at hand.

In the distance, between the dust that rises and the trucks that block his vision, he sees the Ford, its new bodywork buried under a thick layer of dust. Christopher has been waiting for this moment since washing up. The pickup truck stops half a kilometer away and he almost starts running to it, but fortunately it's headed toward him once again, and the emboldened boy beckons to it, standing close to his classmates so that Don Emmanuel may take pity on them and pick them all up.

The truck brakes with tires squeaking. The children laugh, delighted, thanking him before getting on. The first to board is the one who asked for the favor, followed by Stephen, Jacob and finally two boys Christopher knows only by sight, who take advantage of the ride. It's not every day that they get one.

A few minutes later, the truck stops in front of the school. From the rear bumper, four students with scratchy throats from screaming so much during the trip on four wheels jump to the ground. The fifth does not get off. The truck resumes its trip. Christopher envisions the town on the other side and really wants to meet the Yoruba warrior of whom his grandfather has spoken. "Yes, everything has a reason for being," he repeats to himself and crosses his foot over the chain that holds the merchandise. He has slid under the canvas that covers Don Emmanuel's cargo, a safe hiding place. The village from which he has never left now lies behind him, becoming increasingly small. Barahona is his destination, where, according to the diary, his father lives.

Chapter 10

THE ARRIVAL IN BARAHONA

> ". . . Slave to
> the slaves, and to
> the masters, a
> tyrant.
> Who could it be? Who couldn't it be?
> Sugar cane"
> Nicolás Guillén

It is dim under the canvas that covers the pickup truck. Outside, the afternoon advances. Christopher's astonished eyes see landscapes that run at such a rapid speed that he cannot catch or retain them. Don Emmanuel makes a short stop after several hours of travel. Christopher realizes, judging by the voices in Creole, that they have not yet left Haiti. He watches outside. A sign announces food at a good price and, above it, a much larger one reads: *Restoran Le Petit Jacmel*.

Christopher resettles his body. He does not know how long the trip will last, although he knows with certainty that it is impossible to turn back. His grandfather, very worried, must be going crazy looking for him. Later, Christopher will ask Don Emmanuel to explain to his grandfather that he has done this to find his father. Since setting out, Christopher realizes how big his country is and how small Miragoâne is. They quickly crossed Gonaïves, the town of Jérémie, Port-de-Paix and perhaps another one while he slept.

Don Emmanuel does not take his eyes off the road, driving to the monotonous rhythm and familiar buzz of the engine. He only slows down when passing through a village where loud music bursts into the pickup truck. Christopher peeks out from under the canvas and discovers, to his surprise, that he is in another world, so close but so strange and distant. He also looks at the products and articles rolling around beside him. Don Emmanuel is hauling many things, and Christopher cannot imagine who the buyers could be. He prefers to concentrate on the landscapes that pass by fleetingly like mirages under the sun's rays—the sown fields, the bushes of the arid plains, a lake in the distance. At the edge of the road, children walk to school, as he usually does, with their uniforms well ironed. He imagines the girls with braided hair falling on both sides of their faces, as in the photo he saw in one of Ms. Edith's books.

It is hot under the canvas, and Christopher feels the sweat soaking his back and the long hours of travel numbing his limbs. He dreams that he is swimming in the waters of a lake and, on the shore, there is a man lying down. He does not see his face but believes with certainty that it is his father. . . . Yes, it is him, and he is waiting on the shore to help Christopher if he gets tired of swimming. Christopher has never gone swimming; he has never before seen a lake or a river or the sea. He has heard that they exist, and he has seen them on the map. At close range, he only knows the Miragoâne desert. In his stupor, he feels Claude's extended hand offering to help him out of the water.

A sudden movement awakens him. The jumps and jolts of the Ford as it rides over potholes cause Don Emmanuel to cuss in French and then repeat these expletives in Haitian Creole. Christopher hears him grunting and imagines the man's face grimacing as he curses. Then he hears isolated voices, speaking Creole and Spanish, and thinks of men returning home after work.

The truck has stopped, and Christopher stretches his arms and legs, awakening his senses, in case he has to run. Then he changes his mind and prepares to face the possible anger of Don Emmanuel. A woman's voice shouts a few words in a melodious Spanish, and he knows they have arrived because he hears phrases with another accent, although he does not understand their meaning. Something tells him it is time to leave his hiding place. However, an argument begins in front of the pickup truck, and Christopher returns to hiding. Beyond the edge of the canvas, he can see a man dressed in a green uniform carrying a large weapon. Although he does not understand what they say, the high pitch of the voices means that some problem is being discussed. At times, Don Emmanuel speaks in broken Spanish. At others, it is the soldier who changes from Spanish to a poorly spoken Creole. Christopher is frightened. He is aware that his trip might end without him completing his mission.

"*¡Madichon sa yo gad pas janm fatige nan mande pou lajan!*" exclaims Don Emmanuel, complaining that the guards never cease asking for money.

Christopher is even more afraid now of what he thinks is coming.

The guard laughs reluctantly. He extends his hand greedily, and another hand comes out to meet it from the driver's seat. A few bills seem to have the last word. The uniformed man has not yet removed his body from leaning against the truck door, and without waiting for him to move, Emmanuel starts the engine. That noise means that Christopher has been saved. But it takes only a few minutes for the truck to stop abruptly yet again. Through the rearview mirror, Don Emmanuel has seen a corner of the canvas flap in the breeze, like a kite in flight. He could wait until he gets to his destination, but that would risk losing the goods, which would further delay the trip.

Don Emmanuel approaches the rear door of the vehicle, still wondering what is moving in there. He places a hand on his waist in an automatic reflex as Christopher emerges with a frightened look, as if he has seen one of those horrifying monsters from his early childhood. Seeing who it is, the businessman is relieved not to have shot at the shadow that emerged from the depths of his freight.

"Holy mother! What the hell are you doing in there! How did you get here? Who got you into my vehicle?"

Then, Don Emmanuel falls silent with surprise, really taken aback, remembering a scene he would rather forget. Not long ago he was assaulted like this in Jimaní. His mouth suddenly fills with bile that he quickly spits out.

"Do not do that again. I almost killed you!"

Christopher does not know how to answer or explain. He is so frightened and embarrassed that he starts crying. Don Emmanuel hugs him, wondering what to do with him.

"I just wanted to see my dad," the boy says. Calmer now, he realizes that the anger in his big friend has disappeared. "I read in a diary that my father wrote that he was going to a town called Barahona, and I heard my grandfather talking about a street called Enriq . . . Enriq something. He left Haiti ten years ago, and I want to find him."

The merchant, not so angry now, is speechless at the boy's courage. Patting Christopher on the shoulder, he considers the risks Christopher has taken. He thinks of how unshakeable bonds of a son's love for his father have moved him to such action. What determination the boy has shown to go and meet his father, and alone. Not many adults would do something like that.

"Come, get on, sit next to me. . . . We are close to Barahona, and it seems to me that there is a street called Enriquillo. It must be the one you remember. As soon as we arrive, we will try to find it."

Christopher is beaming. He forgets his fear, the fatigue of the trip and the banging and rattling of the truck. He feels that his adventure has been worth it.

"Look, Don Emmanuel," he says, handing him a sheet torn from the school notebook. The handwriting is uneven, but clear, with just three lines as the only clue to find his father.

Don Emmanuel slows down, stops at the side of the road and turns on the light. He checks the paper, remembering that the street is near the market. The setting sun will not be of much help. He turns corners, asking here and there, until he reaches a narrow, unpaved street named Enriquillo. The street looks familiar . . . surely, they are close. He starts counting the few numbers that do not follow any sequence.

"Tell me again the number we are looking for," Don Emmanuel asks without taking his eyes off the humble houses. "I think it's here. I hope we can find your father, boy."

Don Emmanuel and the boy get down from the truck, and the merchant knocks on the door. Someone approaches. Christopher grabs the rough hand of his grandfather's friend and prepares to see the longed-for face of his father. At the threshold appears a man with his shirt tied around his waist and trousers cut beneath his knees. His eyes are suspicious. A hand remains behind his back; the old man suspects the man holds a knife in it.

"What do you want, sir?" asks the man with a horse voice, as if he just woke up.

Christopher realizes that they are not welcome, and so surely does his protector, who hurries to end the encounter quickly.

"I'm sorry, I'm looking for a friend named Claude, and this is the address that was given to me."

The man seems to leave the knife in his belt. He understands that there is no danger and relaxes his stance. "No, your friend does not live here. I just moved in. . . . I don't know who lived here before. Maybe Doña Nenita knows something. She's the owner and lives near the center of town."

"Do you know how I can get there? It's getting late."

"Yes, look . . . just follow this same street. When you arrive at the end, turn right. After the dry bridge, you'll see the San Miguel grocery store. She's the owner. Sometimes she's there. If not, ask the manager. His house is nearby."

A folded paper passes from one hand to another. Without moving from the door, the man has extended his hand, and in a different voice says, "Don't tell her that I gave you the address. She doesn't like it. . . ." And he adds, to soften the request, "You never know."

Back in the pickup truck, Don Emmanuel grumbles. "One more stop," he says to Christopher and adds expectantly, "Don't worry, we'll find it."

Meanwhile, Christopher thinks about what might be happening far away in Miragoâne, about his grandfather whose grandson has been missing for many hours now. He misses Old Jean and feels remorse . . . and, although he does not even remember his father, Christopher also misses him.

Chapter 11

WHAT DO I SAY TO OLD JEAN?

"I have spent two months in a nameless sugar refinery,
because the founders of this factory, in their eagerness to
save time and thoroughly depersonalize people, places
and things, have numbered everything."
Ramón Marrero Aristy

The San Miguel grocery store is a family home made of
wood and adapted to include the shop. On the tin roof there are
all sorts of junk: flat tires, old shoes, pieces of broken plastic,
rusty cans, headless dolls, a bike with no rear wheel, pieces of
wood and a chair with only three legs.

Two large bolts hold the doors of the grocery store open.
The wider, middle door is blocked by a ramshackle bicycle with
a basket on the handlebars. A very black boy with a scar that
crosses his face from the left eyebrow to the hairline attends the
counter and deals with customers looking to buy rice, sardines,
tomato sauce, chicken meat and cleaning products. The door on
the right is in front of the refrigerator, where a man with very
straight hair and an anchor tattooed on his forearm with the ini-
tials MR handles the shelves with alcoholic beverages.

Don Emmanuel parks the pickup truck in a free space in
front of the grocery store. He does not let Christopher get off the

truck as he pursues the conversation through the driver's side window. He focuses carefully on the faces of the people he talks with under the bright, artificial light.

"Good afternoon," he says in a slow Spanish. "I'm looking for Doña Nenita. Someone told me I can find her here."

"May I know who's looking for her?" the boy with the scar replies with suspicion.

"My name is Emmanuel, and she may have information about a person I'm looking for, a man who lived in one of her houses."

The boy inspects the appearance of the stranger and weighs the stranger's words to decide if he will help him.

"Godmother!" he shouts in a voice that struggles to be heard over the raised volume of the radio playing *bachata* music that entertains men drinking beer at one end of the counter.

"Godmother!" he repeats. "Someone's looking for you."

Behind the boy is a small door. It is painted the same color as the wall. Bags of cookies and *pan sobao* hang from a nail. Don Emmanuel notices that the door leads to the inside of the house. A short, middle-aged woman appears at the door. She's wearing three rings on each earlobe and a thick gold chain around her neck from which a simple cross hangs.

"Who is looking for me?" she asks, bored, searching among the regular customers to see if she recognizes someone.

"It's me, ma'am," says Don Emmanuel. "I need to find a person who lived in one of your houses, not long ago. . . ."

"Who is it?" asks Doña Nenita.

"His name is Claude. He came from Haiti. We have been friends for a long time, and I urgently need to find him."

Doña Nenita pauses as if weighing how to respond to the stranger. It was from her that the godchild learned to be suspicious. Despite the comings and goings of the town's sugar mill workers and others who travel outside of town, a new face does not arouse much curiosity. For Emmanuel, the minute the woman takes to think is too long to wait.

"I know him. He lived on Anacaona Street. He had an argument with a soldier and decided to move."

"And do you know where he moved to?" Emmanuel insists with urgency.

"Oh, yes, I got him another place I have. On Duarte . . . two blocks from here, down the street."

Doña Nenita leaves to go and see what is happening at the other door of the grocery store. It sounds like a fight: two voices insult and curse. The woman restores order; it is normal in a place like this that tempers flare over nothing. She soon returns to face Emmanuel.

"If you see him, tell him that the rent is due tomorrow. I will not give him another chance!"

Don Emmanuel nods and returns to the pickup truck.

Despite the fatigue and hunger that tightens his gut, Christopher is still alert. "Did you get my dad's address?"

"I think so, boy. Let's go. I hope we can find him."

Don Emmanuel is glad to be able to help the boy, and Old Jean will be happy to receive the news that his son is alive. He really wants to know about him and to have him back home. If he can bring good news to his friend, Old Jean won't feel so bad about his grandson stowing away in Emmanuel's pickup truck. Jean will surely blame him, because he is the adult, not his grandson.

They have found the address that Doña Nenita gave them. Remembering previous unfortunate experiences, Emmanuel knocks on the door slowly as a precaution to what it can bring out. No one answers for a while, but then there is a slight noise inside. It is so faint he barely hears someone approaching. Shoe soles crawl to the door, and the newcomers step back a little so as not to give the impression that they were peering through the cracks in the planks. The door creaks open halfway, and a woman appears, she's tidying up her hair with one hand. Don Emmanuel greets her politely.

"Excuse me, ma'am, for knocking on the door so late at night," he says, apologizing.

"Hello, what can I do for you?" says the voice that still has no face for Christopher, as it is hidden behind the old man.

Don Emmanuel takes his hat off for the first time during the whole trip, revealing an incipient baldness. "Excuse me," he repeats. "I have . . . we have a real emergency."

"Emergency?" asks the woman, filling the whole doorway. Christopher can see her face now.

"Yes, an emergency, you could say. . . My name is Emmanuel and I am a friend of Jean Morisseau. I come from Miragoâne, you know?" For a moment his eyes roll over the well-shaped body of the woman and then he continues. "This boy is looking for his father, Claude, a tall, strong man. We were told in the grocery store that this is where he lives . . . with a woman by the name of Mercedes."

The woman looks at Christopher, astonished, then relaxes.

Emmanuel holds Christopher by his shoulders. "See here. I am not the one who brought him. He got into my pickup truck on his own, and I discovered him just as I was driving into town. He made the trip alone, and I'll return to Miragoâne in a week. Do you understand me?"

"Come in, come in," the woman says, inviting them to step aside.

She knew that this moment would come, although she did not imagine that it would be like this. "I am Mercedes, and Claude is my husband. He's not here right now. . . . And you, you must be Christopher. . . ."

Mercedes makes a gesture with her right hand, inviting the unexpected visitors to sit. There are only two chairs in the room.

Don Emmanuel chooses the one that seems strong enough to widthstand his weight. Christopher sits down on a corner of the other ramshackle chair, which is covered by a cloth with an embroidered trim.

"I'm going to prepare some juice and something to eat for the boy."

The old man nods, noticing how Mercedes' hips move rhythmically toward the little room that serves as a kitchen. But she is Claude's wife, the son of his friend Jean, so he looks away reproaching himself for the fleeting, although unavoidable, attraction to a beautiful young woman.

When Christopher hears the word food, he opens his eyes wide, suddenly alert from the drowsiness resulting from the fatigue of traveling and the jolts of the truck bouncing over potholes.

The improvised kitchen is only a few steps away. Mercedes calculates in her head where she will place a cot for Christopher, a nail to hang his backpack and how to buy a toothbrush for him. She also thinks that their intimacy will have to be accommodated some other way. Suddenly she shakes her head and puts aside her selfish and inopportune thoughts.

Christopher looks at Mercedes. She does not exactly match the image that he had of his mother, whom he never met. But something makes him believe that Mercedes will perfectly fill the empty space left by his real mother. When he hears the sounds coming from the small kitchen, where Mercedes prepares snacks, Christopher remembers his grandfather with loving gratitude. It is the same devotion Old Jean shows him in preparing him to get to Ms. Edith's classroom early.

Mercedes returns with the largest dish she has on a tray covered with the red cloth she uses to grab the hot pots. On the cloth are two simple sandwiches made with the bread and sausage she was saving for Claude's dinner, along with two small glasses of dark lemonade, sweetened with the unrefined sugar he brings from the sugar mill. The child's eyes meet the woman's, a smile on his lips as proof of new-born affection.

Don Emmanuel takes the bread and a glass of lemonade, barely lifting his grateful eyes, just so as not to be rude to the person who has fed him. He still feels guilty about those thoughts.

Mercedes interrupts his wonderings. "Claude, your dad," she says, approaching Christopher, ". . . he's working on the road and will not come back until tomorrow, but you can stay with me." And to Don Emmanuel, "If you want, you can leave the boy with me, he will be safe."

"He could be . . . but . . ." he answers with a pleading tone, looking askance at her. "Tell me, Mercedes, what I am going to say to Old Jean about why Claude has not come back with me?"

Mercedes has always believed that news, good or bad, should not be left for later. To tell the truth is the shortest way to get out of the difficulties of life. She takes a deep breath to give herself courage and tell a story that does not belong entirely to her.

"Tell Old Jean that Claude has had a hard life east of Haiti. He has survived doing odd jobs, but has never, ever, turned away from the advice of his father or forgotten the love and respect he feels for him. Let him know that since he arrived in Barahona—although I warned him many times it was not convenient for him to do that—he did not listen to me and started to meet with other Haitian migrants. Claude did not waste any opportunity, however small it was, to meet and talk with the cane cutters and mill workers, who continue under the exploitation of their managers, working in very harsh conditions. Tell the old man that he has thought more about his oppressed brothers than his own family, so much so that it has been very difficult for us to have a child, despite the time we have together. His son has paid dearly for his decision to defend what Claude believes is fair, to denounce injustice and abuse and try to create awareness among the workers. Tell him exactly how it is. And if you see the old man become very sad, then leave the story at that. Although I remember how strong the old man was . . . tell him that Claude is still the same, he has not stopped loving him and always mentions him. And that I love him, too."

Mercedes pauses in her story, which is more than a relief to someone who knows Claude's family. She has released the weight that has oppressed her heart for a long time. She looks at the child with a spark of illusion . . . surely, he looks like the son she wants to have, his little arms and his eyes identical to those of his father, jet black, awake and bright. Although she lost a pregnancy, more chances at pregnancy will come and, in any case, Christopher will now be her son, too, and she will raise him and see him grow. She has long wanted to be a mother.

Then, Mercedes fleetingly recalls Claude's clandestine political movements in those times of struggle and demands for social freedom, her arrival in Haiti as an unknown, the collaboration with the team of journalists, the reason she was saved, the day she met Claude and fell in love and how she encouraged him to read the books of great Haitian writers and politicians, and then pushed him to write down his experiences and thoughts. She recalls the dark days of her wandering outside the country, her moving to Barahona, everything she left behind, her life beside Claude, his efforts to defend the workers, the risks they ran and how much they have paid.

Don Emmanuel interrupts her thoughts, saying that he will carry the message as she told it. No doubt his friend Jean will feel hope is born again, after receiving the news of his son. He then puts on his hat as a sign that he is leaving.

Christopher's eyes are almost closed with sleep, but he is happy, overflowing with happiness. He has found his father and to-morrow he will be able to meet him, hug him and talk to him about so many things! He did well to embark on this adventure with Don

Emmanuel. He looks at Mercedes with some shyness and rests his head on the chair in which he's sitting and falls asleep.

"I'll tell Old Jean that his grandson is already with his father," says Don Emmanuel. He is satisfied, having fulfilled the mission that the good God put in his way. "Tomorrow, I have many things to do. I hope to meet the child's father on another trip."

Mercedes smiles, nodding to give the man the confidence that the boy is in good hands. She asks him to put the child on the cot in a corner of the room. Then he heads to the door, says goodbye, bowing his head, goes out, climbs into the truck and heads toward the center of town.

The Barahona Mill's sharp whistle announces that the first shift of twelve hours of work has ended. It's nine o'clock at night, and a second whistle sounds, shorter than the previous one. It means that a new group of workers will begin working in the giant mill that squeezes out the life of those men like the sugar it squeezes from the stalks of cane.

Mercedes is so concerned about what has happened that she thinks she'll be unable to sleep. She caresses the hair of the child who is resting after his tortuous journey and now seems disconnected to the world around him. She checks the small backpack that lies to one side and finds three notebooks. At the bottom there is a book with a thick, brown, worn cover. It captures her attention because she knows very well of Claude's interest in this type of book. It is an interest she herself aroused and stimulated in him so long ago, as well as in writing. She turns to a random page in the middle and a strange, cold air envelops her as she realizes that it is Claude's diary. Quickly she turns the pages, eager to know what it contains. She realizes that the diary was interrupted at some point when she reaches a blank space. Almost at the end, she finds another very different writing, with irregular strokes, short lines and a calligraphy that undoubtedly belongs to a child who is learning to write. Some of it is unintelligible, and there are spelling errors. She looks again at the sleeping child and realizes that her husband probably forgot the diary when he left Haiti, and that later, his son began to write his emerging history.

Sunday
Grandfather is talking to Don Emmanuel, the man with the pickup truck. He says that tomorrow he goes to Barahona where my grandfather thinks my father lives. If he takes me in his pickup truck and we look for my dad, I'll be very happy.

Monday
I got up first before my grandfather. I started to write in the diary what I am going to do. If I find my dad, I'll show it to him. He's going to be happy because I do the same thing as him, write. Ms. Edith helped me a lot, I would like to be a teacher and write like my dad. I want God to help me and Don Emmanuel to take me to school, and then I'm going to hide in the back part of the truck. I must find my dad. . . . It's time to go. God help me.

Mercedes closes the diary abruptly. From her eyes drop abundant tears that wash her face as she sniffles. A feeling of relief and joy swells her chest, something she has not felt in a long time. Was it worth it that the boy dared to look for his dad, regardless of the risks? How brave he is! She stands beside Christopher and then lies down close to him, trying not to move too much. From now on, she will give him all her warmth and affection, along with Claude, she has no doubt. She also realizes that she too needs the tenderness and joy that only children can give.

Chapter 12

BACK TO PAIN

"Yes, blood has been shed, I know,
but water will wash the blood away.
The new crop will grow out of the past
and ripen in forgetfulness."
Jacques Roumain

The sun rays of Miragoâne are less intense, and people are grateful for the goodness of the weather. They come and go about their daily chores, hurried or tired—with the exception of Old Jean, who has aged ten years in a single day, and whose gaze is bleaker than the falling evening. He can barely speak. He enters and leaves the room with the false pretext of fixing something to eat, approaching the door of the hut and entering again, circling endlessly.

At noon, when his grandson does not arrive, he waits a couple of hours. Jean begins to worry even more than usual. His heart, which always warns him in advance of misfortunes to come, today strikes his chest walls early. But he ignores it.

Old Jean sends one of Christopher's playmates to find out if the boy is playing soccer in the vacant lot, but the boy comes back and says no one has seen him. On the table rests the dish with *malanga* and some slices of fried salami next to the food that old Jean has also not eaten. How could he be hungry!

On two occasions he asks Jacob, another friend, to go and see if Christopher walked by old Martine Boyer's store; they do not know of his whereabouts either. Someone said that he had been seen scampering around the place where he used to get food for the pig, but it was not Christopher. The old man feels the suffering grow, choking him. His hands tremble and his eyes fill with tears, like when Claude left. Thick, sour spittle forces him to spit from time to time until his mouth is dry and he only spits out air. He tries to stay busy, but does not know what to do. When he sees Christopher's classmates and others he encounters on his desperate search through the streets of town, he asks if the teacher gave them homework that would justify staying in school longer. "No," they say, and they tell him they did not see him at school all day.

One of the neighbors bring news that a boy about the age and size of his grandson was hit by a vehicle on the way to Petionville, although they do not know for sure who the boy is. Two neighbors, worried to see the anguish and nervousness of the grandfather, offer to take him to the medical center. They take him with their souls hanging by a thread from anxiety. He takes off his hat and puts it back on a dozen times. The neighbors see how the features of the old man, marked by pain, are disfigured. Sometimes Jean babbles words that no one can understand, because he says them to himself. They believe that he is praying to Bondye or another deity, asking protection for his grandson so that nothing happens. They imitate him, taking off their hats for a moment as a sign of respect.

At the medical center, they say that the injured boy is not Christopher, and a fleeting relief soothes the heart of the old man. The accident was not serious: the boy has a broken leg and scrapes on the rest of his body. A woman, his mother or grandmother, wets his mouth with water while his leg is immobilized in a cast. Old Jean looks at the child and does not know whether to rejoice or cry again. He feels ashamed of that little inner joy of knowing that it is another boy, and not his, who has been so close to death. But that intimate joy lasts only a few seconds, because his grandson still does not appear, and in his heart and head there is space only for the anguish that consumes him.

He has returned to the door of his hut, and the neighbors return to their homes. Each person has their own troubles, and Old Jean's misfortune is just one more story of tragedy in the town. Jean thanks them for their support and company, bowing his head. Words come from his heart, but do not make it out through his lips to give thanks as he should. He gets to the door, trying to get comfortable while waiting. He does not know how many hours he will be there without moving.

Old Jean takes off his hat, as rumpled as his clothes, rubs his face with his hands and cleans his spectacles by breathing on them and rubbing the glass with the hem of his shirt. The streetlights come on in the distance. Night is falling like an indifferent blanket on the tragedies of men. The voices and noises of the day are fading, although not completely. Despite projecting a certain calm on the outside, on the inside his heart tells him that his grandson will not return. Back in the shack, his food waits, cold, on the table he built ten years ago. The old trunk no longer holds any promise for him. Then, Old Jean sees everything clearly. This terrible night is identical to the one that still appears in his dreams, when Claude departed, never to come back. The dusty street on which a few trucks pass by, and the cries of fights erupting each nightfall, are just the same as that time long ago. On the checkered tablecloth, two dishes wait unnecessarily for guests. A dagger of renewed nostalgia pierces his chest, into his soul. He looks at the sky where no stars are shining. Yes, he once lived this same vertigo of painful uncertainty and abandonment. From tomorrow on, he will have to fight only against the night and wait for his two Yoruba warriors to return.

Chapter 13

UNDER ANOTHER SKY

"From far away, the sugar train smoked,
coughed, spat and howled; amid a clanging of
piston rods, it rushed on toward the huge chimneys
of the gray mill that could be seen on the horizon.
Even the air was sugary."
Jacques Stéphen Alexis

A bright sun, like a ripe orange, invades the hidden corners of the town of Barahona. A mulatto man dressed in khaki gently knocks on the door, which is locked with a bolt from the inside. The house is marked with the number "23" on Duarte Street. Mercedes opens the door cautiously to avoid making noise. Claude looks at the smiling face that comes out to meet him. He kisses her tenderly on the cheek, and she returns the kiss, to Claude's surprise. He has not seen her so animated in a long time.

"What is it, *mon amour?*" he asks as he enters the house, unbuttons his sweaty shirt and takes off his work boots.

Full of emotion, Christopher crosses the small room. The figure he envisioned in his mind so often is there, in front of his very own eyes. Christopher is all smiles as he runs across the small room and rushes to hug his father.

"*Mon père! Mon père!*" he exclaims, his skinny arms embracing Claude.

Claude's whole body trembles when he hears the child's voice. It fills Claude's soul, and he cannot contain the tears so long suppressed. He has waited for this moment for so long. Claude has mixed emotions, and cannot explain why, but if he were to do so, he would have to use words like grief and hope, nostalgia and gratitude, orphanhood and family. With his heart galloping in his chest, he presses the child against his body and then holds him out to see him well, again and again, several times. He kisses him on the forehead and hair.

In the child's eyes there is only light, no trace of the tired eyes of his father, whom he wishes to have back in his life for good. Christopher is speechless, his words stacked on the tip of his tongue before he can express how much he has missed Claude and explain the details of the journey that brought him to his father. He wants to tell him every little thing, however insignificant it may be. Christopher also wants to tell him that he knows him better than he realizes, but at this moment he prefers to hug him and feel the safety of a father. There will be an opportunity later to tell him that he has read his entire diary and that his grandfather told him the same stories he used to tell Claude. He will also talk about Ms. Edith, her passionate expression when speaking about history and poetry, the tapping of her footsteps in the hall preceding her arrival. He will confess with pride that he knows how to prepare *tassot* and *griot* like his grandfather does.

In the afternoon of that first day under another sky, Christopher goes out on the sidewalk and has fun with a group of children playing cops and robbers, screaming and guffawing. Inside the house, Claude and Mercedes work on the plan of sending him to school as soon as possible, so he does not lose the whole year. Mercedes thinks it is a good idea for Claude to go instead of her, since it's his last name, "Morisseau," that appears on the temporary residency card he bears as a worker in the sugar industry. If there is a problem, it will be easier to prove that Christopher is his son, and, if necessary, they will ask Don Emmanuel to bring back on one of his trips from Barahona a document that proves the relationship between Claude and the boy.

Claude welcomes the plan, although in another sense he worries that his son will be at a disadvantage in the new country, where a strange language is spoken and the people are unfamiliar. But Christopher is already here and he has shown enough courage to face the unknown. Just then, he remembers a phrase that Old Jean repeated many times: *"Nan tan grangou Patat pa gen po,"* In times of hunger, sweet potatoes have no skin. That saying has never left him; it comes back every time he remembers his father's determination to prepare him for the changes and difficult times of life. Something about that refrain makes him immune to grief and struggles. Now he wants to offer his son another paternal voice, one that does not leave him and talks about fighting and resistance, and also joy.

Claude decides to write him a letter . . . no more diaries, and give it to him when the boy turns eighteen. That letter will begin by saying, " . . .

Only a great abyss can prevent a love like mine, for my land, my father, my loved ones—from returning to its origin. I wanted to be faithful to my dreams, no matter what happened, and I also managed to cross that abyss without leaving behind my roots. When I came to this land, I spent eight years defending my brothers crossing the border against the abuses and outrages of the official authorities and the powerful landowners. Even Mercedes had to pay a high price for that struggle with scarce results. She lost our son going to prisons and hospitals on the border, not knowing if I was alive or dead. I was arrested for being an "agitator" among the workers and confronting authority, when all I did was tell them about their rights and fair demands. I was full of rage, much more than in Haiti, finding the same pain I thought I had left behind engraved on those faces. The poor suffer the same everywhere. The day I was released, I was very thin and suffering from incipient tuberculosis. I had been treated very badly: I was beaten, my body anchored in a hole, eating only old bread . . . I almost died. I spent my savings on lawyers who did not help much; they went to the Haitian Embassy to see if they could help me but were told they could do nothing. I tell you these sad things, my son, so that you know the story. But you have before you another way: you can study, you will have friends in this land and you will be able to do other work, not cutting cane as I had to do. I know that you are clever and that warrior blood runs through your veins. Life opens its doors to those who have the boldness to pursue their dreams, without stopping before the obstacles that may arise due to having been born in a poor country that lacks everything. I know you will do well at everything that you set out to do. You will see that the future holds for you what my heart now predicts."

Christopher understands the words he hears around him. By the gestures of the children, he recognizes the game they play animatedly. Then he takes a chunk of limestone from the street and draws on the sidewalk a large well-defined hopscotch. He begins to whistle and yell to attract the attention of the children, and when they look in his direction, he starts jumping from box to box. They leave their own game and approach the new neighbor. They know the game of hopscotch, although it is not their favorite. One of the kids takes the initiative, puts himself in front and throws a stone in the first box. He throws again, and again, yet the next time he does not hit the target, the stone falling outside the box. Christopher thinks of the friends he left behind: Jacob, Paul and Stephen. His turn is next. Taking a provocative look at the boys, he throws the stone and starts to count confidently: *"Yon, de, twa!"* He pauses in the third box to catch his breath and smiles eagerly. Then, he remembers the face of his grandfather, his wrinkles and his calm voice. He keeps jumping: *"Sèt, uit, nèf, dis!"*

His new friends do not understand the words that come from those thick lips. But they understand immediately that he is shouting numbers and they begin to count with him. Nobody hears the street vendors announcing bananas and eggs. Christopher has won. Everyone claps hands, and a boy who introduces himself as Jovanni makes a sign to challenge the winner. He jumps almost to the end, and Christopher laughs as he did at the beginning. Now the laughter enters through the window to the table where Claude is sitting. That sweet and happy sound begins to fill his life.

Untiring, Christopher begins another round. Although the hopscotch grid is drawn on the sidewalk of Duarte Street, he is actually jumping on an imaginary street, a narrow path that leads from Miragoâne to Petionville. Overhead, a bird crosses the cloudless sky. He has an enormous desire to tell Old Jean: "Grandfather, I stopped being a turtle. I am also a dove."